Scared Stiff

by RAMSEY CAMPBELL

from Tom Doherty Associates

Scared Stiff

TALES
OF SEX
AND
DEATH

RAMSEY
CAMPBELL

A TOM DOHERTY ASSOCIATES BOOK

NEW YORK

SCARED STIFF: TALES OF SEX AND DEATH

Copyright © 2002 by Ramsey Campbell
Introduction copyright © 1987 by Clive Barker

Book design by Mark Abrams.

A Tor Book
Published by Tom Doherty Associates, LLC
175 Fifth Avenue
New York, NY 10010

www.tor.com

Tor® is a registered trademark of Tom Doherty Associates, LLC.

Library of Congress Cataloging-in-Publication Data

Campbell, Ramsey, 1946–
    Scared stiff : tales of sex and death / Ramsey Campbell.
       p.   cm.
    "A Tom Doherty Associates book."
    Contents: Dolls—The other woman—Lilith's—The seductress—Stages—
Loveman's comeback—Merry May—The limits of fantasy—The body in the
window—Kill me hideously.
    ISBN 0-765-30004-4
    1. Horror tales, English.   2. Erotic stories, English.   I. Title.

PR6053.A4855 S28   2002
823'.914—dc21

                                                         2002068474

First Edition: September 2002

Printed in the United States of America

0   9   8   7   6   5   4   3   2   1

for Jenny
a pillow book
with all my love

COPYRIGHT ACKNOWLEDGMENTS

CONTENTS

THE BARE BONES:
AN INTRODUCTION
by Clive Barker

DEATH AND THE MAIDEN. It's an eternally popular subject for painters, and in a sense for writers and filmmakers too. What does the image conjure? A woman, naked perhaps, or nearly so, gazing at us with horror (or, on occasion, with a sublime indifference) while Death stretches a rotted paw to touch her breast, or leans its worm-ridden skull towards her as if to ply her with kisses.

Corruption and sexuality in a marriage of opposites.

The motif is echoed whenever a movie monster takes beauty in its arms, or at least attempts to. Sometimes, of course, the Maiden keeps Death at bay; as often, she's claimed. Whichever, the sexual *frisson* generated by her glamour is increased tenfold by the presence of the foulness that shadows her.

But the drama of the image—with the Maiden representing innocence and life, and Death the joyless evil that threatens her— is only one aspect of a fascinating confrontation. There are countless sophistications of that theme, the most complex of them more readily rendered in prose, I believe, where the writer can describe both the outer *and* inner conditions of his characters, than in any other medium.

Stories that can show us the flesh in all its sensuality, then reveal the bone beneath; or uncover the decay at the heart of an apparently wholesome passion; that take us into the wildest realms of perversion, and into the fever of obsession. It's a fruitful area.

But for a genre that derives much of its power from the tres-
passing of taboos, horror fiction has been remarkably coy when it
comes to talking of sex. In an age when characters in all manner
of fiction have forsaken their blushes to fornicate, horror fiction
clings to its underwear with a nunnish zeal.

There have been, it's true, many masterworks charged with erot-
icism (indeed there's an argument that says much of the genre is
underpinned by repressed sexuality) but it has remained, for the
most part, sub-text. We can take our werewolf with a touch of
Freud or without. As long as he doesn't sport an erection (the
werewolf, not Freud) as well as snout and tail, we can interpret the
image shorn of its sexual possibilities.

For my part, I tend to be of the opinion that such willful naïveté
is perverse, and that art is best enjoyed, as it should be made, *to
the limit.*

Turning a blind eye to what an image may signify—either because the interpretation distresses or confounds us—is not what
good fiction should do, nor should it be the response it elicits. It's
doubly regrettable, therefore, that so little horror fiction has taken
the challenge of sexuality by the balls.

I've talked of this with writers and fans alike, and many of them
evidence some fear that if the undertow of sexual meaning were
made manifest the fiction would lose some of its power to persuade.
I have argued in return that any fictional forum that requires a
willful suspension of the reader's spirit of intellectual inquiry (as
opposed to his disbelief) doesn't deserve to survive, and have put
my pen where my mouth is (as it were) with sex in a number of
my pieces.

Mr. Campbell has done the same, with great success. Here, gathered in a single volume, are several of his stories that marry the
horrific with the sexual. I don't use the word *erotic* here, for I think
the sexual material in these tales serves a far more complex func-
tion than straightforward titillation.

For one thing, it is never a narrative aside—an overheated fuck before the horrors begin afresh—but rather a central and eloquent part of the story's texture. For another, the actors in these scenes (when human) are seldom the deodorized stuff of fantasy, but the same pale-buttocked, stale-sweated individuals we all of us greet each morning in our mirrors. Thirdly, and most pertinently, the sexual material is marked by Ramsey Campbell's unique vision, just as everything in his fiction is marked.

Most of you will know that Mr. Campbell has earned his considerable audience, and countless critical plaudits, by creating a world in which much remains unsaid and unseen, and the fear he creates is as much wed to our individual interpretation of what the prose is implying as derived from anything the author explicitly reveals.

This being the nature of his gift, it might seem that graphic sexual descriptions—and believe me, graphic they are—would not sit happily with such obliqueness. Far from it. One of the delightfully unsettling things about these tales is the way Ramsey's brooding, utterly unique vision renders an act familiar to us all so fretful, so strange, so *chilling*. As elsewhere, his pithy prose responds to the challenge of reinventing experience with subtlety and resilience, never slipping into cliché, but always asking us to make fresh sense of the acts set before us.

And so we should, for sexuality is all too often the territory of the sentimentalist or the pornographer, too seldom that of the visionary. Yet it's a transforming act, literally. It remakes our bodies, for a time; and our minds too. For a little space we know obsession intimately; we are at the call of chemical instructions which sharpen our senses and at the same time narrow our focus, so that our perceptions are heightened and refined.

Horror fiction has traditionally had much to say about all these subjects: transformation, obsession and perception. Sex, with its ecstasies and its *petit mort:* its private rituals and its public corruptions; its way of reminding us that all physical pleasure is rooted in the same body that shits, sweats and withers, is the perfect stuff for the horror writer, and there can be few artists working in the genre as capable of analyzing and dramatizing such territory as the author of the volume you hold.

As I said earlier, horror fiction has traditionally dealt in taboo. It speaks of death, madness and the transgression of moral and physical boundaries. It raises the dead to life and slaughters infants in their cribs; it makes monsters of household pets and begs our affection for psychos. It shows us that the control we believe we have is purely illusory, and that every moment we teeter on chaos and oblivion.

And to that list of taboos I now add another list: the forbidden substrata of sexuality. The obsessions with parts and people we keep in our private thoughts; the acts we dream of but dare not openly desire; the flesh we long to wear, the pains we yearn to endure or inflict in the name of love.

Here are fictions which unite subjects from both the above lists. In which the dead don't simply rise—they rise to *fuck*.

To some of you, these stories will seem portraits of Hell. But if you're honest, your dreams may tell you differently.

Who knows, maybe the Maiden hasn't been startled by Death at all; maybe that cold touch on her breast is what she's been waiting for all her life.

People desire stranger things, as the extraordinary Mr. Campbell is about to prove. . . .

London; 29th June, 1986

Scared Stiff

DOLLS

COLD AS THE FEBRUARY WIND, the full moon blazed over
the fields. Anne Norton heard the wind ruffle the wheat a moment
before it plucked at her naked body. She shivered, but not from
the cold, which hardly touched her. Already the power was cours-
ing through her; already the belladonna and the aconite were shivering through her genitals and her legs. She ran behind her
husband John through the gate in their stone wall.

Once out of the garden she glanced back at the cottages of
Camside. Some were empty, she knew, and so was the Cooper
farmhouse at the edge of the village. The rest were dark and sleeping, without the faintest gleam of a rush-light. Across the common,
the high voice of a sheep joined her in derisive mirth. Ahead of
her, John had reached the edge of the wood. Shadows streamed
down his naked back.

The wood was quiet, muffled. Only the Cambrook stream gos-
siped incessantly in the darkness. The others must already be waiting at the meeting place. Now the ointment seemed to pour hotly
down her legs. She ran more swiftly, gliding through splashes of
moonlight, as the trees began to toss in their sleep. The wind
stroked her genitals, which gulped eagerly.

She plunged into the Cambrook, shattering the agitated ropes
of moonlight. Beneath her feet pebbles gnashed shrilly, with a hard
yet liquid sound. When she reached the bank she looked back

sharply, for she'd heard the stream stir with more life than belonged to water. But the water was flowing innocently by.

As if the gnashing of the pebbles had been the earth's last snatch at her she felt herself leave the ground. She saw the luminous ground race by beneath the skimming blur of her feet. Ranks of trees danced beside her, huge and slow but increasingly wild, branches about one another's shoulders. She felt all the strength and abandon of the trees flood through her.

In a moment, or perhaps an hour—for the wood seemed to have swelled like fire, to cover the whole countryside—she had reached the glade.

Everyone was there. The four Coopers were standing in a row at the edge of the glade, waiting impatiently, restless as the trees. Elizabeth Cooper glared at Anne with open hostility. Anne grimaced at her; she knew it was John at whom the old woman wanted to glare, jealous of his power. The Coopers had preserved the witchcraft for so long alone that now they were unwilling to allow power to anyone else. But they dared not oppose John. Giddy with borrowed power and borne up by the fierce ointment, Anne strode into the glade, feeling her feet sink to earth.

John had been halted by Robert Allen. The man's eyes were rolling out of focus, so that he seemed to address someone behind John's shoulder. "Celia Poole called my Nell a witch," he said. "She meant it as a joke, till she saw how Nell looked. She thinks slowly, but she'll come to the truth."

John nodded. He seemed to withdraw from his eyes, sinking down to a secret center of himself, leaving his eyes glazed by moonlight. Watching, Anne flinched away. Though his power sustained her, it was unthinkably terrifying; it was something she dared not ponder, just as her wedding night had been. "Celia Poole," he said. "By the time she is sure, she will be unable to tell."

Adam Cooper stepped forward, defiantly impatient, almost interrupting. "Introibo," he shouted.

At once Elizabeth Cooper began to chant. It was in no language Anne knew, she wasn't sure it was even composed of words: a howling and yodeling, a clogged gurgle. Sometimes sounds were repeated monotonously, sometimes Anne recognized no sound that she'd heard from the previous meeting. She suspected the old woman of making up the chant. None of this mattered, for the Coopers had linked arms and were dancing wildly around the glade, the outermost dragging the bystanders into the dance as they passed.

Anne was snatched away by Adam, almost overbalancing. John had been caught by Jane Cooper, scarcely fifteen but already plumply rounded. Anne felt a hot pang of jealousy. But now that John had joined the dance they were whirling faster, spinning her away from her jealousy, from everything but the linked circle of thirteen turning about the axis of the center of the glade, whizzing above the ground.

Clouds shrank back from the moon; light washed over the glade, and the shadows of the capering trees grasped at the earth. Anne felt her husband's power surging through the circle, lifting her free of the ground. When she opened her mouth the chant spilled out, incomprehensible yet exhilarating. Beside her Adam's penis reared up, unsheathing its tip, enticing her gaze.

Suddenly the dance had spun her out of the circle; she rolled panting over the damp grass. The circle was breaking up, and Adam ran to the edge of the glade, where he'd hidden a basket. From the basket he produced a black hen, which he decapitated, squeezing the body between his thighs to pump the gory fountain higher. "Corpus domini nostri," he shouted, elevating the head towards the moon.

He'd changed the ritual again, Anne realized; last time they'd eaten fish which he'd consecrated, and the time before there had been biscuits like flattened communion wafers. All the Coopers' magic changed from month to month, largely because of Elizabeth's failing memory. In this case it didn't matter, for the meaning of the ritual remained the same. "Amen!" Anne cried with the rest as they lay on the ground, hearts pounding. That would show Parson Jenner how frightened she was of him.

"Amen!" they shouted. "Domini nostri! Domini nostri!" And nodding to Robert Allen, John rose to his feet and left the glade.

The twelve fell silent. The moon hung still and clear. Even the trees were subdued, like uneasy spectators holding their breath. Their shadows wavered to stillness, as if the frightened anticipation of the twelve had gripped them fast. Anne's heart scurried as time paced, slow, slower.

Before John returned his power had filled the glade, cold and inhuman as the moonlight. Nobody looked at his face. Everyone gazed at his hands, where all his power was focused. His hands displayed a knife and a faceless wooden doll.

Robert Allen refused to take the doll at first. He gazed at it, and at the immobile moon-bright hand that held it out to him, with something like dread. Not until Nell gestured furiously at him did he clutch the doll, closing his eyes and squeezing his face tight about a silent curse.

As soon as Robert handed back the doll, John slashed at its head half-a-dozen times with the knife. His movements seemed casual, negligent, practically aimless. But now there was a face on the doll: low brow, long blunt nose, high cheekbones and wide mouth: Celia Poole's face.

Though she had watched him carving before he had turned to witchcraft, Anne was terrified. His carving had the economy and skill of pure hatred. That, and more: carving, he became a total stranger—not the man who had courted her, not the man she'd lain coldly beneath on their wedding night, not the man their marriage had made of him. When he strode away into the trees, gazing at the doll, she felt exhausted with relief. Even had he not forbidden them to watch his curse, she could never have followed.

John was hardly out of the glade when Elizabeth Cooper seized Robert Allen. She slid down his belly and thrust her head hungrily between his legs. To Anne it looked as if a gray hairy spider had fastened itself beneath Robert's belly and was plucking at its web. His entire body strained back like a bow from the arrow of his genitals. His face glowed coldly with moonlight as his mouth gaped wider, wider.

Elizabeth's action released them all from their dread. Adam pushed Jenny Carter against a tree and thrust into her from behind as she clawed at the trunk. James Carter was tripped by Alice Young and Nell, who fastened on him with their genitals as if they were famished mouths. Arthur Young had pinioned Mary Cooper to the ground with her arms stretched wide, but she lifted her hips higher to shackle him too, gasping.

Jane Cooper lay on top of Thomas Small, her plump young breasts crushed against his chest as his thick arm pressed her to him. He'd torn up a bunch of nettles and was flailing her round buttocks with them. Her buttocks churned, pumping him, as her hands yanked frantically at his hair. She cried out as he did, almost lifting herself free of him.

Elizabeth lifted her head and looked at Anne as Robert Allen slumped to the ground, spent. "Your John never shows his face now, does he?" she taunted. "Does without, does he? You mark my words. No man has that kind of power."

There was nothing behind her words but envy, Anne knew. Envy had made her seize Robert Allen as soon as John had gone. Nevertheless, Anne suddenly felt rejected by the others, as she had tried not to admit to herself while she waited for a partner. She grabbed Adam as he left Jenny Carter still clinging to the tree, and dragged him on top of herself. Deeper in the wood she heard a creaking, as of trees flexing in the wind. But there was no wind.

Her body closed on Adam's penis, sucking him deeper, quickening his thrust. Her thighs crushed his ribs, her toes arched upward, straining him closer still. Her buttocks rolled against the damp grass, and the ointment blazed through her legs, exploding in her genitals almost at once. At her third orgasm his penis seemed to double its size, pumping long and uncontrollably.

As she lay beneath him she heard the tread approaching through the wood, creaking.

She tried not to think. She tried to feel nothing but Adam's heavy body crushing her against the grass; but he pushed himself away and sat waiting, suddenly subdued. She tried to hold the cold bleached glade still, empty except for the twelve. She tried to fend off what was approaching. What the orgiasts had been trying to ignore was unthinkable. Since she couldn't think it, it couldn't happen.

She was trying to convince herself when the devil stalked creaking into the glade.

He surveyed the twelve, sneering, and his head brandished horns that could gore a bull. His eyes, his wide mouth and the hollows of his cheeks were thick with shadow. So much Anne saw before she wrenched her gaze away. But it was no use averting her eyes, for she could feel his body massive as an oak dominating the glade, and smell the fetid leather of him. She looked up.

He was beckoning. One finger thick and knotted as a branch hooked towards them, creaking faintly. Perhaps that was the most terrible aspect of him: that he never spoke, because he had no need. Anne felt a sudden wound gouged out where her stomach had been. It must be her turn now. Then she realized he was not beckoning to her, but to Jane. His enormous penis stood ready before his featureless belly, glistening with moonlight.

He waited, finger hooked, while Jane went trembling to him in the center of the glade. His presence seemed to weigh down time; her paces were hours long. When she reached him and at last touched his shoulders timidly, he threw her to the ground.

At once he was on her, his knotted fingers pinning her shoulders down. As the huge penis entered her she gasped as though it had clubbed all the breath from her. Her stinging buttocks struggled wildly beneath him, on the grass. He drove himself deeper into her, with long slow deliberate strokes. Even when she tore at his back with her nails and bruised her thighs against his sides, his sneering mouth neither spoke nor moved.

When she fell back exhausted he thrust her away and strode out of the glade, creaking slowly and massively as the trees.

Parson Jenner was screaming.

"The carnal mind," he screamed, "is enmity against God! To be carnally minded is death!"

The church hurled his voice back behind Anne. She dwindled into herself. He wasn't looking at her. He couldn't know.

"This is God's word," the parson said quietly, intensely; then screamed "Will you silence him with the words of men? Will you tell him lust is natural, God-given? Wallowing in filth is in the nature of animals! Is that your nature? Will you glorify your own slime and call it Christian love?"

Anne wished she dared cover her burning face. She knew he was right. She knew it more certainly every time he preached on the subject. She'd known it on her wedding night, as soon as she'd seen John's uplifting penis. She'd known as he drove it into her, dry and hard and rough, for no better reason than that Parson Jenner had licensed him to. Her body had stiffened against the intrusion and grown cold, and so it always behaved with John.

Yet it hadn't behaved so when she was sixteen, when she'd joined (she had to hurry her mind past the words, lest God and Parson Jenner overhear) the coven. The ointment had helped her then, initiating her into ecstasy; it had always done so since. Only at home, on her bed with John, did her body feel rigid and grimy. After much thought she had decided why. In the village the parson's power was everywhere. She was free of his power only in (she thought it loudly, defiantly) the coven.

The entire coven was here in church, subdued by Jenner's power. Anne glanced about surreptitiously. There was Adam, sitting stiffly upright as if held to attention by his long black jacket, his genitals muffled beneath the folds of its full skirts. There—Anne felt an inexplicable violent surge of jealousy—was Jane, her breasts laced tightly into a corset-bodice, her buttocks surely throbbing still beneath the many petticoats and long skirt and apron; they could hardly have recovered in less than a day. And there were all the others, hiding behind their intent respectful faces. In the gallery at the west end Anne saw Robert Allen and Arthur Young, Robert's oboe and Arthur's horn at their sides ready to accompany the next hymn.

"Did Jesus Christ Our Lord," Parson Jenner screamed, "bring shame upon His Blessed Mother's virgin flesh by lusting after woman?"

This must be the only time he ever felt passion, Anne thought in a bid to reassure herself. But that made it worse. It meant that the force of the whole man was behind his words. She snatched her gaze back to the altar, trying to pretend she'd never looked away.

His power was too strong for them. By hiding their bodies and their thoughts from him they had acknowledged his power. The coven was nothing but an escape from him, an escape dictated to them by the whims of the full moon. The rest of the month they were his.

She knew that the Carters and the Youngs had joined the coven simply in order to escape the sermons by which Jenner had restricted their marriages. She imagined his furious contempt if he ever found them out. She felt diminished, ashamed. She could hear him telling her that the coven was nothing but a delusion.

She shook her head; at least, it trembled. Her thoughts were confused. She tried to force her way through the gray mist which always descended on her mind after each coven and hung about her until the next full moon. There was more to their witchcraft than delusion. Once, running through the Cambrook at midnight, she'd heard the entire stream rise up behind her, a glittering mantle coldly boiling in the moonlight, sweeping forward to follow her to the coven; but when she'd turned the water had been playing aimlessly between its banks. She was sure she'd heard that.

And there was something she had seen. Once, at the height of the coven's ecstasy, she had looked up to see a gigantic white moonlit face grinning at them from the sky. Its eyes and mouth had been full of night; their tattered rims had smoked slowly. As it had gradually spread to encompass the whole of the sky, still gazing down and grinning, horns had streamed from its forehead.

"Lust is a delusion, a trick played on us by the devil!" Parson Jenner screamed. "Did Our Lord Jesus Christ feel lust? Did His Blessed Mother?"

A delusion, Anne thought. If the devil could make her feel what she felt at the coven, he could certainly make her see faces in the sky. Her face grew ashen. The coven had no power except the power of delusion.

But it had, she thought suddenly. It had real power, terrifying power. For the first time that day she was able to look up at Parson Jenner's face. "We shall sing in praise of God," he declared. She rose to her feet, buoyed up beyond the music. The coven and the parson had battled within her. And the coven had won, because it had John's power.

Color flooded back into her mind and into the church, and for the rest of the service she felt as if she were caught in a blaze of light: until, as she emerged from the church, she saw Celia Poole walking ahead of her, unharmed.

At once John, strolling beside her powerful and secret behind his calm face, became what the others had been in the church: a hollow puppet skulking behind a God-fearing expression. He'd said Celia Poole would be struck down before she could speak. But how could he be sure unless he silenced her immediately? His power had failed. Parson Jenner had won.

At their cottage she sat wordlessly. The parson's power was here too. While others enjoyed a Sunday stroll she and John must sit at home, insisting on their piety. Her stomach ached dully. Having starved herself for the coven she must now abstain on the Sabbath. She gazed towards her spinning wheel, then looked away. She could not even mend their clothes, lest the parson chance to call.

Her mind felt dark as the earth floor. The grandfather clock marked off the approach of the evening service, loudly, lethargically. She imagined Celia Poole springing to her feet in the church, not for a public penance but to denounce Nell. Then Nell would break down and implicate them all. And Parson Jenner would have them, his voice surrounding them, binding them with a noose of villagers. Never mind George II's Witchcraft Act. That kind of leniency wasn't for Jenner, nor for the village he had made his own.

She watched John place wood on the fire, carefully, untroubled. She refused to be deluded by his calm. Behind his discreetly secretive face there was nothing. He was the only one who could have saved her from Jenner. She'd thought the parson's first victory over him, years ago, had filled him with cold hatred—the source of his power. But that power had faded.

He sat opposite her, his face unchanging. For a moment she realized that his days outside the coven might be as gray as hers. But at least she had her ecstasies beneath the moon. What pleasure could he have that carried him through life?

It didn't matter, she thought, shrugging dully away before the thought took shape. Neither of them could look forward to pleasure, now that Jenner had won. A wind forced smoke out of the fireplace towards them, billowing darkly up to the rafters.

On her way to the later service she stumbled continually in the deep ruts of the road. It was as though they were forcing her feet towards the church. The red-brick cottages stood back from her in their large gardens. The sun hung low over the wheat, and her shadow bumped over the ruts, dragging her along.

Before she reached her appointed place in the pew she passed the Coopers. None of them looked at her and John, nor did she dare look directly at them. The parson's power was absolute; they dared not even acknowledge each other. She wondered whether they were as numb with dread as she.

Then she saw that the Pooles' places were empty.

She didn't dare hope yet. But she felt the possibility of hope for the first time in church since Jenner had taken up residence. The Pooles were almost always half an hour early for the service; they preferred not to suffer each other's awkward silences alone.

Kneeling, she gazed about. The church had been neglected in the previous parson's day. Then Jenner had come and blamed them all, fastening his words deep in their most secret flaws. Some of the villagers had welcomed him, as the solution to what they saw as the laxity of the time; the others had not dared oppose him, for his contempt was spreading through the villagers like an epidemic. Most of the villagers infected themselves before the contempt could be turned against them.

Then Jenner had called them to clean and renovate the church, to renew its whitewash. It gleamed around Anne, in the evening light. But now she felt that perhaps this was not the victory Jenner thought it was. After all, it was Jenner who preached the unimportance of earthly things. The real victory was over Celia Poole, and that was John's—

When Anne heard the footsteps approaching down the aisle she knew without turning that it was Celia Poole.

Turning with the rest as they disapproved of the latecomer, Anne saw Celia take her place unruffled in her pew—in the pew which, like the rest, had been built to Jenner's order by John. In Celia's eyes, biding its time, Anne saw the denunciation. Beside her Richard sat, red-faced and puffed up by their recent argument. Celia's eyes showed that she had won.

As if he had been awaiting his moment of triumph Jenner strode to the altar, robes flying. His Latin rang through the church, hard and imperative. Anne responded dully, though the words were virtually meaningless to her. They sprang from her, bypassing conscious thought, as the chant at the coven had done. But these words were closing on her like a trap. Each word Jenner or the congregation spoke held her more tightly, binding her in readiness for Celia's accusation. She felt Celia behind her, ready to pounce to her feet.

There was a clattering and a heavy thud.

The Latin broke off. Everyone looked round. There was something in the aisle, writhing helplessly as a baby. Its face was black and strained about a protruding silent tongue; the mouth worked, but only foam emerged. It was Celia Poole.

"Be vigilant!" Jenner screamed, pointing. "Because your adversary the devil, as a roaring lion, walketh about, seeking whom he may devour!"

Anne could hardly contain her smile. She knew this was not the devil's victory. It was the coven's.

Then, as Richard looked up from his writhing wife, his eyes blank and moist with fury, she realized he knew also.

It was the day before the next full moon that Elizabeth Cooper's words began to grow into Anne's suspicion.

Anne was mending clothes. Unafraid now, her mind moved smoothly as her needle through her memories. For the first time since her marriage she found herself spontaneously enjoying her work. She dwelt on it. She remembered the initiations of the Carters and the Youngs, remembered their wild writhing and cavorting as they had experienced their own untrammelled sexuality.

Her mind snagged on that. Suddenly she wondered what had happened to John's sexuality.

She tried to think. John wasn't sexless, quite the contrary; his fierce desire had terrified her on their wedding night, when sex had confronted her unsteady with rush-light rather than luminous beneath the full moon. When he knew he was unable to coax or bludgeon a response from her he had withdrawn his desire into himself, but she couldn't believe it had vanished entirely. "No man has that kind of power," Elizabeth had said.

Of course. That was where his sexuality had gone: into his magic power. Elizabeth's jealous words had inadvertently shown Anne the truth. But somehow Anne wasn't entirely convinced. She heard John in his room, finishing a piece of furniture. She'd often caught him looking at her when he thought she was unaware; she'd seen the desire in his eyes. She'd shudder then: she couldn't, that was all, it was no use trying to force her. Now, thinking about it instead of hurrying past, she couldn't believe that he had managed to translate his desire so easily into his power. Surely the ecstasy of the coven must inflame him beyond control.

Besides, she was sure John had always had the power. It had

been Parson Jenner who had channeled it into hatred. John was an expert furniture-maker, as his father had been; he worked cheaply yet with style, and many of the farm laborers boasted a canopied bed rather than a trestle or a flock mattress on the floor. But John's genius had been for the figures he carved; tiny riders, shepherds, farmers, animals—even, in his room, an entire miniature Camside populated with minute replicas of the villagers. He'd used to take some of his carvings to Brichester; he had seldom brought any home.

Near Christmas he had used to display his work at the edge of the road outside their cottage. Since their marriage he had devoted more time to his carvings; that last Christmas he had displayed more work than was likely to be bought even by the villagers and the folk who made a special journey from Brichester.

He had been standing by his display, and almost the entire population of Camside had been admiring his work, when Parson Jenner stalked up. He stared at the display as if it confirmed the rumor of some awful sin. "Thou shalt not make unto thee any graven image!" he'd shouted at John. "Do you not understand the word of God? A graven image is a carved image. It is not for man to steal perfection from God."

Anne had felt the crowd change in an instant from admiring to condemning John's work, had felt their disapproval seize her too, almost palpably. She'd felt frightened but safe; John would overcome them. But then he'd betrayed her. He had given in to Jenner and asked what he could do. "Burn them," Jenner had said, "and give thanks to Almighty God for your salvation."

Half an hour later John's work had been a cone of flame. Anne had felt contemptible, hollow. When John had retreated into the cottage she had thought he'd gone to hide his miniature Camside, or mope over it; but he'd brought it out in pieces and had thrown it on the fire.

Since their marriage she had avoided the coven, for she'd thought that John was becoming suspicious. The Coopers had let her lapse, for the other couples had recently been initiated. But that month, desperately pursuing her sense of self, Anne had obtained the ointment from the Coopers and had gone to the meeting. Running through the nodding wood, leaving behind the cottage and its air of terrible defeat, she felt released at last. Behind her, urging her on, she'd heard the faint padding of the wood's heart—except that when she'd reached the glade and had turned to see what everyone was looking at, she'd realized the sound had been John's footsteps.

"I thought so," he'd said, though he'd gazed in surprise at some of them. "Well, I have more reason to hate the pratings of the religious than any of you. You had better let me join you."

"And then we shall be thirteen at last," Anne had said, suddenly sure that he'd saved himself for this victory over Jenner.

"You would have been more use to us," Elizabeth had said, "when you had it in you to carve your dolls. They would have given us power over the ones you carved."

He'd taken a knife from his pocket; Anne had seen decision flood his eyes, like the moonlight that spilled over the blade. "Perhaps they still may," he'd said.

Within the week Jonas Miller had smashed both knees beneath his wheel. Jonas had helped John throw his dolls on the fire, with virtuous relish; John had carefully gouged out both knees from the image of Jonas he'd carved in the glade. After that, the coven had called John to strike down their enemies at whim, but he had cursed a victim only for good reason, lest a spate of injuries and afflictions betray the presence of the coven. Roger Place, the Brichester landlord, had been prevented from enclosing land in Camside by a chronic urinary infection that had confined him to his house, so that Arthur Young had kept his job day-laboring on the widow Taylor's land. And those who John heard had begun to suspect the witches were silenced: most recently, Celia Poole.

As she remembered Celia's fate Anne's doubt faded. To wield such power John must draw on the whole of himself, on his frustrated desires too. Such power must be capable of subsuming all of him into itself. Her needle moved easily again.

Musing on Celia, Anne felt pity for Richard Poole: a timid man, anxious to avoid unpleasantness and bad feeling; no doubt he had tried to argue Celia out of her proposed denunciation. Now that his wife had been stricken with epilepsy, Anne imagined that he would withdraw further into himself, poor man. Still, the coven had had to protect itself. Able to feel comfortable again, Anne encouraged the fire with the bellows.

She was warming her hands gratefully when Jane Cooper arrived to collect the chair that John had finished. Anne felt an almost habitual jealousy at the sight of the girl. A moment later, when Jane had gone into John's room, Anne felt ashamed; she was too much at peace with the world to spoil it with such unworthy emotions.

One luxury John's work afforded them was tea, something Jane was unlikely ever to have tasted. A pot full of water stood ready by the hearth, and Anne hung it over the fire. Then she hurried to tell Jane to wait.

When Anne entered the room John scarcely bothered to conceal his expression. He was gazing at Jane, his eyes full of the memory of coupling and the promise of more. After what felt to Anne like many minutes, he glanced at her with weary impatience and put away his feelings, like a master brusquely hiding a book when a maid enters.

Jane went out, the upturned chair on her back. Anne returned to her own room, stumbling, and stood aimlessly. For a moment she battled with the truth. John couldn't have touched the girl. He never had done so at the coven, and the elder Coopers would never allow it under any other circumstances. They were as strict as Jenner on that point. Indeed, she thought (or almost thought, for her mind shied away), if they were able to take each other at will, there would be no need for the coven.

But the truth was waiting patiently for her to look at. John was the devil that appeared at the coven; that was how he gratified his sexuality.

Even now, urged on by that insight, she had to struggle in order to think of the devil. He had appeared eight full moons ago, creak-ing out of the wood as if the trees and wind and moonlight had combined in him. Since then he had always appeared at the height of their ecstasy. He had never been seen before John had joined the coven; they had taken that as proof of the power of thirteen, and of John's power. The women had cried that his penis was hard and unyielding, as Elizabeth had said it would be, remembering the covens of her childhood. Everything had seemed to show the old magic had returned to them. Now Anne saw there was another explanation.

The devil had never taken her. She had been unthinkingly grateful to be spared, so grateful that she dared not think of her good fortune lest thinking bring the devil upon her next time. Sometimes she moaned and writhed in her sleep as the massive sneering face weighed on hers, the enormous penis conquered her. At the last two covens she had been sure the devil must take her, and she'd locked away dread deep in her mind; but he had chosen Nell and Jane again. At last she knew why she had felt instinctively jealous of Jane.

Within her mind, memories bound themselves into a certainty. The devil never appeared until John had vanished into the wood to curse his dolls. Even when nobody had petitioned him to curse, he said he must renew the existing curses so that their power would not weaken. Always the devil appeared from the direction in which John vanished. And—remembering this, Anne realized that the truth had always been in her mind—whomever John danced with before the sacrifice, the devil later chose.

Before she had time to be terrified of him, she strode into his room. He was carving the leg of a chair, with a lover's delicacy. "The devil who comes at the full moon," she said, tightly aware that they had never discussed the coven outside its time before. "I know who he is."

"He is our master," he said, not looking up.

"He is not mine. He is you in disguise, so that you can have all the women at your mercy. That's how you get your fucking."

"I would not touch any of them," he said with a contempt as profound as Jenner's.

She recoiled, back into her own room. Yet somehow, when she reflected, his words hadn't quite the power she was sure he intended. He hadn't said he wasn't the devil. Of course he wouldn't touch other women, since his head-to-toe disguise would always intervene between their touching bodies: not if he meant "touch" that way.

She might have contented herself with that, with the sense that he was having to strain at his words in order to deceive her, since that was a kind of victory: she'd trapped him into a position where he couldn't use his power directly. But all at once "I would not touch any of them" turned and insulted her. Not "any of you"; he excluded her out of pity, out of indifference; she was beneath even his contempt. She was sure in her bitterness that there could be no other reason. The water rose up in the pot, hissing, brimming over. She snatched it away from the fire, coldly, calmly. She knew what she was going to do.

Later she told John that she was going to church. Jenner had been looking at her oddly, she said, and she wanted to head off his suspicions. She hurried down the road, towards the church. As soon as she was out of sight of the cottage she doubled back, into the wood.

She strode into the coven's glade and halted, confused. The sun was a silver wafer decomposing into a gray pond, and beneath its light the glade looked bare and cramped, hemmed in by denuded trees: not at all like the expanse of ground about which the trees danced deasil. But she recognized the gnarls of the trees between which the devil always emerged. She hurried toward them, calming her heart. Around her the wood creaked slowly and deliberately, like the pendulum of an enormous wooden clock.

She knew that John never brought his dolls with him to the coven: that he hid them and his knife beforehand, somewhere in this area. The devil-disguise was here also, she was sure. That was the proof she needed.

Someone was coming towards her through the wood. She hushed the creaking trees frantically with an unthinking gesture, but they swayed slowly on, interrupting her view of the depths of the wood with a dense net of branches. The branches made passes over each other, like the hands of a conjurer she'd seen in her childhood. Within the slow net of sound and black wood, someone was approaching.

After a long breathless time she told herself that it must have been a stroller, and went on. She peered between the trunks, anxious to find John's disguise, anxious to be gone. The trunks moved apart stolidly as she walked, revealing trunks beyond. Twigs groped blackly against the dull blurred sky. The trees swayed in unison, creaking with the effort, but their roots stayed firmly buried. Someone was following Anne through the wood.

She twisted around, glaring through the trees. There was nobody. At last she turned back, and came face-to-face with the devil.

He was sneering sightlessly out between two close-grown trees. He was almost hidden within a pile of twigs and branches, which had slipped down from his cheeks and left his face protruding, as from an impossible beard. His fixed mouth sneered; his eyes were sockets from which all but deep darkness had been gouged.

Even immobilized as he was, his massiveness was terrifying. But she forced herself closer and began to pull away the branches. At once she realized that the devil's leather hide was stretched over a wooden frame. No wonder he was massive. She remembered the tale she'd heard that a large quantity of leather had been stolen from a Brichester cobbler's; she didn't need to wonder where the wooden frame came from. As she separated the branches, she saw that the devil had no penis, only an orifice. She nodded grimly.

She was preparing to touch the devil, to prove that she could do so, when a movement back in the direction of the coven's glade caught her attention. Her imagination had not deceived her, after all; someone else was in the wood. It was Richard Poole.

She wrenched the branches together over the devil, and shrank back behind the trees. Peering out, she glimpsed Richard's face. He was no longer timid. His gaze was blazing with hatred. She knew he was searching for signs of the coven.

As she slipped between the trees and fled, she heard a creaking as if the devil had stirred in its sleep. Startled, she stumbled, snapping a branch. When she regained her balance she saw Richard staring at her. She nodded casually to him and strode away, ignoring her frantic heart.

When her heart slowed she found she was able to plan, and smiled wildly. Everything had fallen in her favor. She felt powerful enough to be reckless. She had hidden the devil completely; she had been too far from it when she stumbled to have betrayed it to Richard. She could afford to wait until tomorrow night. Already she had two plans, and she wanted to enjoy them both to the full.

It was the next night. Anne was running behind John. The full moon had cleared the sky; its light seeped through the hard ground, the starved trees, the restless grass furred with frost. When the branches stirred their movements lingered on Anne's eyes, like trails of luminous mist. Even John seemed to glow coldly from within. The weeks since the previous coven felt like a dream from which she had awakened at last.

But the weeks weren't so dreamlike that she could not interpret them, or plan from them. As she entered the glade she saw that everyone was waiting again, and realized why she and John always arrived last: in order that the others should feel bound to wait, to confirm their faith in his power. Very well, she thought. She could make an entrance too.

Loudly enough for everyone to hear she said to John "Make me a doll of Parson Jenner."

Before he turned inward, towards the core of his hatred, she thought he looked at her in something like admiration. "Why should you curse him?" he demanded.

"He saw how I smiled when Celia Poole was taken by her fits," she said. "Now he watches for me to betray myself. Every night I dream that I have. Soon it will be true."

John's eyes stared at her, and within them was someone old and overwhelmingly vicious, famished of everything save hatred. "He will never watch you again," he said.

A confusion of emotions welled up through her: satisfaction, terror, admiration, a poignant sense that they could admire each other only in this moment of inhuman power. She had often wondered why he had never cursed Jenner. At times, with a contempt as deep as that she'd felt when he'd burned his carvings, she had believed he was terrified of the parson. But perhaps, she had thought yesterday, he was too afraid of being engulfed by his own power ever to use it for himself. Yesterday she had seen that she could both test him in this and render Richard Poole harmless. If Jenner were destroyed, the villagers would never dare move against the coven. She smiled at the cold bland moon.

Elizabeth Cooper was chanting impatiently, almost shouting— scared, Anne thought, of the enormity John had undertaken to perform. The Coopers were dancing, stamping defiantly like animals. She ran to join the chain of dancers, holding fast to Jane's arm. Elizabeth frowned spitefully down the chain at her; it had always been the Coopers who chose the order of dancers. But Anne smiled back triumphantly and dragging the others with her, danced to John and took his arm. She let the chant seethe through her and pour from her mouth.

Her legs felt aflame with the ointment, urging her to dance more wildly. She gripped John's arm and capered, anxious to exhaust the dance, willing him to go in order to return to her—as the devil, if he must. Her heavy breasts rolled with the dance, their nipples taut and tingling; her genitals smacked their lips eagerly. She looked down at herself as her hips flexed powerfully. She would make him forget Jane and the rest. Beyond John she saw the circle of dancers close, as he took Alice's hand.

Anne was lying at the edge of the glade, legs loose and trembling. Adam had ripped open a fish and was displaying it to the moon. "Domini nostri," they shouted. All of a sudden John wasn't there; they were all huddled close to the trees, waiting amid the rusty creaking of the wood, and Anne's stomach suddenly felt as empty and cold as the glade.

John was striding towards her through the trees. His face was fixed and bland as the moon. His glowing colorless hand thrust a doll towards her. As she grasped the doll she stifled a cry. It had seemed to move in her grasp, as if Jenner were trapped in the wood, struggling frantically within her curse, his buried struggles making the surface crawl.

She closed her eyes to curse, and found panic waiting. If they tried to curse Jenner he would know; God would tell him; he would destroy them. She gripped the doll fast, hearing it creak. She entrusted herself to John's power. She squeezed everything from her sight except burning red, and cursed.

When John had taken the doll from her she opened her eyes. She didn't see him carve the face; Jenner was already there when she looked, glaring up from the wooden head, tiny but vastly contemptuous of her. It was if the core of Jenner had burst out of the wood and was staring at her from John's hand, all the denser and more concentrated for its size. For a second she felt its power take hold of her. Then she stared back at the paralyzed mannequin, and felt colossal with triumph.

John vanished into the wood, fading as he walked, only feebly luminous now, entirely dark, gone. Silenced by what he had done, the twelve waited unmoving. They needed their master to appear, to reassure them that their presumption had not destroyed him; all except Anne, who lay untroubled as her excitement grew, spreading through her thighs. When she heard the creaking among the still trees she knew it was John, returning to take her. Her genitals gasped with excitement.

The devil stalked into the glade, bearing his immobile sneering face towards them, beneath the moon. His deep eyes rolled with shadow. For the first time Anne dared look closely enough to see that his feet were cloven. The leather of his limbs gleamed dully as it wrinkled, creaking. Above his thighs his penis stood like a swollen rod of moonlight.

Anne was on her feet before she saw that he was beckoning to Alice Young.

As Alice rose Anne knocked her sprawling and strode towards the devil. The others gasped in outrage, more loudly as she took hold of his penis with her hands. It was far bulkier than any of the men's, and stiffer; it seemed wholly unlike John's, as she remembered it from the beginning of their marriage. The inhumanly still face leaned towards her, the shadows of its great horns drooping over its forehead. Within the staring sockets she could see no eyes at all.

Then the devil gripped her shoulders, bruising them cruelly. He twisted her about and threw her down. The thawing grass struggled beneath her breasts and legs. She felt his icy knees forcing her thighs apart, and strove to hold them closed. But his hands closed on her shoulders like vises, trapping her before she tried to crawl away, and his penis thrust peremptorily between her buttocks.

She began to cry with pain and rage—with a frustration she hadn't felt since her wedding night. Her legs shoved helplessly at the earth; her feet clawed at the crackling grass. He was riding her, butting deeper into her, his body creaking stiffly as the trees. The heavy smell of leather clogged her nostrils. His movements rubbed her nipples against the ground. She sobbed, for the ointment was responding to him in defiance of her will, causing her to squeeze him deeper into herself. She could not distinguish the blaze of her pain from the fire of the ointment.

Suddenly he withdrew and released her shoulders. She began to crawl swiftly towards the edge of the glade. When she heard him creaking slyly above her she turned on her back to fend him off. He had been waiting for her to do so. As she kicked out he lifted her knees and forced them wide, then, as her genitals and her mouth gaped, he slid himself into her.

She shouted in protest, writhing like an impaled moth. She felt stretched to breaking, on the lip of pain, but as she waited for the pain, a slow explosion began to spread through her from her genitals. The huge unyielding bludgeon rubbed within her, lifting her from the ground at each stroke. The sneering mask pressed against her face. She pummeled his unresponsive chest with the heels of her hands.

Suddenly something broke deep within her, in her mind, as the explosion reached it. It was as if the pent-up blaze of the ointment had engulfed her all at once. She was inundated by the force of the explosion, blinded. She tore at the brittle grass and earth with her hands as her knees dragged him closer again, again.

She fell back, drawing long slow hungry breaths. The devil was raising himself from her when she saw Richard Poole rush into the glade.

She screamed a warning, but the devil still moved slowly, unheeding. The watching eleven stared blankly at her, then at the man who had already dashed through their midst. Moonlight streaked across the blade of Richard's axe.

The devil regained his feet, and was turning when the axe swooped. Perhaps the sight of the sneering shadow-eyed face reminded Richard he was timid after all; for the axe, which had been aimed at the devil's neck, faltered aside and lopped off the devil's right arm.

The coven screamed, and Anne screamed the loudest. The arm fell across her legs. Richard whirled the axe and buried it between the devil's shoulders; then he fled into the wood, snapping branches. The devil tottered and began to fall beside Anne. She kicked the severed arm away hysterically. Then she stared at her legs, searching for spilt blood. There was none, for the arm was made entirely of wood.

She was so furious at the deception, furious with herself for having responded to this dummy, for having even feared for its life, that she gave herself no chance to wonder how it had been made to move. She turned on the devil, lying on its back next to her. She wrenched at its brandished penis. It was a shaft of young wood carefully pared to smoothness. As she twisted it violently, it turned in the socket and came away in her hand.

He'd made sure the wood was as moist as possible by renewing it each time, she explained to her startled heart. How thoughtful of him, she thought viciously. In her hand the penis now felt exactly like wood. But a sound was intruding on her musings. As the clamor of Richard's flight faded, they all heard someone moaning nearby.

John had ceased moaning by the time they found him. He lay on the ground close to where Anne had discovered the devil. He seemed to be sinking into what at first looked like an enormous expanding shadow, that surrounded him completely. He was lying on his right side in the undergrowth; they could not see his right arm. His left hand was gripped deep in his crotch, and the blood pulsed uncontrollably between the fingers.

He was not quite dead. He gazed at them with a last surge of power, and Anne felt his contempt condemn them all. She hadn't believed him when he'd said he would never touch any of them. She saw him watch her realization, and begin to smile mirthlessly. Then all the power drained from his eyes, and it was as if the entire wood drooped.

A chill wind carried to them the sound of Richard fleeing towards the village, shouting Parson Jenner's name.

THE OTHER WOMAN

OUTSIDE THE WINDOW, in the park, the trees were glossy with June sunlight. The sky floated in the lake; branches were rooted in the water, deep and still. Phil gazed out, then he glanced back at the strangled woman and pushed her aside. He had painted her before. She wouldn't do.

He read the publisher's brief again. *Throttle* ("racing driver by day, strangler by night!"). You could see the sunlit racing car, and the moon sailing in a splotch of night, behind the woman. But that was it exactly: it was the details that caught your eye. The woman wasn't at all compelling. She looked like just another murder victim on the cover of another book.

And why shouldn't she? Art didn't sell books—not this kind of book, anyway. People looked for the familiar, the predictable, the guaranteed product. There would be tense scenes on the racetrack, a girl with her dress ripped away from one nipple would be strangled (and probably more that the cover couldn't show); that was enough for the commuters glancing hastily at the station bookstall. But it wasn't enough for Phil. He'd painted this victim before, on *Her Dear Dead Body*. He was copying himself.

All right, so he was. There was only one way to halt that tendency, and he had the time. He'd left the rest of the day clear so that he wouldn't be tired tomorrow in London. Two satisfying checks had arrived that morning. He felt more than equal to the task. Gazing out the window, he began to rethink the cover, and to sketch.

A woman screaming at a hand groping into the picture—no; he tore that up impatiently. A corpse with a bruised throat—no, too static. A woman's throat working between intrusive thumbs—no! He'd just painted that! "God's bloody teeth!" he shouted, hurling the crumpled sketch across the room. "God damned bleeding—" He went on at length, until he began to repeat himself. Thank heavens Hilary was at work. If she had been here he would only have found an excuse to lose his temper with her, wasting half his energy.

When he'd calmed down he stared at the branches hanging limply into the depths of the lake. He felt himself draining into the view. Suddenly he closed his eyes and tried to imagine what it would be like to strangle a woman.

You would throw her down on the floor. You'd lie on top of her so that she couldn't kick, you'd pin her flailing forearms down with your elbows. You'd lean your weight on your thumbs at her throat. Her throat would struggle wildly as a trapped bird. Her eyes would widen, trying to spring free of the vise: one blue eye, one brown.

At once she was there in his mind, complete. Her lips were a natural dark red and very full; they strained back now from her large white perfectly even teeth. Her nose and cheeks were long and thin, gracefully simple. Her red hair rippled as her head swung violently from side to side, uncovering her small delicate ears. He had never seen her before in his life.

He was painting furiously, without wasting time on a preliminary sketch. She wasn't Hilary. Some of his women were: Hilary running in terror across a moor on *Murder by Moonlight,* Hilary suspended in the plight of falling in front of a train (though looking unfortunately like a displaced angel) on *Mind the Doors.* It didn't matter who this woman was. Because she wasn't anybody, of course: she was a fantasy his imagination had released at last, when he needed her. He painted.

When he'd finished he stepped back. It was good, no doubt

about it. She lay between the patches of day and moony night. She might be dead, or might be writhing in the clutch of an invisible attacker; though she was corpse-like, there was still a suggestion of life in her. Standing back, Phil realized that whoever looked at her became the attacker; that was why he'd painted her alone. Her legs were wide beneath the thin dress, her heels digging into invisible ground. Her nipples strained at the white fabric. It was as though she were offering herself for choking.

Eventually he looked away, confused. Usually when he'd finished a cover he felt lightened, hungry, freed of the painting. Now he felt inexplicably tense, and the presence of the painting loitered in his mind, nagging him. He signed the painting Phil, and his attention wandered from the corner back to the woman. Perhaps it was that she was so alluring; his covers of Hilary never had been. He felt an irrational conviction that the woman had somehow been put into his mind, at the precise moment when he was susceptible to her. And why shouldn't she turn me on? he shouted himself down. Only hope it does the same to the readers.

He was still musing vaguely when Hilary came home. "That's good," she said, looking at the cover. "It's really good. But frightening."

"What do you mean, *but* frightening?" he demanded.

He ate dinner tensely. Hilary read his mood and tried to soothe him with her talk, her movements, her silences. Awareness of what she was doing made him more tense. He found he was anxious to photograph the *Throttle* cover and develop the slide with the rest. Of course, that was what was keeping him on edge: the thought of meeting publishers tomorrow. Yet he'd met one of them before; he hadn't been tense then. It must be the anticipated strain of meeting two in one day. He gazed at the victim as he photographed her, and felt his tension ease. With her to show to the publishers he had nothing to worry about. Gladdened and relieved, he hurried to make love to Hilary.

He couldn't raise an erection. He'd masturbated on Friday, when she'd begun her period, but it was Monday now. "Never mind," she said, pushing his head gently away from her thighs. "Tell me about what you did today."

"What do you mean, what I did today? You've seen it, for God's sake! You don't want to hear what a bloody strain it was to paint, do you?"

"If you want to tell me."

"I'd rather forget, thanks." He crawled into bed. "Surely to God you can understand that," he said.

"There was a woman in the shop today wanting to know the best vintages for claret," Hilary said after a while. "I said I'd get the manageress, but she kept saying I ought to know." She went on, something about the end of the year, while a woman reached up to Phil. He tried to make out her face, but she was growing larger, spreading through him, dissolving into his sleep.

"That was remarkable, that murder victim," Damien Smiles said. "Let's see her again."

Phil recalled the slide of the cover for *Throttle*. "That's amazing," Damien said. "If you do anything as good as that for us you'll be our star artist. Listen, if Crescent don't use it we'll get someone to write it a book."

He switched on the light and the basement office flooded back around Phil, startling him out of his euphoria. He wished he hadn't to go on to Crescent Books. Apollo Books were offering him better rates and the security of a series all to himself; even the lunch Damien had bought him was better than Crescent's. But at least Apollo were offering him all the work he could handle. If Crescent didn't increase their offers, they'd had him.

"Something else you might think about," Damien said. "We'll be going in for black magic next year. Take this one to read and see what you can get out of it, no hurry. Awful writing but good sales."

The Truth about Witches and Devils. Phil read snatches of it in the Underground, smiling indulgently. That foulest of secret societies, the coven. Every possible filthy excess diseased minds could conceive. Are today's hippies and beatniks so different? They could have a point there, Phil conceded, with abnormal people like that. Satan's slaves, human and inhuman. The vampire, the werewolf. The succubus. Here was the station for Crescent Books. Phil hurried off, almost leaving the book on the seat.

Crescent Books took the *Throttle* cover and fed him drinks. They were sorry they couldn't increase his fees, sorry to see him go— hoped he would have every success. Phil didn't care that they were lying. He meandered back eventually to Lancaster Gate. With the money that was coming to him he could have afforded a better hotel, if he'd known. Still, all he needed was a bed.

Surveying the rest of his room, he decided the curtains must have been bought secondhand; they were extravagantly thick. He struggled with the window until it developed lockjaw, but the room's heat leaned inertly against the heat outside. He found that if he left even a crack between the curtains, an unerring glare of light from the streetlamp would reach for his face on the immovable bed. He lay naked on top of the bed, amid the hot dense cloud of darkness that filled the room, smelling heavily of cloth and, somewhere, dust. Once or twice a feeble gleam crept between the curtains and was immediately stifled.

It might have been the alcohol, or the disorienting blackout, or the heat; quite possibly all of them. Whatever the reason, the darkness felt as if it were rubbing itself slowly, hotly over him, like a seducer. His penis levered itself jerkily erect. He reached for it, then restrained himself. If he held back now he would have no problem with Hilary tomorrow—except haste, maybe! He smiled at the dark, ignoring his slight discomfort, hoping his erection would subside.

The darkness moved on him, waiting to be noticed. His penis twitched impatiently. Still no, he insisted. He continued to smile, reminiscing; he refused to be distracted from his contentment. And all thanks to the *Throttle* cover, he thought. That was what had sold Apollo on him. At once the slide clicked brightly into place in his mind: the limp helpless body beneath the thin dress. The blue eye and the brown gazed up at him. In his mind he picked up the slide and gratefully kissed the tiny face. Somehow it was like kissing a fairy, except that the face was cold and still. She was receding from him, growing more tiny, drawing him down into darkness, into sleep.

It must be sleep, for suddenly she was struggling beneath the full length of his body. She was trying to drive her knees into his groin, but his thighs had forced her legs wide. His elbows knelt on her forearms; her hands wriggled as though impaled. His hands were at her throat, squeezing, and her eyes welcomed him, urging him on. He closed his mouth over hers as she choked; her tongue struggled wildly beneath his. He drove himself urgently between her legs. As he entered her, her genitals gave the gasp for which her mouth was striving. He drove deep a half-a-dozen times, then was trying to hold back, remembering Hilary: too late, too late. He bit the pillow savagely as he came.

Next day, on the train home to Liverpool, he was preoccupied. Trees sailed by, turning to display further intricacies, slowly glittering green in the sunlight. He should have saved his orgasm for Hilary. He was sure she looked forward to sex; they were closest then, when he could give all his time to her. He had the impression, from odd things that she'd said but which he couldn't now remember, that she wasn't entirely happy working at the wine shop—all the more reason for her to value sex. But he couldn't always manage two erections in twenty-four hours: particularly when, now he tested himself, even the most elaborate fantasy of Hilary couldn't arouse him. Still, there was no point in blaming himself. After all, he had been half-asleep, susceptible. The theme of last night's fantasy didn't bother him; it wasn't as if it had been real. In fact, that was all the more a tribute to the conviction of his painting. Unzipping his case, he turned from the streaming grain of the fields to *The Truth about Witches and Devils*.

A few miles later the cover was ready in his mind: a nude woman resting one hand on the head of a smoldering gleeful snake. Her genitals were hidden by something akin to the reptilian stage of a human embryo, appearing between her legs, conceivably being born between them. In her free hand she held a wand with a tip like a sparkling glans. He read the briefs on the Apollo crime series and began to plan the covers, though he had yet to see the books. His mind urged the scurrying of the wheels as he finished each cover: hurry up quick, hurry up quick.

Hilary must have been waiting for him; she opened the door of the flat. "Did it go well?" she said eagerly, already having read his face.

"Yes, very well," he said. "Very well," and hurried into his studio.

He was painting by the time she brought the coffee; she stood watching, hovering at the edge of his attention, nagging silently at him like a difficult statement whose difficulty grew with silence. Perhaps something of the sort was keeping her there but for God's sake, he hadn't time now. "Thanks," he said for the coffee. "Just put it there. Not there, damn it, there!" He could feel his temper slipping. Not now, please not now, not when he had so much to paint: bloody woman, get out. He painted with deliberate intensity for a minute, then he realized with relief that Hilary had gone.

If she had wanted to say something she didn't take the chance to say it at dinner, which had to be postponed twice while he painted out the last of his ideas. "Sorry I spoiled dinner," he said, then tried to step back from his *faux pas*: "I mean, it's very good. Sorry I kept you waiting." He told her about Crescent and Apollo, but didn't quote Damien Smiles; he realized he would be embarrassed to repeat the praise to anyone, except to himself as encouragement. "What did he say?" she asked, and Phil said "That he wanted me to do some work for them."

As he'd feared, he couldn't summon an erection. When Hilary realized she ceased caressing him. Her genitals subsided, and she lay quiet. Come on, help me, he thought, good God! No wonder he couldn't will life into his penis. At that moment there seemed to be less life in Hilary than in the strangled woman. She turned on her side above the sheets to sleep, holding his hand on her stomach. With his free hand he turned out the light. Once she was asleep he rolled quickly away from her. He heard their bodies separate stickily. In the summer humidity she'd felt hot and swollen, tacky, actually repulsive.

When he entered his studio next morning to photograph the covers, he gasped. The woman with the blue and brown eyes was waiting for him, four of her.

He had painted so intensely that he hadn't realized what he'd done. He was bewildered, unnerved. She gazed at him four times simultaneously: wicked, submissive, murderous, cunning. So why need he feel disturbed? He wasn't repeating himself at all. The woman brought life into his paintings, but also infinite variety. The ease with which he'd painted these covers proved that.

He photographed a group of earlier unpublished covers to show Damien next time they met, then he went into his darkroom, behind the partition, to develop the slides. The red glow hung darkly about him like the essence of the summer heat made visible, not like light at all. The tiny faces swam up from it, gazing at Phil. He remembered kissing the slide. That was the truth of the woman, that cover; all the others were derivations. He remembered strangling her.

He was strangling her. Her body raised itself to meet him, almost lifting him from the floor; her throat arched up toward him, offering itself. The breathless working of her mouth sucked his tongue deeper, her struggles drew his penis into her. Suddenly all of her went limp. That's it, he thought, stop now, wait for tonight, for Hilary. But he had only begun to stoop to peer at the slides, in order to distract himself, when the orgasm flooded him.

He leaned weakly against the partition. This must stop. It wasn't fair to Hilary. But how could he stop it, without risking his new and better work? Depression was thickening about him when the doorbell rang. It was the postman.

The parcel contained five American crime novels. We're considering reprints, Damien's letter told him. If you can give us your best for them that should swing it. Phil shook his head, amazed and pleased. He made himself coffee before sitting down to read the first of the books. He took the letter into his studio, then carried it back into the living-room: Hilary might like to see it.

"That's good, isn't it?" she said when she came home.

"It's promising," he said. "I'll be with you in a few minutes. Just let me finish this chapter."

He was painting the second of the covers, afternoons later, when the underbelly of a storm filled the sky. He painted rapidly, squinting, too impatient to leave the painting in order to switch on the light. But the marshy dark swallowed the cover, as if someone were standing behind him, deliberately throwing a shadow to force him to notice them.

As he hurried irritably to the light-switch he realized that was no use; if he switched on the light now he wouldn't be able to paint. There was something he had to do first, an insistent demand deep in his mind. What, then? What, for God's sake? The limp body rose toward him, offering its throat. Don't be absurd, he thought. But he couldn't argue with his intuition, not while he was painting. He took hold of his penis, which stiffened at once. Afterward he painted easily, swiftly, as the storm plodded crashing away beyond his light.

The August evening faded gently: gold, then pearl, merging with night. Hilary was reading *Forum*, the sex education magazine, which she had recently taken to buying. Phil was dutifully finishing *Necromancers in the Night*. When he glanced up, he realized that Hilary had been gazing at him for some time. "Aren't you ever going to paint anyone except that woman?" she said.

"There's bound to be a book sometime that needs a man."

When he looked up again impatiently she said "Aren't we going to have a holiday this year?"

"Depends on whether the work eases off. I don't want to leave it when it's going so well."

"The atmosphere at the shop's terrible. It's getting worse."

"Well, we'll see," he said, to satisfy her.

"Don't you want to go away with me?"

"If you let me finish my work! Jesus!" All right, he thought. Let's talk this out once and for all. "I want to finish what I'm doing before I see Damien next month," he said. "He likes my stuff. The more I can show him the better. I've got some ideas he might be able to use. He was talking before about getting writers to do books around covers. Right? So don't say I never tell you about my work. Just let me finish what I'm doing, all right? I'd like a chance to relax sometime too, you know."

"You don't even talk to me at weekends now," she said.

Well, go on, he thought irritably. She said nothing more, but gazed at him. "This *is* the weekend!" he shouted. "Have I just been talking to myself? Jesus!" He stormed away, into his studio.

But Hilary was there too; her photograph was, gazing at him mildly, tenderly. He avoided the unassailable gaze. He knew what was wrong, of course. They hadn't had sex for almost three months.

He threw the book into his chair. God knows he'd tried with Hilary. Perhaps he'd tried too hard. Each time there had been a gray weight in his mind, weighing down his limp penis. As the weeks passed Hilary had herself become less and less aroused; she'd lain slack on the bed, waiting to be certain she could say "Never mind" without enraging him. Occasionally she'd been violently passionate, but he had been sure she was manufacturing passion, and the feeling had simply made him more irritable. For the last few weeks they hadn't even bothered with the motions; she had begun reading *Forum*. All right, he thought, if it kept her happy.

He was happy enough. Each time he failed with her he would masturbate later. He needed only a hint to bring him to the boil: the sleek submissive throat, the thin dress ready to be torn down, the struggling body beneath him, the invitation hidden in the blue eye and the brown, hardly hidden now. The first time he had masturbated wildly in bed; he had been on the brink of orgasm when Hilary had moaned and rolled over, groping for his hand. He'd held his twitching penis as if it were a struggling creature that might break free and betray him. When she'd quietened he had inched his hand out of hers and had hastened to the bathroom, barely in time. He always crept there now when Hilary was asleep, carrying his victim with him, in the dark.

He felt no guilt. If he were frustrated he couldn't paint. He'd felt guilty the first time; the next night he'd failed with Hilary he'd lain for hours, refusing to think of the woman in his dream, trying to clear his mind, to let sleep in. In the morning he'd been on edge, had spilled paint, had broken a brush; the inside of his head had felt like dull slippery tin. He had never risked controlling himself after that, nor could his work afford the luxury of guilt.

But he did feel guilty. He was lying to himself, and that was no use; the lurking guilt would only spoil his work eventually—sometimes he felt he was painting to outrun it. Hilary made him feel guilty, with her issues of *Forum*. You read those things as a substitute, he told himself. But that wasn't why she left them lying around. She scattered them in the hope that he would read them, learn what was wrong with him. Nothing was wrong with him! Sex wasn't everything. Jesus! He was rushing from success to success, why couldn't she just share in that? Why was she threatening to spoil it, by her pleading silence?

As he glared at her, at her tenderness trapped beneath glazed light, he remembered kissing the slide.

He had never kissed Hilary's photograph. Yet she was at least as responsible for his success. It was she who made the effort to stay out of his way while he was working, so as not to distract him; and the job she'd taken for this reason was clearly less enjoyable than his. Yet he had never thanked her. He stepped forward awkwardly and, resting his palms against the wall, kissed her photograph. The glass flattened his lips coldly. He stepped back, feeling thoroughly absurd.

So he'd kissed her photograph. Well done. Now go to her. But he knew what frustration that would lead to. He couldn't give up the victim of his dream; even if he did, there was no reason to suppose that would reunite him with Hilary. Maybe, he thought— no more directly involved with the idea than he had been with the novels of which it was a cliché—he could see an analyst, have

Hilary substituted back in his mind. But not now, when he needed his dream for his work. Which meant that he couldn't go to Hilary. He had learned that he couldn't have both Hilary and his dream.

Then his eyes opened wider than her eyes beneath the glass. Unless he had Hilary and the dream simultaneously.

The solution was so simple it took his mind a moment to catch up. Then he hurried out of the studio, down the hall. He knew he could do it; the strength of his imagination would carry him through. As he hurried, he realized that his haste wasn't like the urgency of needing to paint; it was more as if he had to act swiftly, before someone noticed. That slowed him for a moment, but then he was in the living-room. "Come on," he said to Hilary.

She looked up from her magazine, puzzled but ready to understand. "What is it?" she said.

"Come on," he said rapidly, "please."

He propped himself beside her on the bed and began to caress her. The intermittent breathing of the curtains gently imitated his fumbling. When she lay smiling hopefully, knees up and wide— smiling bravely, infuriatingly, he thought—he began again, systematically stroking her: her neck, her back, her buttocks, her breasts. Veins trailed beneath the pale skin of her breasts, like traces of trickles of ink; a hair grew from one aureole. At last she began to respond.

He stroked her thighs, thinking: woman struggling beneath me, eager to be choked. He coaxed out Hilary's clitoris. Her thighs rolled, revealing blue veins. He thought: sleek throat straining up for my hands. It wasn't going to work. All he could see was Hilary. When she reached for his limp penis her hand was hard, rough, rubbing insensitively, unpleasantly. He almost pushed her hand away to make room for his own.

Suddenly he said "Wait, I'll turn out the light."

"Don't you want to see me?"

"Not that," he said urgently, irritably. He hadn't much time, he didn't know why. He must be near orgasm without feeling so. "It might help," he said.

The dark gave him the woman at once. She was lying helpless, and immediately was fighting him off to draw him on. Her tongue was writhing about her lips, eager to be squeezed out farther; her dress slipped back over her stomach as her hips clutched high for him. She struggled violently as his penis found her. Somewhere he could feel himself working within Hilary. The sense of division distracted him. There was a barrier between him and his orgasm. He was going to fail.

Then he found himself thrusting deep within the woman. Her throat was still; so was the rest of her. Only his furious excitement moved her, making her roll slackly around his penis as he quickened. Yet he knew there was life within her somewhere, for otherwise she couldn't return to him, as she always did. The thought made her lifelessness all the more exciting; he drove brutally into her, challenging her to stay lifeless. But she was still limp when he came. When he heard himself shouting, he became aware of Hilary's gasps too.

She didn't even blink when he switched on the light. She was staring up at him in exhausted gratitude. He felt enormously pleased with himself. He loved her.

When Phil boarded the Underground train he was preoccupied.

There was tension in him somewhere. There had been since he'd succeeded with Hilary. Since that night he had determined never to masturbate. But the first time he had entered his darkened room he'd succumbed. Since then he had used a commercial firm of developers, though it was more costly, and had restricted his dream to his sex with Hilary. The woman was still there in his new paintings, of course, though she had begun to look more purposeful, consistently menacing.

Perhaps that was the source of his tension. No, it wasn't that. He suspected the source was Hilary. He was sure she was happy now he could make love to her; certainly he was. But he'd sensed a tension in her whenever he'd mentioned this trip to London, as if she disliked the idea, almost as if she were suspicious of him.

He'd begun to feel something disturbing would happen to him in London. Rubbish. She felt he shouldn't be going away so much when he hadn't promised her a holiday, that was all. Well, maybe they could manage one after all.

He glanced up, and discovered that in his preoccupation he'd sat opposite a girl in an otherwise empty carriage.

She was staring at him. Her head swayed with the rocking of the carriage, her glossy black shoulder-length hair swung against her cheeks, but her brown eyes were still. They stared at him in undistinguished challenge. You dare, they threatened. Within the sheath of her thin short skirt her thighs clung together, clipped but rubbing softly, inadvertently. She reminded him—her expression particularly—of the woman in his dream.

He couldn't get up now. That would look even more suspicious. Besides, she had no reason to suspect him: he wasn't going to let her will him to move. He felt uncomfortably hot, frustratingly tense. The wind through the Underground seemed to touch the September heat of the train not at all; the heat pressed on him, oppressive as the grimy yellow light. He toyed with the zipper of his case, gladly aware of the slides within, while the girl gazed at him. He was still distracting himself when, at the edge of his eye, a shape leapt past him and then past the girl.

He stared and met her gaze. She must have seen what it was, although he had seen nothing but movement. But the challenge in her eyes remained unchanged, and he felt she wasn't pretending not to have noticed. Perhaps the movement had been an aberration of the lights. As he thought so, the lights of the carriage went out.

Phil grabbed his case to him with both hands. He was rushing forward, borne by clattering hollow darkness. For the first time he was aware of the girl's breathing, rapid, harsh. It was near his face, too near. He had just realized that when her nails jabbed into his shoulders.

She was struggling with him. She was fighting him off. Yet he knew that if she were genuinely afraid of him she would have groped away down the carriage, however painfully. She was fighting him so that he could find her. The force of her struggles, the jerking of the train, threw him on top of her on the seat. Her arms were flailing at his face, but not so viciously that he couldn't trap her wrists in one hand. His penis was pounding. With his free hand he dragged up her skirt.

He could see her now, could see the welcome in the blue eye and the brown. That wasn't her. It didn't matter. That was the woman he was raping. The swaying of the train rolled her violently on his penis. He came almost at once.

He was lying face down on the seat, and she had somehow vanished from beneath him, when the lights flickered on.

He was still gasping: but the girl was standing at the other end of the carriage, gazing at him in open disgust. Her hand was on the communication cord. It didn't seem possible that she could have moved so far so quickly. At the next station she left the train, or at least changed carriages, leaving him a last contemptuous glance.

He sat with his case on his lap, retrieving his emotions. He was stunned. He'd read of women who needed to pretend to be raped, in Hilary's *Forum*, but he had never expected to encounter it. It could only happen in London, he thought.

He didn't feel ashamed. Why should he? Once she'd touched him his orgasm had been inevitable; he couldn't have prevented it. If anything he felt self-righteously pleased. Despite her pretense of contempt, it had been she who had approached him. She hadn't been a fantasy, a self-indulgence, but a real woman. He was concerned only that she might have infected him. But he didn't think so; she had looked clean, no doubt she needed to be especially clean to keep up her pretense. When he reached the station for Apollo Books he was smiling. There was no need for Hilary to know; he would be able to satisfy her too.

"Here are some of your covers printed," Damien said. "People have been saying good things about them."

Phil smiled and admired the covers while Damien examined the

new slides. "I'm sure we can get some books for these," Damien
said. "They're the Phil woman again, I see."

Phil smiled more broadly, amazed at himself. He'd always tried
to paint as well as he could, but he'd never realized that he wanted
to be recognized for a personal style. Now Damien had shown
him—no, the woman of his dream had shown him. He was kissing
the slide.

"Will you have time to see a film tomorrow?" Damien said. "I
want to get a book out of it, and I'd like you to do the cover. I'll
fix it with the film people for you to go. *Father Malarkey's Succubus*,
it's called. It's French."

They went out to a nearby pub. Phil was pleased he got on so
well with Damien, despite the man's long hair and mauve silk shirt.
Afterward Phil wandered about the shops, buying himself a book
of nudes, and an Indian necklace for Hilary; she liked Indian paintings. Then he had dinner at his hotel, after enjoying his private
shower-bath.

Oddly, he found that most of all about his room he enjoyed the
light which penetrated the pale curtains. Indeed, he left the bedside lamp on that night. He was unwilling to sleep in the dark.
Perhaps it was just the strangeness of luxury. He felt too euphoric
to spoil his mood by pondering. He lay smiling, remembering the
girl on the train, until he fell asleep.

Next morning he misjudged the trains; the supporting film was
under way when he arrived at the cinema. He could no more piece
a film together that way than he would begin reading a book in
the middle; he strolled around Soho, and bought the latest *Forum*.
Hilary wouldn't have been able to buy it yet in their local news-
agent's.

"I'm Phil Barker," he told the girl in the pay-box. "You're expecting me." She called a doorman to usher him past the queue,
to the manager's office. This treatment pleased him immensely; it
was part of his success. The manager, a dapper man with a black
moustache shiny as his dress shoes, gave Phil a glossy folder of
information about the film, which had originally been called *Le*

Succube du Père Michel and had run four minutes longer, revised in ballpoint. The director had previously made *Le Chant des Peto-manes*. The manager asked Phil about his work. "I'm best known for my women," Phil began. Eventually it was time for the film.

It took place in a small rather featureless film studio, scattered with stateless anachronisms. Father Malarkey, a French priest trans-lated into American Irish, was lusting after the nuns in the nearby convent. Frustrated, he began to masturbate. Stop that, the censor said, snipping. Afterward, when the priest went to bathe, his stained robe started jigging about his room; eventually a girl's face faded into the cowl, grinning gleefully. Bejesus, now what's this, he said the first time she visited him in bed. I want to confess, she said. Not here, he protested, huddling beneath the blankets. But otherwise I'll have nothing to confess, she pouted, slipping her hand under the uncontrollably rising blankets. That's enough, the censor said. Her name was Lilith; she visited him every night, encouraging him to rape her, spank her, and so on. Later, when he succeeded in sneaking into the convent, she forced her way be-tween him and his unseeing bedmates. Eventually the priest en-tered the cell of two entangled nuns. Now look here, the censor said. Discovered, the priest and Mother Superior were defrocked and, disapprovingly, married. But Lilith clung to his other arm. As far as Phil was concerned she had one blue eye and one brown. He could see the cover now.

He sat and waited for *The Fall of the Roman Knickers*. An ush-erette was chasing a cat which persisted in sharpening its claws on the purple furry walls. Though it was a small cinema, one of a unit of four, the cat was eluding pursuit. An old man snarled and hurled an ice-cream carton at it. The usherette stopped to remonstrate, and Phil began to leaf through *Forum*. The secret sexuality of the outsize woman. Sex can prevent heart attacks. Rub him up the right way. He turned to the letters, which he liked reading best; they made him glad to be normal. A heading caught his attention at once: *Promiscuous painter?*

My husband paints pictures. Until recently he used to paint
me. Then he began painting a woman I have never met, and
now he paints nobody else. He often goes away on business
trips, and I'm sure he met this woman on the last one he
took before he began to paint her. I know it is a real woman
because her eyes are different colors

No, Phil thought numbly. No, no.

and he must have based that on someone real. He still makes
love to me—more passionately, if anything—although he
was impotent for a while after meeting her, which must have
been caused by guilt. Now I feel he is thinking of her even
when he makes love to me. What can I do to keep him? I
would never leave him.

H.B.
(Address withheld by request)

Oh Christ, Phil thought. Tell her it isn't true. Don't make her
believe it. She's wrong, tell her. The lights were fading. He peered
desperately at the reply.

*If you have no more evidence of your husband's "affair" than you
describe in your letter, I really don't think you have much to worry
about. You say you are sure he is thinking of the woman in his
paintings when he makes love to you; does this really mean that
you feel estranged from him when he paints? Perhaps, since apparently you can't ask him where he got his idea for his painting,
you need to involve yourself more in his work. (I assume it is his
work, rather than a hobby.)*

   *As for the woman herself—our artists tell me they would be
very surprised and bewildered if anyone thought they had affairs
with all the women they paint! Doesn't your husband use his
imagination in his work? Then why, if he had a particularly good*

*inspiration and wants to make the most of it, does it have to be
based on some unknown rival? I suspect that you see the woman
as a rival simply because she is unlike you, or unlike your image
of yourself (the two aren't always the same, you know). If you
are sure your husband isn't involved with you in your love-
making, perhaps sameness is to blame. Is there some fantasy he
would like you to act out? If you become*

But the page had dragged his head forward and down into the
darkness. He started, completely disoriented. He was floating forward on the darkness, sailing toward a band of chattering men
running through the dark Roman streets. He clung to *Forum*, to
his case, to anything. He was at the mercy of the waves of darkness.
He couldn't think. He must get out. He was preparing to stand up
when something caught his leg.

He looked down. In the dark, amid the crumpled cartons and
the spilled ash sticking to stains of orange juice, a woman was
reaching up to him. Her nails tore at his hands, pulling him down
among the cigarette butts, into the secret darkness. Her dress was
up; her thighs yawned on the dusty floorboards; her head lolled on
the bruised snapped neck. "Jesus!" he screamed. "Get away!"

The usherette's torch-beam swung toward him along the row.
At his feet the floor was bare; nothing moved but the shadows of
rubbish. "It was the cat," he stammered. "I didn't know what it
was." He stumbled out. Of course it had been the cat; no wonder
he had turned it into his dream, after what he'd read. He'd dropped
Forum beneath the seat. Thank God, he thought. He must reach
Hilary before it did. She mustn't think he'd read it and was taking
her on holiday to deceive her. There was time.

The train was nearing Liverpool when Phil realized how like the
succubus his experience had been.

Exactly like. Well, no, not exactly: of course there weren't such
things. But his dream had come between him and Hilary, just as
the succubus had behaved in the film. It was almost as if it had

been deliberately blinding him to her. When he tried to visualize Hilary he could reach nothing but a dull blank in his mind.

The dream had come from inside him. He had to remember that. The notion he had had originally, that it had been put into his mind, was nonsense. That must have been his mind, trying not to admit the truth. Since the dream had come from him, he could destroy it. What they advised in *Forum* was wrong, that you should act out your fantasies; that was wrong.

All at once he saw how much of a mute appeal Hilary's issues of *Forum* had been. He felt admiration and compassion; she suffered a good deal, without burdening him with it. Only because he wouldn't let her speak! My God, he thought numbly. With that insight came another. She didn't go out to work so that he could paint undisturbed. That was a sentimental lie. She went out in order to stay away from his temper. He'd driven her out of the house.

He felt lightened by his insights, buoyant, capable of anything. At last he could see Hilary as she was. But he couldn't; still there was only the dull blank. Overhead the rush hour traffic clogged the bridge. Deep in his mind there seemed to be a gray vague weight, waiting. Never mind. Once they were on holiday the last of his depression would lift. No time to think further. Here was Lime Street Station, home.

At the flat he packed their cases. He'd booked their hotel before leaving London. When he'd finished he glanced at his watch. Hilary would finish work in an hour; tonight was early closing. They could catch a train at once. He took a taxi to the shop, amid the Jaguars and Japanese front gardens.

The shop was open for half an hour yet. He was sure they'd let Hilary go when they saw the taxi waiting. He could see her behind the counter, watching a woman who was talking to the manageress. Good; he wouldn't have to wait to speak to Hilary. He strode into the shop.

"This is absolutely ridiculous," the woman was saying loudly.

"That woman knows nothing about her job. If you're so hard up for staff my daughter is looking for work."

Only when he saw Hilary's expression—mutely furious, ashamed—did he realize the woman was talking about her. "That's my wife you're insulting," he said.

The woman turned to examine him. "Then your wife is igno-rant," she said.

"Not ignorant where it counts, like you." He tried to hold onto his temper, but couldn't deny himself the pleasure. "Go on, you fucking old whore," he shouted.

The woman whirled and stalked out. "There's the taxi," he told Hilary. "Your holiday begins right now."

"Do you want me to lose this job?"

"We can do without it. Come on," he said, restraining his irri-tability. "Don't you want to go to the Lakes?"

She smiled as broadly as she could. "Yes, I do," she said. She was about to speak to the manageress, but he headed her off. "The least you could have done was stick up for her," he told the woman. "You've been paying her little enough, God knows."

In the taxi Hilary said "I told you I was going to give that job until the end of the year."

"I never heard you."

"You never hear anything I say."

He gazed at the taxi-driver's attentive neck and succeeded in focusing his irritability there. "I know I've been drifting away," he told Hilary. "I'm sorry." He said loudly, "I'm going to get close to you tonight."

It was still light when they reached the hotel. Streamers of mist were caught in the branches on the hilltops; a mass of mist was groping down toward the nearby lake. From their window Phil could see perfect trees in the lake, reaching down into the sunset water. The corridors were thickly carpeted: hushed, gentle. He read the same feelings in Hilary. He felt she had had to make an effort to be happy—to forget the scene in the shop, of course. Never mind; she was happy now.

They were late for dinner, but somebody cooked them a meal. They had a cobwebbed bottle of wine. Afterward they drank in the bar and played billiards, which they hadn't played since before their marriage. When the bar closed they went up to their room. The corridor closed softly about them.

Phil gazed into the night. The mist had reached the road now, greedy for headlights. It felt like the gray blank that was still in his mind. He tried to grasp the blank, but it wouldn't come out until it was ready. He turned as Hilary emerged from the bathroom naked and lay down on the bed. Quickly drawing the curtains, he smiled at her. He smiled. He smiled. He felt no desire at all.

"Are you going to get close to me now?" she said.

He nodded. "Yes, I am," he said hurriedly, lest she sense his mood. Undressing, he gazed at her. Her breasts lay slack, faintly blue-veined; the golden hair still grew from one. The gray blank hung between his penis and his mind. He had to make love to her without the dream. If he relied on the dream it would estrange them further, he was sure. But so, he realized miserably, would failure.

"Will you leave the light on?" she said.

"Of course I will," he said, but not for her reason.

She smiled up at him. "Do you want to do anything different?" she said.

"Like what?"

"I don't know. I just thought you might."

At once he knew what he'd seen back home at the flat as he'd packed: a copy of *Forum* lying on the settee. It had been a copy of the issue he had bought in London. In his hurry he hadn't realized. She had read the reply to her letter.

She gazed up, waiting. His mouth worked, suddenly dry. Should he tell her he knew? Then he would have to explain about the dream—to tell her everything. He couldn't; it would hurt her, he was sure. And he didn't need to. She had already suggested the solution. His penis was stirring, and so was the gray blank. "I'll rape you," he told Hilary.

He knelt above her. "Go on, then," she said, laughing.

That wasn't right. If she laughed it wouldn't work. "Put your legs together," he said. "Fight. Try as hard as you can to stop me."

"I don't want to hurt you."

The gray was returning, seeping through his mind; his penis was shrinking. "Don't worry about that," he said urgently. "Defend yourself any way you can." His penis was hanging down. God, no. He pinched her nipple sharply. As she cried out and brought her hands down to protect it, he seized both her wrists. "Now then," he said, already inflamed again, thrusting his knees between hers.

She was struggling now. The bed creaked wildly; the sheets snapped taut beneath them as her heels sought purchase. She had ceased playing; she was trying to free her hands, gasping. His hand plunged roughly between her legs. In a moment she was ready. This is the way she liked it, he thought, and he'd never known.

On the lip of her, he hesitated. The gray blank was still there in his mind, like a threat. He could hear people in the corridor, the television in the next room, the cars setting off into the mist, intruding on his passion, distracting him. He was sure his penis was about to dwindle.

Then he knew what he'd omitted. He dragged Hilary's hands up to her shoulders and, digging his elbows into her forearms, closed his fingers tightly on her throat. She was panting harshly. The sound of her breath tugged him violently into her. The presence was gone from his mind at once. His penis pulsed faster with each stroke, his fingers pressed, her eyes widened as his penis throbbed, her hands fluttered. He strained his head back, gasping.

Like the sound of a branch underfoot betraying the presence of an intruder, there was a sharp snap.

He came immediately, lengthily. His breath shuddered out of him. His hands let go of Hilary and clawed at the sheets. He closed his eyes as he finished, drawing deep breaths.

When he looked down Hilary was gazing at the wall. One cheek rested on the sheet; her head hung askew on her broken neck.

Phil began to sob. He took her cheeks in both hands and turned her face up to him. He rubbed her cheeks, trying to warm life back into her eyes. He stroked her hair back from her eyes, for it lay uncomfortably over them. He grasped her shoulders, shaking them. When her head rolled back onto its cheek he slumped on her body, grinding his fists into his eyes, moaning.

Then her legs closed over his, and he stared down to see her eyes gazing up at him: one blue eye, one brown.

LILITH'S

PALIN MUST HAVE NOTICED the shop shortly after it opened. He rode home that way every weekday evening. The district depressed him; its sameness did—the same colorless tower blocks everywhere on the slope above the river, the same slow procession of derelict terraces as the bus ground uphill, the same hostilities scrawled on walls, attacking the nearby travelers' camp. The January rain on the glass of the bus made the view worse, more the same: the houses were smudged brown blotches, the boards in their windows were bedraggled slashes of dark crayon; huge pale unsteady lumps of tower-blocks floated past. Palin sat swathed in layers of tobacco-smoke, coughing; the driver had driven him upstairs when he'd tried to stand, bloody little Hitler. The bus throbbed throatily at a stop. As Palin glanced about, trying to blink the smarting from his eyes, he caught sight of an unfamiliar protrusion on a terraced house, like a railway signal at STOP but written on: the streaming letters said— The bus shook itself and breasted the headlong rain.

The next day the gray sky was saving up its rain. LILITH'S, Palin read before the bus whipped the sign away. The window of the terraced house contained a display; many of its neighbors were plugged with bricks or boards. The main road framed the side street with an anonymous dilapidated shop and an abandoned gap-toothed WO LWO TH'S. Palin craned back as the progress of the bus closed the side street. What on earth was that in the window beneath the sign?

For the rest of January he made sure he sat upstairs, on the right side. He opened the window to clear the glass, despite the protests of coughing smokers. If the bus failed to stop by the street, angry frustration welled in him, threatening to explode his silence—it felt like his impotence with Emily. The morning journeys began to frustrate him too, for then the bus used another road, higher up the slope. But even when the bus dawdled, and daylight spread further into the evenings, Palin couldn't make out what was sitting in that window.

It looked something like a person. It sat pinkly in the display, wearing a woman's black underwear. Around it were books, posters, vaguer objects. Perhaps it was only a mannequin—of course that was what it must be. But why did it have a huge white blossom in place of a head?

In March, determined to know, he got off the bus opposite the shop.

It was only two stops before his. Nevertheless he'd had to argue himself off the bus. It was a long walk home, his mind had reminded him. He didn't like the area, he just wanted to rest after wrestling with people's taxes and their complaints all day; it was raining, it was absurd to give in to his impulse. One evening he'd determined to get off, but his arguments had carried him past the stop. The next day, despite drizzle, he hustled himself to the doors of the bus.

Beneath the bus stop's metal flag he felt isolated, faintly ridiculous. Among the paved paths between the tower blocks rectangles of unkempt grass lay juicily stranded, like life thrown away by a sea. Children spied on him from concrete balconies. A doll with a trampled head lay at the foot of a stack of balconies; the doll's mouth was burst wide. Down the slope men plodded home, stopping to threaten the travelers' camp.

Palin crossed the road. On one corner of the side street, within the anonymous shop, a dog biscuit lay on bare boards, gathering dust. He hurried along the blinded terrace. LILITH's signal waved him on, gesturing in the moist wind. The pink figure sat waiting, its face lost in white convolutions like coral.

It wasn't a mannequin. It was a Love Mate; the carton against which it rested said so. Its title on the carton was clumsily stenciled, but its limbs and body were well-shaped, even attractive if that kind of thing attracted you. Its head was wrapped in tissue paper.

Palin shrugged wryly. At least he knew now; it wouldn't bother him again. Behind the display he could see what looked very much like the front room of a terraced house, patched with astrological posters. Bare floorboards supported a counter of bare boards, piles of books about witchcraft, odd objects beneath cloth; on a book a girl held a carved man toward the carving's living subject, who stumbled toward her, glassy-eyed. There was something deeper in the dimness, Palin saw, between the books and Tarot decks and phallic ornaments. It was a girl, dim beyond the counter. Her large dark eyes gazed from her heart-shaped face. Her beauty shivered through him.

What beauty? He could hardly see her. He shook his head, frowning. He didn't intend to be lured in. He'd had enough of feminine allure, that promised but frustrated; he'd had enough with Emily. So stop gazing at this dim girl. He was still trying to see what was so beautiful about her when something tapped him on the shoulder.

Only rain. But when he turned, a man was staring at him from the steps of the house opposite, front-door key in hand. As he gazed at Palin, his expression burned with hatred and disgust. Palin tried to stare him out, then strode toward the main road; he felt the stare following him. At the road he looked back. The man was staring at the shop now, a crusader in dirty overalls; his stance was a furious threat.

A fortnight later Palin returned to the shop.

It was spring, it was pleasant to walk home a little way. If he got off the bus here he needn't sit upstairs, suffering smoke for the sake of a glance. He might see a present for Emily in the shop. None of these was his real reason. For a fortnight he had been trying to fathom what had made the girl so beautiful.

It wasn't just her large eyes, her small softly rounded heart-shaped face. Then what? He never saw her body; she always wore a long dress and the dimness. Her full lips and her eyes smiled at him, an encouraging smile, promising, mysterious. Promising what, for heaven's sake? He snorted at his eager fantasies. But the next evening he went back, peering for her slight smile.

Often he was watched from the house opposite. Once, when children stood in an alley to gaze at the shop, the man rushed out and chased them away. Sometimes Palin saw the man's head displayed in a small upstairs window above the front door, a hostile Toby jug. Let him try to chase Palin away, just let him try.

But it was absurd, this fascination. What could come of it? Traffic droned along the main road, dust and fumes swirled. Perhaps he should buy Emily a present and be done with the shop. She'd been aloof from him today—her period, no doubt, some such excuse. Among the plain-wrapped books—*Joy of the Body, Glory of the Flesh*—and unlabeled vials and what he guessed from the coy pictures on their closed boxes to be penis candles, Palin saw several packs of Tarot cards. They were the kind of thing she might like. He didn't: too inexplicable, unpredictable.

No. He wouldn't buy her a present for being moody. When she was friendlier, maybe. If she ever was. He and Emily were drifting apart, slowly as flight in a nightmare, each making timid attempts to break it off, giving hints of impatience and boredom; neither was willing to make a decisive move. He couldn't be sure they had drifted too far to reunite. But it was so much work, judging her moods, trying to keep her happy, to know what she was thinking. It was always work, with women. The girl gazed smiling from deep in the shop.

That was the girl's appeal. He gasped; his face hung open-mouthed on the window. She wasn't like Emily, she hadn't encouraged him only to make him struggle to please her. She simply waited, displaying her smile on the velvety dimness, an intimate smile if he wanted it to be. She would be willing, anxious to please, peaceful and quiet and submissive. She was there if he wanted her. All that was in her smile, her eyes.

Nonsense. It was only his fantasy. For a moment he wondered whether she had fantasies. She was always sitting behind the counter in the dimness; what could she think all day? But it would be wonderful to have a woman who would do exactly what he wanted, whenever he wanted it. Like the Love Mate. Oh no. He didn't need that sort of thing.

Why not?

His answers to that seemed weaker each day. On the neck of the figure was a bulb of coralline convolutions, as if white brains had boiled from the head: but beyond that shock the body was beautiful—the long slim arms and delicate hands, the smooth thighs mysteriously closed, the round full breasts that he was sure were clothed for decency, not for support. The figure looked soft, not rubbery at all; even the pink flesh no longer looked unnatural, simply new, young, virgin. The girl's body beneath the long dress could be no more beautiful. It was as if she veiled herself in the dimness the better to display her body in the window.

He couldn't. It wasn't the florid glaring Toby jug that held him back; but he couldn't go into the shop and ask. Asking a girl would be all the more difficult. She knew whose face was beneath the blossom of tissue paper; somehow that would be most disturbing of all. But to have a body waiting when he came home, ready for whatever he'd worked up during the day—He'd feel absurd, a fool. He listened to his mind debating, astonished. That he, of all people, should be trying to counter argument with feelings! The girl's face flickered softly on the dimness, smiling.

It was Emily who decided him.

He'd invited her home to cook dinner. She had offered him dinner at her flat earlier that week, but he found her flat intimidating: the old warmly dark furniture, inherited or bargained for in obscure shops; a huge soft smiling lion; Kafka, Mick Jagger, *The*

Story of O, women's magazines for recipes, *Taxes: the Journal of the Inland Revenue Staff Federation*, *The Magus*—too many contradictions, they bewildered him. He blamed her flat for inhibiting him sexually.

The first time there he'd been too eager; he had barely entered her before ejaculating. Then for weeks his erections had dwindled nervously; her flat had watched like a crowd of critics. When he managed erections again he felt sure Emily was growing bored with his lack of consistent rhythm, the time he took to come—sometimes she was dry before he came. In his house he felt easier, more in command.

But he hadn't felt easier this time. All day Emily had kept glancing at him from her desk. He sensed that she wanted to call off their evening; perhaps she was waiting for him to give her the chance. He avoided talking to her, except briefly.

On the bus they were silent. Around them conversations shifted beneath the laboring of the bus. LILITH's signaled, then sank back into the side street. Bricks of Palin's house glowed orange, painted amid the dark terrace. The hall carpet welcomed him, borrowing orange from the Chinese lampshade.

They'd planned an elaborate dinner. "I know, shall I cook you something simple, a surprise?" Emily said now. She glanced at his face. "If you don't mind," she said.

No, no, he didn't mind: but why couldn't she have said before instead of skulking around the subject all day? Still, a simple meal gave them more time to get to the local cinema, as they planned. "Oh, do we have to go out after dinner?" Emily said. "Let's just stay in."

He enjoyed dinner. He drank just enough wine and felt mellow. He was glad they were staying in. When they'd washed up he switched on the light over the stairs and waited for her. "Oh, not tonight," she said.

"What do you mean, not tonight?"

"I can't. You know. My period," she said irritably. "What do you think I mean?"

That really made the evening, that did—her having that now, of all nights. And she looked at him as if he should have known, have kept count! There was nothing to do except switch on the box, and he could have watched that by himself. He'd tried talking to Emily over wine before, but she didn't seem very interested in model soldiers or even war games. Abruptly, halfway through a film he was watching, she said "I'm going." She didn't wait for him to see her out.

Next day brought a raise in salary. Emily went out at lunchtime to buy clothes. She didn't speak to Palin all day, not even to show him what she'd bought. At her desk she presented her back to him; her long blond hair looked defiantly indifferent, shaking at him when she shook her head.

He sat downstairs on the bus home. Why shouldn't he get off at the shop? He did so, although the day was overcast: the sky was like dishwater, spilling into the river. The dog biscuit was still displayed, unattainable beyond dusty glass.

He dawdled toward LILITH's. Should he buy Emily an apologetic present—Tarot cards, perhaps? No, he was damned if he would. He'd bought her too much already just to get her in the right mood, and then half the time it wasn't worth the effort. This time he was going to pay for something assured, for pleasure he needn't struggle for. The white coralline bulb went by. Before he was quite ready Palin's strides had carried him into the shop.

Dimness floated over him. It felt as if he'd walked into someone's front room by mistake, where they were musing in the dark; the room was full of the girl, it didn't feel like a shop at all. Though it was irrational, Palin almost fled. But he could see the counter now, which helped make the room a shop. The girl's smile formed from the darkness. Very slowly her heart-shaped face began to glow.

Her smile waited for him to speak. Could he really ask to buy the figure? He needn't commit himself yet, he realized gratefully. "How much is the, the er . . . ?" he said, waggling his fingers toward the window.

"What thing do you mean?"

Her voice was low. He had to strain to perceive it, like her face. But straining, he heard how appealing it was: its musical lilt, its rich huskiness; welcome, readiness to please, a mysterious sexual tension. Perhaps more of that was in his strain than in her voice.

"The thing in the window," he said. "The er . . ." What was it called, for God's sake? "The Love Mate!" he remembered, almost shouting with relief.

"How much will she be worth to you?"

He'd wanted her to tell him. He didn't want to commit himself yet, to admit he wanted to buy the thing. But she smiled from the shadows, glowing, waiting. "Well, I don't know." Then he must guess. "Ten pounds," he said, hoping that wouldn't offend her, hoping she'd name a price now; haggling with a woman made him uncomfortable.

"Ten pounds for her?" She seemed sad but resigned. Her face rose through the dimness; she stood up from her easy chair behind the counter. She was very tall. "I must take your offer," she said. If she sounded as if she were submitting to the inevitable, somehow her tone included Palin too.

As she moved toward the window he realized with an unpleasant shock that she was crippled. Beneath the long dress she was hobbling unsteadily, lopsidedly. He could see nothing of her except her face and delicate hands.

She lifted the pink figure gently from the display. Then she pulled off the underwear and threw it into a corner of the room. Palin realized she had dressed the figure only so as to avoid possible prosecution. Naked now, the figure glowed.

The girl straightened the figure's arms at its sides, then pulled the legs up until the feet rested under the armpits. Palin saw the hairless genitals gape in shadow, and was momentarily excited. The girl was opening the carton. He must ask her to unwrap the head. But he couldn't; he was sure it was her face, on the perfected body; he could only buy so long as the knowledge remained unspoken between them, unacknowledged. He fumbled in his wallet. The open genitals slid into the carton. Beyond the window he saw the Toby jug, frowning down.

As he handed her the notes the girl clasped his hand deliberately. Her smile seemed a promise. But what did her clasp mean? *Au revoir*, an appeal to him, a gesture of friendship? He saw her long body twist lopsidedly beneath her dress as she sat down in the easy chair. Suddenly he felt oppressed, a stranger who'd strayed into a house that had too strong a personality. "Goodbye," he said curtly, and was out amid the comforting gray of sky, pavement, river. The gaze of the Toby jug turned on him.

He was glad to escape the gazes, from the shop and from the house opposite. He felt the figure shifting within the carton. Buses carried friezes of faces beside him, staring. It was all right, they couldn't see into the carton. He draped his coat wider over the stenciled name. As the Love Mate thumped against its box, he felt absurd. What on earth had persuaded him to buy this dummy? Well, it was only ten pounds. He wondered how one went about selling such a thing.

The damn thing was heavy. He dumped it on the front doorstep while he groped for his key. Suddenly he remembered he had yet to see the face. All at once he was excited: to have that face waiting for him in the dimness, mysterious, welcoming—perhaps it was money well spent, after all. He hurried into the front room to open the carton. He halted; then he carried the carton to his bedroom and drew the curtains.

The pink genitals yawned from the box. He found the bare pink hole unnerving, so still in its cardboard frame. After a while he grasped the upturned buttocks to pull out the doll. They felt velvety as peaches, and shockingly warm; he couldn't imagine what they were made of. He pulled the doll out as far as its knees, then shook it onto the bed. It landed on its splayed buttocks and rolled back; he almost expected it to roll upright again. The bandages of tissue faced him. He could see her face already. He arranged the limbs, arms limp at the sides, knees high and wide; they resisted him a little, but stayed placed. Then he reached for the convoluted paper mask. His fingers dug beneath it at the chin and tore it upward. He recoiled, almost slipping off the bed. The head was bald and faceless.

The doll lay ready for him. The front of the head was smooth, pink, slightly flattened. The smooth vacancy lay turned up as if gazing at the ceiling. Palin thrust himself off the bed and shoved the doll's limbs roughly together, then he stuffed the doll into the carton and threw it into the spare bedroom. As he hurried downstairs he felt cheated, uneasy, vaguely angry, somehow disgusted.

But why? He mused as he cooked his fish fingers. Suppose it had had a face? The face would have been stiff, lifeless, gazing with fake eyes. A mask of the girl's face would have been dismaying. His dreams were supposed to give the doll a face, the face he most wanted; only he could provide that. He hadn't been cheated. It was just that he doubted it would work.

There was only one way to find out. By the time he'd eaten, the sun had sunk beyond the roofs opposite. He drew the squashed figure from its box. He was sorry he'd been so brutal; the body was beautiful, it seemed a pity to spoil it. He straightened the limbs and carried it into his bedroom. The curtain filled the room with orange twilight. Instead of a pink blank, the face was a vague oval orange glow.

He raised the knees wide. As he undressed he gazed at the figure. All right, Emily. I'm going to have you as you've never been had before. He didn't believe a word of it. Emily's thighs were looser, a little flabby; her breasts flattened somewhat when she lay back. His penis dangled unconvinced.

The body glowed warmly, enticing. It looked unnatural only in its perfection. It was wrong for Emily, for her contradictions. Suddenly he remembered the girl's face in the dimness, her body hidden beyond the proffered body. That face on that body would be perfection. He stared, astonished by a coincidence: the figure's right hand lay almost in the shape of the girl's clasp on his.

He gazed. As its glow flickered with his gaze, the unfeatured head seemed to shift. He imagined the heart-shaped face, her glowing smile, gradually gathering light to its outlines, gazing intimately at him. Her smile formed from the orange glow. The slow growth of his imagination made the prospect more arousing. She lay waiting for him, arms and legs wide. His penis jerked erect at once.

He knelt above her. Impulsively he clasped the hand. A shock ran through him; her hand was soft and warm, firm in his—indistinguishable from the girl's hand, for the moment anyway. He raised her hands above her head. He stared at the wall behind the bed; her face glowed vaguely. Though his penis jerked impatiently, thumping in time with his heart, he was putting off the moment of entry. He was sure disappointment lay there, in the bald pinkish crevice. At last he lowered himself on her, and gasped.

It wasn't like Emily's slick ridges, sometimes rough. He didn't have to thrust. It gave softly as he slid in; it felt like velvet. It seemed to ripple back over the shaft of his penis, kissing each nerve. As his crotch touched hers her legs closed softly, warmly over his back. He lay in her, feeling the ripples of sensation along his penis.

She waited. He could take as long as he liked, move her any way he wanted. He wouldn't have to suffer an unsatisfactory position, as had happened with Emily; it annoyed him to have to direct her, he felt she should know when she was wrong. Now he could have exactly what he wanted.

The thought excited him. His penis swelled, filling the velvet more snugly; pleasure trickled through his nerves, intensifying. The velvet rippled over his penis; as he thrust wildly, the ripples became waves. He clutched the velvety shoulders, he pressed his face against the smooth cheek. The ripples were velvet lips around his penis, drawing out his orgasm as he clawed at her shoulders, biting the pillow.

He lay in her. Her breasts were firm beneath his chest. The velvet stayed snug on his dwindling penis. Her legs clasped him.

Her face was a dark glow now; it smiled warmly. Suddenly he gasped. For the first night of his life he was achieving a second erection.

The dark blot hung almost still on the blue sky. Everyone on the bus gazed ahead at it, wondering. It was black smoke, spread wide and thin on the sky above the terrace. Palin gazed; anxiety swelled in his stomach. The smoke filled an enormous patch of sky over the slope down by the river. It grew; its formlessness hardly shifted. Its tail hung down toward a terraced street. It wasn't that street, it couldn't be. But it was.

He thrust aside the closing doors of the bus. There was little to see except smoke and charring. The houses on both sides protruded bricks and blackened struts. Between them lay a black tangle from which poked sooty metal, bits of glass coated with smoke, crumbling bricks, most of LILITH's signal.

The man stood on the steps opposite. As he recognized Palin, something like triumph filled his eyes. "She was in there," he said grimly. His voice rang flatly in the dilapidated street. "She's dead. Burned alive."

Palin thought the man intended him to hear how right that was. But he grinned at the man; he'd destroyed his triumph. "Oh no she isn't," he said, and walked away. He felt no sorrow at all. She was still alive, in his mind. Somehow the burning would bring her more alive, in the submissive body. He would keep her alive.

He hurried home. He need feel no guilt about his lack of feeling. He could hardly say he'd known the girl; only the image he kept in his mind. But he was anxious to make love to her body—because it *was* her body, he'd wished it on her. He felt she would like to be remembered so.

He'd left the front-room curtains drawn. That was foolish, it told thieves the house was empty. He hurried into the room: a bit late now, but never mind. Sunlight fanned through a gap. His model soldiers glittered on the mantelpiece on a bookcase; he glimpsed bright pink where the sunlight fell on the chair facing the window. He turned, frowning.

The faceless head met him, shining bright pink in the sunlight. It was as if the face had been lopped off cleanly, leaving the smooth chopped flesh. "God!" He flinched back; his fist thumped the window through the curtain.

He'd carried the figure downstairs this morning. Of course, he'd been half-asleep. He'd arranged the body in the chair, knees parted, hands on knees, face upturned slightly. Why, for God's sake? Because, because he'd thought she might seem welcoming when he returned.

She did. He drew the curtains and gazed at her—her long legs, her soft firm breasts. Beautiful. He hadn't grown too used to her, over the weeks. Yet he flinched from her. "I'm sorry," he said, seeking the smile in the orange glow.

He gazed at the naked slightly parted lips of her vagina. She sat waiting for him. He picked her up tenderly. As she lay on the bed, compassion and excitement mingled in him: he wouldn't let her die, he'd keep her with him, make sure she would never slip from his memory.

While he undressed, an idea excited him further. He'd often wanted to ask Emily but had never dared. He turned her over and spread her buttocks gently; they glowed, soft, warm. His breath hissed between his teeth as he slid in. The sensation of velvet streamed along his penis. Around the bed, soldiers glittered coldly.

When he went up to bed that night she still lay there. He lifted her, she lay warm in his arms. After a moment he slid her between the sheets. She seemed welcoming among the cold stiff soldiers, too welcoming for him to put away: there was welcome even on the smooth head, its perfect curve, its softness. In the dark he drew her clasping hand around his chest. Her face nestled warmly against his shoulder, a large constant kiss.

A few weeks later he gave away his soldiers. He couldn't stand them now. They looked dwarfed, tinny, absurdly unreal. When he thought how painstakingly he'd painted in each historical accuracy, it seemed childish. It was childish to work to make them lifelike, when he had her.

He sent them to John Hulbert, as an apology for cutting short their postal war game. Palin had been enjoying the game; it relaxed him, the leisurely research, the long slow pondering, the week-long rests between moves. Now he found she distracted him. As she sat near him, in her chair within the orange curtained glow of the front room, her empty face seemed like a mute reproach, a plea. He became impatient with the game. He left Napoleon hanging about outside Waterloo, and sent the model soldiers. When he took her to bed that night he felt enormously virtuous.

It was the tea break. Palin cleared a space among his work as best he could; he was helping someone slower to move all their post over seven days old off their desk before the 5CI count. Piles of paper lay on the floor among the cabinets, where the clerical assistants were searching for the misfiled files. One of Palin's colleagues was showing a letter around the office; another taxpayer had written to H. M. Inspector of Taxis—the joke would appear in *Taxes* eventually, if it hadn't been printed there too often. "Are you going to the Lakes this year?" Palin's neighbor asked.

"Yes, that's right." It was always restful in the Lakes. Palin realized with surprise that he hadn't thought about his holidays for weeks. Usually by this time of year he was anticipating them eagerly, even impatiently. He must be relaxing more at home.

Emily was answering her phone. She came over to Palin. "It's one of yours," she said, handing him her scribble of the taxpayer's name. There had been a time when she and Palin would deal with each other's telephone inquiries. Now they never did; they would have been too nervous, wary of making a mistake on each other's territory. In fact Emily hardly spoke to him now, although she made sure he overheard her phone conversations with her new boyfriend. Palin found the file and went to the phone. He was uneasily aware of Emily, sitting beside him.

The caller was a married woman. She'd bought some life insurance, but her tax code hadn't changed. Palin explained patiently that it had been allowed for in her husband's code number. He explained patiently again. Again. Yes, madam. Yes, you see. The point is. I'm afraid there's nothing I can do. "I'm sorry, madam. As far as the Inland Revenue is concerned, once you're married your money is your husband's."

Emily was gazing silently at him. What was wrong with her? How could he ever have been involved with a woman who stared like that? "What's up with you?" he demanded.

"Oh, nothing. It just sounded so much like you."

"What did? What the hell do you mean?"

She gazed at him for a pause, then said it anyway. "Your attitude to women."

"It's the Revenue's attitude." She gazed at him. "Seems to me that when a woman gets married," and his rage rushed him past whatever he'd meant to say, "she ought to know her place."

"Marriage doesn't enter into it as far as you're concerned."

"And just what's that supposed to mean?"

"I'll tell you what it means. It means," though he tried to hush her, "that women are fine so long as they don't have feelings. They're good to have around to cook your dinner. And for stuffing, when you're capable of it. But by God, don't let their feelings get in your way. Who are you kidding that that's the Revenue's attitude?"

It was as if he'd lifted a lid and couldn't replace it. Well, his own lid was off now. "I've a girl at home who's a damn sight more willing!" he shouted.

"God help her, then." Everyone was listening. The Tax Officers (Higher Grade) watched, frowning; one stood up to intervene. Palin hurried back to his desk, ducking his hot red face. "A damn sight more willing," he muttered. And a hell of a lot cheaper to take on holiday.

He was at home and staring at the pink figure in her chair before he wondered how on earth he was going to take her.

The carton was too cumbersome, and there wouldn't be room in his luggage. How could he get her to the hotel—post her ahead? No, that would be heartless. Suddenly he imagined the chambermaid finding her in his room, in his bed. God, no. He stared at her dim glowing face. He would have to hope a solution came to him. If none did, he'd simply have to stay at home.

Everyone from the office stood around his bed. Emily was pointing, laughing. As his penis thrust violently, desperately, the doll's body parted; a pink split widened up the belly, through the chest; it opened the head wide, cleaving a flat pink vertical mouth. Palin fell into the chill plastic crack, and awoke. A weight rested on his shoulder, against his cheek: smooth, slick, chill. He flinched, and the blank head rolled limply on its pillow. He calmed his breathing, then embraced her, angry with himself. But it took him a long time to call forth the girl's smile, and sleep.

Emily was transferred to another section of the office. When Palin saw her moving he was glad. But next day everyone seemed to glance persistently at him, even the girl who had taken Emily's place. Were they blaming him? Couldn't they see the scene had been Emily's fault, her and her moods?

His dull anger grew. When he reached home he had to let it out. "I've had a bloody awful day. All because of women, bloody women. And you're not much bloody good, are you? Don't have my dinner waiting, do you?"

He'd said too much. He'd filled the punk bulb of a head with misery; he could feel the misery swelling unbearably, because it had no outlet. "All right, I'm sorry, I'm sorry," he said. He was just depressing himself, that was the misery he felt. He needed a holiday. "Can't even take you on holiday, can I?" he shouted. "You'll just have to sit at home for a couple of weeks. It won't do you any harm."

He was being a swine. He felt worse as he cooked and ate dinner. Leaving her alone after a scene like that—When he found he was gobbling, he restrained himself. Don't be ridiculous. She could wait. He'd nearly finished dinner.

She hadn't moved. As he sat her face was turned aside from him a little. He leapt up and turned her head, but then she faced him only because she had no choice. Her still head reproached him. Cowboys galloped tinily on a twenty-inch desert; the dim face nagged at the edge of his vision. "Oh, for God's sake. Can't I even watch television now?" No need to shout; he lowered his voice. "Look, I've said I'm sorry. But I've got to have a holiday."

He leapt up and shoved her head away. She faced the wall, unprotesting. Minute steers stampeded. Her bare pink shoulder held still. "Can't you see I'm sorry?" he shouted. "God almighty, are you trying to make me feel worse? Can't you say anything?"

He hurled himself forward and switched off the television. "Satisfied now?" he shouted. He was throwing the silence at her, challenging her to maintain her aloofness. He waited, already triumphant. Then, in his silence, he heard what he had been saying.

God, had he had such a bad day that he was talking to a bloody dummy? That was all it was. "That's all you are!" he shouted. It was alive only when he made it live. But he knew that wasn't true, for he could feel its presence now.

Only because he'd worked himself up. That, and the way he'd given the dummy the girl's presence. Well, the girl was very dead. "You're dead," he told it, and wondered why he'd been so morbid as to sit a corpse in his front room. No, not a corpse—something that had never been alive. He was beginning to dislike the sight of it. "You're going in your box for a while," he said.

Couldn't he stop talking to it, for God's sake? No, not while he was oppressed by so much stifling emotion—mute reproach, wounded rebuff, heavy as gas in the air. Even the dim orange light seemed thicker. He hurried from the room, slamming the door.

Standing aimlessly in the hall, he knew he must get rid of the figure. He had been overworking, he needed a holiday—when he allowed a dummy to make him think twice about that, it was time to get rid of it. God, it had made him give away his soldiers, call off the war game. That was more than enough.

He'd grasped the door handle when it occurred to him to wonder why he'd bought the doll at all. He had never found such things attractive. He remembered the witch on the book in the window, the stumbling glassy-eyed man. Had the girl learned something from the books to lure him into the shop? In that case, what might she have meant the Love Mate to be?

It didn't matter. He didn't believe in that sort of thing. The Love Mate was just a doll, and the girl was dead. He shoved the door open.

The figure sat glowing in the orange twilight, face turned aside. He strode to the curtains and wrenched them wide. Now the figure's long legs, slim arms and delicate hands were unnaturally pink; the genitals gaped like a split in plastic. But when he went to pick up the figure, the girl's face began to settle on the head at once, smiling reproachfully, trying to be brave. Palin brought an opaque plastic bag from the kitchen and dragged it over the blank head.

He carried the figure into the backyard. Grass straggled, squared by concrete; a vague cat scurried away from the dustbin. He couldn't burn the figure, it might be too violently inflammable. Instead he thrust it into the bin, tangling its limbs. He pressed down the plastic lid on the bagged head and turned away.

He heard the lid spring off. As he whirled, the doll popped up like a faceless Jack-in-the-box. It sat in the bin, dim pink in the twilight, its white faintly fluttering head turned up to him.

It was only the spring in its limbs. Palin thrust it down again, clamping the lid tight. But the head pushed the lid up; the white bag stared at him. He needed to settle the lid more firmly. He found a saw in the shed.

But he couldn't bear sawing through the neck. He couldn't stand the sight of the head rolling from side to side in its bag as the throat began to part. He disentangled the figure from the bin and sawed half through the left arm at the shoulder and elbow. That'd keep her down. He thrust the head into the garbage, stuffed in the limbs. This time the lid stayed clamped. Ten pounds down the drain, he thought. Cats spied warily from the alley walls.

He gazed from the kitchen window. The lidded bin looked reassuring, actually calming. Palin felt enormously relieved, free at last. He'd never fall for anything like that again. By God, he was going to enjoy his holiday. That was what he needed. Cats were staring down at the bin. Let them fish in it if they wanted to, they'd be disappointed.

The gathering darkness was warm. Soon he went to bed. He missed his soldiers; the room looked bare. Could he beg them back from John Hulbert? He didn't see how. Even that didn't seem to matter. He sank easily into untroubled sleep.

He was making love to a girl. Her eyes sparkled; she panted; she smiled widely, laughing—he made her feel alive as she never had before. As soon as he was free he'd gone to her. He'd dressed and run to find her. He was laughing too, as they worked together toward orgasm. He'd found her and carried her easily to bed. Her left arm lay carelessly above her head, carelessly twisted, impossibly twisted. He'd found her and dragged her out the rest of the way, as cats struggled from between her limbs.

When he awoke screaming he was lying face down on the bed, in her.

The bag had gone. Dawn twilight crawled on her face. For a moment it gave her a face, a charred fixed grin, eyes like holes in coal. Then he was screaming again, struggling with her slippery limbs; his erection nailed him in her. He began to wrench at her head. The neck gave way almost at once. The head rolled from the pillow; he heard it thud on the floor.

The thighs clamped about him in a last convulsion, stiff as rigor mortis.

THE SEDUCTRESS

HE HADN'T TAKEN HER HOME before. His mother was out tonight, he told her, smiling a secret smile. "Which is your room, Alastair?" she said eagerly. "Oh, let me see." She heard him call out behind her; he must have been telling her not to go in—but she had already opened the door. After a while she went closer, to be sure of what she was seeing. When she came out she pushed him aside violently, saying "Don't you touch me!"

He followed her through the empty twilit streets, plucking timidly at her sleeve. "It's not what it looks like, Betty. I only did it because I wanted you." She slapped his hand away as if it were an insect, but couldn't stop his voice's bumbling at her. "I'm not interested!" she shouted. "I don't want anything to do with that sort of thing!"

Her voice seemed small between the blank walls. She had never seen the streets so deserted. She hoped someone would come to a door to see what the noise was, but nobody did. "Get away or I'll go to the police!" she shouted. But he followed her to the police station, pleading.

When she emerged, having pretended to a policeman that she'd lost her way home, Alastair had gone. He must have fled as soon as she'd gone in. He wouldn't dare to lie in wait for her, he must be worrying about what she might have told the police.

The streets were darker now, yet they made her feel oddly secure.

Her father would never have let her walk through these streets. There were too many things he wouldn't let her do. She was free of him now, and of Alastair. She felt free, ready for anything—for anything she chose.

As she came in sight of her flat, the ground floor of the last house in the Georgian terrace, she smiled. The empty rooms, the spaces between her posters on the walls, were waiting to be filled with new things: as she was.

Next morning she found Alastair's note.

The unstamped envelope lay on the hall floor, on a tray of sunlight. It bore only her name. Should she tear it up unopened? But she was free of him, free enough to be able to read what he'd written. It might give her insights. Insights were what a writer needed.

She walked upstairs, reading. The stairs shook the page in her hands. Halfway up she halted, mouth open. In her flat she read the note again; phrases were already standing out like clichés. Was it a joke? Was he trying to disturb her?

> I suppose you told the police everything. It doesn't matter if you didn't. I've never seen anyone look with such contempt as you did at me. I don't want anyone to look at me like that again, ever. When you read this I shall be dead.

What an awful cliché! Betty shook her head, sighing. His note read like an amateur's first story. But did that mean it wasn't true? Could he have killed himself? She wasn't sure. She had realized how little she knew about him when she'd opened the door of his room.

At first, peering into the small dim cluttered room, she had thought she was looking at a mirror on a table beside the bed: she was there, gazing dimly out of the frame. But it wasn't a mirror; it was a photograph of her, taken without her knowledge.

Venturing into the room, she had made out diagrams and symbols, painted on the walls. Magic. The unknown. She'd felt the unknown surrounding her dimly, trapping her as she was trapped in the photograph: the many shadows and ambiguous shapes of the room, Alastair looming in the doorway. But she'd strode to the photograph. Herbs were twisted about it; something had been smeared over it. It stank. She swept it to the floor, where it smashed.

Alastair had cried out like an animal. Turning, she had seen him as though for the first time: long uneven mud-colored hair, a complexion full of holes, a drooping shoulder. All of a sudden he looked ten years older, or more. Had he managed to blind her in some way? When he tried to block the doorway she shoved him aside, unafraid now of him and his furtive room. "Don't you touch me!" She could see him clearly now.

But could she? Could she tell how true his letter was? Of course she could—if she wanted to; but she wasn't interested. She buried the note beneath her notebooks. It was time she worked on her new book.

She couldn't. Her notes gave her no sense now of the people she'd talked to. The void of her room surrounded her, snatching her ideas before they formed. One strong emotion remained, where she'd pushed it to the back of her mind. She had to admit it: she was curious. Had Alastair really killed himself?

To find out she would have to go near his home. That might be what he'd intended. Still, she would be safe in daylight: good Lord, at any time of day—he couldn't harm her. Early that afternoon her curiosity overcame her apprehension.

Alastair's home was one of a terrace of cottages in central Brichester, washed and dried by April sunlight. Betty ventured along the opposite pavement. A cyclist was bumping over cobbles, a van painted with an American flag stood at the end of the terrace. Sunlight glared squarely from the cottage, making Betty start. But in a moment she was smiling. None of the curtains in the cottage was drawn. Alastair had been bluffing. She'd known that all along, really.

She was walking past the cottage—it would be silly to turn, as if fleeing—when the door opened.

She gasped involuntarily. It was as though she'd sprung a trap, snapping the door open, propelling a figure forward into the sunlight. But it wasn't Alastair. It was a tall woman, somewhat past middle age, wearing a flowered flat-chested cotton dress. She gazed across the street and said "You're Betty, aren't you?"

Betty was still clutching at her poise; she could only nod.

"You must come in and talk to me," Alastair's mother said.

Betty was aware of her own feet, pressed together on the pavement, pointing like the needle of a compass—halfway between Alastair's mother and flight. She could feel the effort she would need in order to turn them to flight. Why should she? The woman seemed friendly; it would be rude to walk away, and Betty couldn't think of an excuse.

"Please," the woman said, smiling bright-eyed; her smile was a gentle plea. "Talk to me."

Perhaps she wanted Betty to help her understand Alastair. "I can't stay very long," Betty said.

The front door opened directly into a large room. Last night the room had been dim; blocks of sunlight lay in it now. Brass utensils hung molten on the walls, jars of herbs on shelves were tubes of light, large containers stood in the corners. There was no sign of Alastair.

Betty sat in a deep armchair; the knees of her jeans tugged at her, as if urging her to rise again. "I'd love to live somewhere like this," she said. Perhaps Alastair's mother meant her to talk without interruption; she nodded, busy with a kettle over the grate.

Betty chattered on, surrounded by silence. Alastair's mother brewed tea and carried the pot to the table between the chairs. She nodded, smiling gently, as Betty drank; her square plump-nosed face seemed homely. Not until Betty had begun her second cup did the woman speak. "Why did you do it?" she said.

Betty had become tense, had been sipping her tea more rapidly because there seemed no other way to respond to the gentle smile. Now her heart felt hectic. "Do what?" she said warily.

The woman's smile became sadder, more gentle. "What you did to my son," she said.

But what was that? Betty felt heavy with undefined guilt; heat was piling on her, though the day was cool. She was about to demand what she was supposed to have done when the woman said "Seducing him then turning him away."

Betty had never had sex with him—thank God, she thought, shuddering a little. "Oh really, Mrs.—" (annoyed, she realized that she didn't know the woman's name) "—I didn't seduce him at all."

"Whatever you choose to call it." The woman's mouth smiled gently, but her eyes gleamed. "It didn't take you long to get him into bed with you," she said.

An odd taste had accumulated in Betty's mouth. Her tongue felt gluey; she sipped more tea, to loosen her tongue for a denial, but the woman said "Perhaps you didn't appreciate how sensitive he was." She smiled sadly, as if that were the best excuse she could find for Betty.

"Perhaps you don't realize what he's been up to," Betty said.

"Oh, I think I know my son."

There was a tic at the root of Betty's tongue. It made her irritable, made her almost shout "Do you know he practices witchcraft?"

"Is that what it was. Is that why you turned him away." The woman gazed sadly at her. "Just because of his beliefs. I thought you young ones weren't supposed to believe in persecution."

"I don't believe in that sort of thing," Betty said furiously. "It's against life. He was trying to trap me with it."

The woman's voice cut through hers. "His body was good enough for you but not his mind, hey? You should like me less, then. I'd only begun to teach him what I know."

She was smiling triumphantly, nodding. "Yes, he'd just begun to learn his craft. And just for that, you killed him."

Betty felt her eyes and mouth spring wide; the odd insistent taste of the tea filled her mouth. "Oh yes, he's dead," the woman said. "But you haven't seen the last of him."

The teacup clung to Betty; the handle seemed to have twined around her finger like a brittle bony vine. She tugged at it. She must leave hold of it, then she would walk straight out. As the cup rolled in her hands the black mat of tea-leaves seemed for a moment to writhe, to grin, to be a man's wet face.

Her hand jerked away from her, the cup smashed against the table. She stood up unsteadily, but the woman was already on her feet. "Come and see him now," the woman said.

She was pulling Betty toward the door to the stairs. The door was ajar on a glimpse of dimness. The dimness was widening, was darkening; it was reaching to pull Betty in. And in the dimness, lying on the bed, or sitting propped on the stairs, or lying ready for her at the bottom—

She dragged herself violently out of the woman's grasp. For a moment fury gleamed in the woman's eyes, as she realized Betty was still stronger. Betty managed to head straight for the front door, although the walls moved like slow waterfalls.

But the door was retreating, moving faster than she could gain on it. She could feel Alastair's mother behind her, strolling easily to catch her, smiling gently again. Suddenly the door surged toward her; she could touch it now. But it was shrinking. The doorknob was enormous in her hand, yet the door was too small for her even if she stooped. It was no larger than the door of a small animal's cage. The door was edging open. Sunlight fell in, over her head. As she staggered into the street, turning to support herself against the door-frame, she saw that the woman hadn't moved from the stairway door. "Never mind," she called to Betty, smiling. "You'll see him soon."

Betty squeezed through the shrinking frame. The street dashed sunlight into her face; the frame pressed her shoulders down, toward Alastair. He lay on the pavement, his head twisted up to her over his drooping shoulder, his huge tongue reaching for her through a stiff grin. The frame thrust her down, thrust her face into his.

It wasn't broad daylight, it was only six o'clock. But as she lay blinking in bed, having fled awake, that did little to rid her of her dream. Her room felt deserted, it offered no defense against the memory. After a while she dressed and went out to the park two streets away.

The tea had been drugged. Perhaps she wasn't yet free of its effects; she felt a little unreal, gliding lightly through the gradually brightening streets. Never mind. Once the drug had worn off she would be free of Alastair and his mother.

Mist shortened the streets. It dulled the railings of the park, lay like a ghost of metal on the lake. The colors of the trees were faded, the perennial leaves were glazed; the most distant trees looked like arrested smoke. Betty felt vulnerable. Reality seemed to hold itself aloof, leaving her menaced by her imagination.

On a rise in the ground within the mist, a sapling moved. It was walking toward her: a slim dark form, swaying a little as it descended the path. It was tall and dim. It was coming leisurely toward her, like Alastair's mother.

When it stepped from the mist onto the clear path she saw it was a man. Her gasp of relief was so violent that the mist snagged her throat; she was coughing as he neared her. He halted while she spluttered silent, except for the occasional cough which she could make sound like an apologetic laugh. "Are you all right?" he said.

His voice was light, soft with concern; his long slim face smiled encouragement. "Yes, thank" (cough and smile) "you."

"Pardon my intrusion. I thought you looked worried."

His tone was friendly without familiarity; it offered reassurance. Did she look more worried than she realized she felt? "Just preoccupied," she said, thinking of an acceptable excuse. "I'm working on a novel." She always enjoyed saying so.

His eyes widened, brightening. "Do you write? What do you write about?"

"People. That's what interests me." She wrote about them well, according to the reviews of her first novel.

"Yes. People interest me too."

In what way? But if she asked, she would be interviewing. That was how she'd met Alastair; she had been searching for someone worth interviewing in a cellar disco, where underground lightning made everyone stagger jaggedly. He had watched her searching, had come over to her; he had seemed fascinating, at the time.

The man—perhaps twenty years older than her, about forty-five—was smiling at her. "What do you do?" she said neutrally.

"Oh—know about people, mainly."

She deduced he meant that he had no job. Some of the most interesting people were unemployed, she'd found. "I'm in Brichester to talk to people," she said. "For my new book."

"That must be interesting. I know some people who might be worth your talking to," he said. "Not the common kind."

Oh yes? But Alastair and his mother still seemed too close for her to feel quite safe in trusting this man. "Well, thank you," she said. "Perhaps I'll see you again. I must be going now."

She thought she glimpsed the sign of a twinge of rejection. He must be vulnerable too. Then he was smiling and raising his hand in farewell, and she was walking away, forcing herself to walk away.

At the gate she glanced back. He was standing as she'd left him, gazing after her. Nearer her, a movement caught her attention: between the trees, against the muted glitter of misty ripples on the lake—a dark figure watching her? There was nothing when she faced it: it must have been the effect of the light. The man waved briefly again as she left the park; he looked small and rather frail and lonely now, on the thin path. She found herself wishing she'd asked his name.

Brichester was disappointing in the wrong way.

She had shown it to be disappointing in her first novel, *A Year in the Country*. She'd shown its contemptuous openly reluctant pandering to tourists; the way decay and new estates were dissolving the town's identity; the frustrations of the young and the middle-aged, the young settling for violence or hallucinations while they yearned for London, the middle-aged extending their sexual repertoire in glum desperation. She hadn't called the town Brichester, but the local papers had recognized it: their reviews had been peevishly hostile. That had added to her sense of triumph, for most reviews had been enthusiastic.

All she'd written had been partly true; the rest of Brichester she'd imagined, for she had been living in Camside. Perhaps she had underrated her imagination. She had moved to Brichester to write her second book, a portrait of the town in all its moods and aspects, based on observation and interviews. But the reality proved to be less interesting than her version of it; it was full of clichés, of anticlimaxes. No wonder Alastair, with his sense of a secret to be revealed, had seemed interesting.

The more she saw, the more it dulled her. In particular the young people were worse than bored: they were boring. She spent the rest of the day after she'd left the park, and the following day, finding that out. Some trendy phrases she heard a dozen times; if she heard them once more she would scream.

She walked home through the evening. Unpleasantly, she felt less like an observer than an outsider. She knew nobody in the town. But she wasn't going back to Camside, to her father; that would be admitting defeat. She nodded to herself, pressing her lips together, trying to feel strong.

Above the roofs the sky was flat; its luminous unrelieved gray was almost white. Its emptiness was somehow disturbing, as though it were a mirror clear of any reflection. The trees that bowed over the pavement, the bricks of the houses, looked thin, brittle, unreal; their colors seemed feeble. All this fed her alienation. The only real thing she could find in her recent memory was the man in the park, and he was distant now. If only she'd talked to him. Dully preoccupied, she took a short cut through an alley behind two streets.

The walls paced by, half as tall again as she. Their tops were crowded with shards of glass, dull as ice. Old doors went by amid the brick, bolted tight, no doubt on rusty hinges. She made her way between double-parked bins, their lids tilted rakishly. The whitish sky glowed sullenly in everything. Someone was hurrying behind her.

He wouldn't be able to squeeze past. She could hear his quick footsteps approaching. She began to hurry too, so that she'd be out of the alley before he reached her, so they wouldn't have to squeeze between the bins; that was why she was hurrying. But why couldn't she look back? Wasn't it silly to hurry as if fleeing? The footsteps stopped, leaving abrupt silence at her back.

He had leapt; he was in the air now, coming down at her. The idea was absurd, but she turned hastily. The alley was deserted.

She stared along the blank walls. There was nowhere he could have turned. She would have heard if any of the doors had opened. Had he leapt onto a wall? She glimpsed a figure crouched above her, gazing down—except that he couldn't have leapt onto the glass. The dead light and the brittle world seemed unnaturally still. Suddenly panic rushed through her; she fled.

She ran past her street. The building might be empty, her flat would feel all the more unsafe for being on the ground floor. She ran to the park. The man was there, at the lake's edge. She had never been so glad to see anyone in her life.

He turned as she came near. He was preoccupied; she thought she saw a hint of sorrow. Then he read her face, and frowned. "Is something wrong?" he said.

What could she say? Only "I think someone was following me."

He gazed about. "Are they still there? Show me."

She could feel his calm, the directness of his purpose; they made her feel secure at once. "Oh, they'll have gone," she said. "It's all right now."

"I hope so." He made that sound like a promise of justice and strength. She was reminded of her father's best qualities; she turned her mind away from that, and said "I'm sorry I interrupted whatever you were thinking."

"Please don't trouble yourself. I've time enough." But for a moment what he had been thinking was present between them, unspoken and vague: a sense of pain, of grief, perhaps of loss. When she'd said goodbye to her father— Perhaps the man wanted to be alone, to return to his thoughts. "Thank you for looking after me," she said.

As she made to walk away she sensed that he felt rebuffed. She had had that sense as she'd left her father: the sense of his mute sorrow, the loss of her like a bond she was stretching between them until it snapped. She thought of tomorrow, of talking to people whom she could hardly distinguish from yesterday's batch, of explaining about her new book over and over until it sounded like an old stale joke, of going to her empty room. "You said you could introduce me to some people," she said.

His name was James; she never tried to call him Jimmy or Jim.

She had no idea where he lived. They always met at her flat; she suspected he was ashamed of his home. His job, if he had one, remained a mystery. So did his unspoken suffering.

She was often aware of his suffering: twinges of pain or grief deep within him, almost concealed. She tried to comfort him without betraying her glimpses. Perhaps one day she would write about him, but now she couldn't stand back far enough to observe him; nor did she want to.

And the people he knew! There was the folk group who sang in more languages than Betty could recognize. They sang in a pub, and the barman joined in; in the intervals he told her the history of the songs, while his casually skillful hands served drinks. There was the commune—at least, it was more like a commune than anything else—trying to live in a seventeenth-century cottage in a seventeenth-century way: six young people and an older man, one of what seemed to be a group of obsessed local historians and conservationists. There was the painter who taught in the evenings, a terrifying woman whose eyes shone constantly; all her pupils painted landscapes which, when stared at, began to vibrate and become mystical symbols.

Betty enjoyed meeting them all, even the unnervingly intense painter. She felt invulnerable within James' calm. But she wasn't sure how much use these meetings would be. Sometimes when she thought of her book, she felt irritable, frustrated; it was changing form, she could no longer perceive it clearly, couldn't grasp it. Surely its new form would be clear to her soon; meanwhile she avoided touching it, as if it were a raw wound in her mind. Instead, she enjoyed the calm.

Sex with James was a deeper calm. She learned that the first time he had to calm her down. He'd taken her to a meeting of the British Movement, addressed by a man who looked like a large peevish red-faced schoolboy, and who spoke in generalizations and second-hand anecdotes. A few of the audience asked most of the questions; later these people gathered in someone's front room, where Betty and James had managed to accompany them. They proved to be British Supremacists. Some were young, and shouted at Betty's disagreements; some were old—their old eyes glanced slyly, suspiciously at her notebook, at her. They examined her as if she were a misguided child. Didn't she believe in her country? in tradition? in helping to make things the way they used to be? Just what did she think she was doing? Eventually, mute with fury, she strode out.

James followed her. "I'm sorry," he said. "I thought it would be worth your meeting them." She nodded tight-lipped, not caring whether he realized she didn't blame him. When they reached her flat she still felt coiled tight, wound into a hard lump in her stomach.

She tried to make coffee. She spilled hot drips over her hand, and dropped the cup. "Bloody fucking shit!" she screamed, and kicked the fragments against the skirting-board, ground their fragments smaller with her toes.

James put his arm about her shoulders. He stroked her hair, her back, massaging her. "Don't get yourself into a state," he said. "I don't want you like that." She nestled more snugly against him; her shaking slowed, eased. He stroked the small of her back, her buttocks, her legs; his hand slid upward, lifting her skirt, slowly and gently baring her. She felt enormously safe. She opened moistly.

He switched off the light as she guided him to her bed. Shortly she felt him naked beside her; warm, gentle, surrounding her with calm. In fact he seemed almost too calm, as though he were an observer, detached. Was he doing this simply to soothe her? But his penis felt hard and ready. Her body jerked eagerly.

He held himself back from her. I'm ready, ready now! she pleaded with him, gasping, but he was still fondling more pleasure into her, until it was almost pain. She tried to quicken him: his penis tasted salty, much more so than her first boyfriend's, the only boy (she'd vowed) her father would ever lose her.

Eventually James raised her knees leisurely and slipped into her: thick, heavily knobbed, unyielding yet smooth. The growing ripples of her pleasure were waves at once; they overwhelmed her; all of her gasped uncontrollably. She didn't feel him dwindle. As she lay slack he kissed her forehead. In a minute she was alone.

That was the only thing she disliked: the way he left her as if he were late for an appointment. Once or twice she asked him to stay, but he shook his head sadly. Perhaps he had to return to his home, however poor, so as not to admit he was ashamed of it. She feared to plead, in case that troubled his calm. But alone in her flat at night, she felt uneasy.

She was disturbed by what she had seen looking in at her. A dream, of course: a pale form the size of a head that was never really there in the gap between the curtains when she sat up, frightened by her own cry. She'd seen it several times, at the edge of sleep: an impatient dream, tugging at her while she was awake. But once, when she'd sat up, she had seen it dimly, nodding back from the window. She'd seen something—a bird, a flight of waste paper, the glancing of a headlight. Or a hallucination.

Perhaps it was the last of the drug. She'd thought it had worn off after the footsteps in the alley; surely it had caused them. But it might still be able to touch her near her sleep. She couldn't tell James about the business with Alastair; she didn't know where to start. That helped her to accept that James was entitled to his own unspoken secret, but at the same time her muteness seemed to refuse the reassurance of his calm, to leave her vulnerable there.

Then one day she saw her chance to be reassured. It was evening; they were walking back to her flat. He had introduced her to an antique dealer whose house was his shop, and who lived somewhere among rooms that were mazes of bookcases. James talked about books now as they strolled: for some he'd had to search for years. Did James keep them all in his mysterious home, she wondered? Houses sauntered by. The cottage where Alastair's mother lived was approaching.

Betty tried not to be uneasy. Nothing could happen, she was with James. The sky steamed slowly, white and thick, low above the roofs; it pressed down the quiet, oppressively, until their footsteps sounded like the insistence of relentless hollow clocks. It held down the flat thin light of the streets. The terraces between Betty and the cottage were full of the mouths of alleys. Any of them might propel a figure into her path.

Abruptly the terrace halted. A railing led to open gates; between the bars grass glowed, headstones and a church shone dull white. All at once it occurred to Betty that she still wasn't sure whether Alastair was dead. Wouldn't he be buried here, if anywhere? She was sure any truth would be a relief. "Let's go in here," she said.

The evening had darkened before she found the stone; it was darker still beneath the trees. The new smooth marble gleamed between stains of the shadows of branches. She had to kneel on the grave before she could read anything. At last she made out ALASTAIR, and the date his letter had arrived.

"Who was he?" James said as she rose.

She thought she heard jealousy, a secret pain. "Oh, nobody," she said.

"He must have been somebody to you."

There was no mistaking the sound of hurt now. "Nobody worth bothering about," she said. "I wouldn't have bothered with him if I'd known you."

She held him tight and thrust his lips open. One of his hands clasped her buttocks hard. She was still kissing him when she felt his other hand at work between their bodies. He freed his penis; she could barely see it, a darker shadow, gleaming. "Oh no, James," she gasped. "Somebody might see."

"There's nobody else about. Besides, it's dark." He didn't bother to conceal his pain. He sounded rejected, as though she were refusing him for fear of offending Alastair. She dug her nails into his shoulders, confused. When he began to strip her beneath her skirt and caress her, she protested only silently.

As he entered her, her back thumped against a tree. His glans stretched her again and again, like a fist, as he thrust. Sections of her mind seemed to part, to watch each other. She saw herself proving she was free of Alastair, to herself and to James. It was as though this were a chapter she was writing, an almost absurdly symbolic chapter.

But she could just see James' face, calm, uninvolved. She wanted him to feel something this time, to let go of his calm. Couldn't he feel her giving herself? She strained her body down on his, she wrapped her thighs about his hips, squeezing; the treetrunk rubbed her buttocks raw through her skirt. But when she'd exploded herself into limpness he took himself out of her at once.

She lay on the grass, regaining her breath. The red flashes her lids had pressed into her eyes were fading. Above her something pale nodded forward, peering down from the tree. A bird, only a bird. Before she could make herself look up it had withdrawn into the darkness, rustling.

She must satisfy him. That goal became clearer every time she met him. She loved his calm, but he shouldn't be calm during sex: it made her feel rejected, observed, though she knew that was irrational. Once she seemed almost to reach him, but felt his unspoken pain holding him back. She felt obscurely that he didn't enjoy sex in her flat, that for him there was something missing. If only he would invite her home! Whatever it was like she wouldn't mind. All she wanted was to feel his orgasm.

Ironically—perhaps because she had been too preoccupied with Alastair to worry about it—her book was taking shape. Now she could see it properly, it excited her: an answer to her first novel, a book about the character of Brichester, about its strangenesses.

She found herself thinking inadvertently of her father. "How can you write such stuff?" he'd demanded. "Oh well, if you *have* to get known that way," he'd greeted the reviews of her novel. They had had a row; she had fled its viciousness, for she'd seen that it could be an excuse to leave him—him and his possessiveness, his cold glum moralizing, his attempts to mold her into a substitute for her dead mother. And now she was contradicting her novel, admitting it was false. She saw her father standing back from his bedroom window where he thought she couldn't see, mouth slack, eyes blindly bright with tears— She didn't need to remember these things. James would be here soon.

He seemed to have run out of people to introduce her to; he was showing her places now. Today's was a church, St. Joseph's in the Wood. They climbed Mercy Hill, which was tiered with terraces. Huge dark stains uncurled sluggishly over the sky. The church stood beyond the top of the slope, deep in trees.

Betty walked around it, taking notes: thirteenth-century; some signs of the Knights Templar had been partially erased; Victorians had slipped stained glass into the windows. The trees surrounded it with quiet. The foliage was almost as dark as the clouds, and moved like them; above her everything shifted darkly, ponderously. In the silence dim vague shadows crawled over the church, merging. She hurried back to the porch, to James. "Shall we go in?" he said.

It was quieter within, and dim. Though small, the church was spacious; their footsteps clattered softly, echoed rattling among the pews. Unstable dark shapes swayed over the windows, plucking at saints' faces. Betty walked slowly, disliking to stay too far ahead of James. But while she stayed close she could feel he was excited, eager. Had he planned a surprise? She turned, but his face was calm.

The stone void rang with their echoes. She stood in the aisle, gazing at the arch before the altar: a pointed arch, veined with cracks but unshaken. On either side of the altar stood a slim window; amber-like, each glass held a saint. She leaned over the altar-rail to peer. She felt James' hands about her waist. Then one was pushing the small of her back; the other was lifting her skirt.

At once she knew why he had been excited. Perhaps that was why he had brought her here. "Not here!" she cried.

His hands stopped, resting where they were. She glanced back at his face. For the first time she saw unconcealed pain there. He needed to make love to her here, she realized; he'd admitted it to her, and she'd recoiled from it—the means to his satisfaction.

"Oh, James." She couldn't help sounding sad and bewildered. Part of her was pleading: anywhere but here. But that was how her father would moralize, she thought. His moralizing had turned her against her childhood religion long ago. If James needed it to be here then that was natural, that was life. Nobody would see them, nobody would come here on a day like this. She turned her face away from him, letting her body go loose. She closed her eyes and gripped the rail.

She felt him baring her buttocks; the cool air of the church touched them. Now he was parting them; her sphincter twitched nervously. Why didn't he turn her? What was he— He stretched her buttocks wide and at once was huge and snug within her. That had never been done to her before. Her shocked cry, an explosion of emotions she couldn't grasp, fled echoing around the church, like a trapped bird.

It was all right. She had reached her goal at last. It was experience, she might write about it sometime, write about how she felt. But she suppressed her gasps; the church mustn't hear. God, would he need this every time? She felt him thumping within her, the sounds of her body were strident amid the quiet. Shadows threshed toward her from the altar; the church frowned darkly, hugely. Someone stood at the window on the left of the altar, watching her.

Only the stained glass. But the figure of the saint seemed to fill, to become solid, as if someone were standing within the outline. He pressed against the glass, dim and unstable as the shadows, gazing at her with the saint's face. The glass cleared at once, but with a wordless cry she thrust her hands behind her, throwing James out of her. Her buttocks smacked shut.

She ran down the aisle, sobbing dryly. When she heard James pursuing she ran faster; she didn't know what to say to him. She stumbled out of the church. Which way had they come? The darkness stooped enormously toward her, creaking; shadows splashed over the grass, thick and slow. Was that the avenue, or that one? She heard the church door open, and ran between the trees.

The dimness roared about her, open-throated. The heavy darkness tossed overhead, thickening. She lost the avenue. Dim pillars surrounded her with exits beyond exits, leading deeper into the roaring dark; their tangled archways rocked above her, thrashing loudly. Someone was following her, rapid and vague. She wasn't sure it was James.

The trees moved apart ahead. The wider gap led to little but dimness, but it was an avenue. She ran out from beneath the trees. Foliage hissed wildly on both sides of the avenue, darkness rushed over the grass, but her way was clear ahead. She ran faster, gasping. The avenue led to an edge full of nothing but sky; that must be the top of Mercy Hill. The avenue was wide and empty, except for a long dim sapling in the middle of her path. A crack rolled open briefly between the clouds, spilling gray light. She was running headlong toward the sapling, which was not a sapling at all: it was a dreadfully thin figure, nodding toward her, arms stretched wide. She screamed and threw herself aside, toward the trees; a root caught her foot; she fell.

———

As soon as they reached her flat, James left her.

When she'd recovered from the shock of her fall she had seen him bending down to her. He had helped her to her feet, had guided her through the hectic darkness, without speaking. There was no sapling on the path. His silence rebuked her for fleeing.

He left her at her gate. "Don't leave me now," she pleaded, but he was striding away into the dark.

He was being childish. Had he no idea why she'd fled? Most women wouldn't have let him get so far. She'd tried to understand him, yet the first time she needed understanding he refused to try. She slammed her door angrily. Let him be childish if he enjoyed it. But her anger only delayed her fear of being alone. She hurried through the flat, making sure the windows were locked.

Days passed. She tried to work, but the thought of the nights distracted her; she couldn't stand the flat at night, the patient mocking stillness. She drifted toward the young people she'd interviewed. They knew she was a writer, they showed her off to friends or told her stories; they were comfortingly dull. Occasionally boys would invite her home, but she refused them—even though often as she lay in bed something moved at the window. If she drew the curtains tight, they moved as if it had got in.

Each morning she went to the park. Flights of ducks applauded her visits, squawking, before they plunged into their washes on the lake. The trees filled with pink, with white. There was never anyone about: never James.

One night a shadow appeared on her bedroom wall. She lay staring at it. It was taller than the ceiling; its head folded in half at the top of the wall. Its outline trembled and shifted like steam. It was only a man, waiting for someone outside beneath the lamp. It dwindled to a man's size; it ceased to be a menacing giant. Suddenly she realized that the dwindling meant he had come to the window—he was staring in, and his head still seemed oddly dislocated. She buried her face in the pillow, shaking. It seemed hours before she could look to see that the shadow had gone.

The next day James was in the park.

She saw him as she neared the gate. He was standing at the edge of the lake, against the shattering light. She blinked; her eyes were hot with sleeplessness. Then she began to pace stealthily toward him, like a hunter. He mustn't escape again. No, that was silly. He wouldn't like her playing tricks on him. She strode loudly; her heels squeaked on the gravel. But he gazed at the sunlight scattered on the water, until she wondered if he meant to ignore her. Only when she was close enough to touch did he turn.

His face was full of the unspoken: the memory or anticipation of pain. "I'm sorry," she said, though she hadn't meant to be so direct. "Please come back."

After a while, when his face showed nothing but calm, he nodded. "I'll come to you tonight," he said. "Do you want me to stay?"

"If you like." She didn't want to dismay him by seeming too eager. But at once she saw the shadow in her room. "Please. Please stay," she said.

He gazed; she thought he wasn't sure whether she wanted him. He mustn't wonder about that. She would tell him all about Alastair. "I'll tell you some things I haven't told you," she said. "I'll tell you tonight. Then you'll understand me better."

He smiled slightly. "I've something to tell you, too." He moved away alongside the lake. "Until tonight," he said.

She ran home smiling. At last she dared think they might have more than half of a relationship. She would cook him meals instead of paying discreetly in restaurants. She could work without slowing to wonder whether she would see him today. She would be safe. Her smile carried her across the park.

She tidied her flat. God, what a mess she'd let accumulate! A poster mapping seventeenth-century Brichester, half-read books by Capote and D.H. Lawrence astray from the bookcases, notes for her own book tangled as the contents of a wastebasket: she'd be able to handle those soon. And all these letters she must answer. One from her publisher: the paperback edition was reprinting. One from the GPO about the delay in providing a telephone: it annoyed her not to be able to phone her friends in Camside—to invite them to meet James, she thought. One from a driving school, offering a free introductory lesson. If she learned to drive it would be worth her visiting friends in Camside: she wouldn't be restricted by the absurdly early last bus back.

When she'd finished she felt exhausted. Her loss of sleep was gaining on her. She checked that the door and windows were locked, smiling: she wouldn't need to do that in future. She'd make sure James stayed with her. She lay down on the couch, to rest.

She woke. The room was dark. But the darkness was shrinking. It had limbs and a head; it was walking on the wall, growing smaller yet closer to her. The ceiling thrust the head down at an angle that would have broken a man's neck. The shadow slipped from the ceiling, yet the head stayed impossibly canted. As she realized that, the shadow was extinguished. At once she felt the man lying beside her. She had to struggle to look; her body felt somehow hampered. But he waited for her. When she turned the face rolled toward her above the emaciated body, like a derisive thick-tongued mask that was almost falling loose: Alastair's face.

She woke gasping. The shadow filled the room; it had pressed against her eyes. She ran blindly to the door and snatched at the light switch. The room was empty, there was nobody outside the window. Night had fallen hours ago; it was past eleven o'clock. James might have come and gone unheard.

Surely he would come back. Wouldn't he? Mightn't he have thought she'd reconsidered, that he'd been right to hear doubt in her voice when she had asked him to come to stay? Might he have taken this as the final rebuff?

She gazed into the mirror, distracted. She must wait outside, then he would know she wanted him. If he came back he mightn't come as far as the door. She tugged at her hair with the brush, viciously. In the reflection of the room, a shadow passed.

She turned violently. There had been a dark movement in the mirror. She felt vulnerable, disoriented by the stealthy fall of night, trapped in unreality. The shadow passed again, dragging its stretched head across the ceiling. Betty ran to the window, but the street was empty. The streetlamp glowed in its lantern.

She couldn't go out there—not until she saw who was casting the shadow. She gazed at the bare pavement, the flat stagnant pool of light. She was still gazing when something dark moved behind her, in the room.

She whipped about, gasping. The shadow was stepping off the edge of the wall, into invisibility. Soon it returned, smaller now, more rapid. Whenever she turned the street was deserted. The shadow repassed, restless, impatient. Each time it was smaller, more intense; its outline hardly vibrated now. Betty kept turning frantically. She heard her body sobbing, felt its dizziness. The shadow was only a little larger than a man; soon he would reach for her. It vanished from the wall, moving purposefully. Her doorbell shrilled, rattling.

Her cry was shrill too. For a moment she couldn't move, then she ran into the hall. It must be James, or someone: not the shadow. The hall rumbled underfoot; the stairs loomed above her, swollen with darkness. She reached the front door and grabbed the light switch. The hall sprang back, bare, isolating her; a shadow stood on the front-door pane, irregular with frosting. She reached for the latch. She wished there were a chain. She opened the door a crack, wedging her toe beneath it, and saw James.

"Oh thank God. Come in, quickly." Behind him the street was empty. She pulled him in and slammed the door.

It wasn't until she had locked them into her flat that she noticed he was carrying no luggage: only a large handbag. "You're going to stay, aren't you?" she pleaded.

Did she sound too eager? His face was calm, expressionless. "I suppose so," he said at last. "For a while."

Not only for a while! she pleaded. She glanced anxiously at the blank wall. Would he see the shadow if it returned, or had it been the drug? "I've got to tell you something," she said. "I want you to know."

"Not now." He had opened the handbag; he took out four

lengths of glossy cord. "Get undressed and lie on the bed," he said.

His calm felt cold. She didn't want to be tied up, she would feel like a victim, she wouldn't feel close to him. She was frightened of being tied, when the shadow was so near. But James would protect her from that. And if she rebuffed him again he might leave her for good. She stripped unwillingly and lay down.

At least the cords weren't rough. But he tied her tightly, spread-eagled. She felt nervous, unsafe. But she didn't dare protest; if he left the shadow would come back. She closed her eyes, to try to soothe herself. He undressed and stooped to her.

His smooth cheeks slid along her thighs. His tongue probed into her, strong as a finger. It was rough; it darted deep, opening her. He mounted her; his penis thrust fiercely. Her hands clutched beyond their nooses, struggling vainly to reach for his back. She felt impaled and helpless. Above her his face gazed at the window, calm, mask-like. Behind his head the blank wall hung.

Her body twitched with the strain of her bondage, humiliated, frustrated. His thrusts tugged at her; she glimpsed herself as he must see her, at the mercy of his penis. Suddenly, by a translation she couldn't understand, her genitals began to twitch toward orgasm. It was all right, after all. She could enjoy it too. She closed her eyes again, beginning to enjoy the straining of her limbs against their bonds. Outside she could hear people walking home, from a club or somewhere; the sound was reassuring, it drove the shadow away. Her limbs strained. She was nearly there, nearly—and then he had left her. He was standing beside the bed, reaching into the handbag.

"Oh, what's wrong?" He was gazing at the darkest corner of the room, beyond the window. She saw something move, but not there: on the wall opposite the window—a shadow dwindling, darkening, advancing rapidly. Her hands struggled against their leashes to point. "James!" she screamed.

He turned swiftly. His hand emerged from the bag. Before she could react, his other hand raised her head deftly. He thrust the gag into her mouth and tied it behind her head. At once she felt his calm lift; his eagerness struck her like an explosion, leaving her limp and trembling. His voice rose, rose impossibly. "Not James," it said gleefully. "Mrs. James."

When Betty lay trembling, unable to look, the face stooped for her to see. It was Alastair's mother, smiling triumphantly. She passed a hand over her face. As though that reversed each aspect of it she was James again; his long face replaced her square one, her small plump nose was all at once slim and straight. She passed her hand upward and was herself, as if she'd changed a mask. The mask smiled.

Beneath the smile and the flat-chested body the penis was still erect. Mrs. James pulled at it. Betty shuddered back as far as she could, but the woman wasn't masturbating; she'd detached the organ and dropped it on the floor. Betty heard rubber strike wood. "Yes, that was all it was," Mrs. James said brightly. "Now you know how it feels to have your body used. You're beginning to know how my son felt."

Choked screams stuck in Betty's throat like bile. The wall was full of shadows now: the twelfth shrank into place, completing the wall's unbroken frieze of dark blank faces. Betty strained back on the bed; her eyes heaved at their sockets, the gag suffocated her screams.

Mrs. James brought her a mirror to show her who was at the window. Betty saw one of the folk group, and the barman; the oldest man from the commune; the art teacher, two of the British Supremacists, the antique dealer; others to whom she had been introduced. Their eyes were bright and eager. Mrs. James smiled at them. Softly, like an articulate breeze at the window, they began chanting.

"You could get the better of my son," Mrs. James told Betty. "He was a novice. But now you'll see what I can do."

She joined in the chanting. The whispering insinuated itself into the room, slow as insidious fumes. Betty lay shivering, her cheek against the pillow. The nooses held her easily, the gag rested in her mouth. The twelve shadows gazed, whispering. Beyond Mrs.

James, in the darkest corner, there was something more than a shadow: the suggestion of a figure, thin and pale as smoke. From the corner came sounds of a crawling among bones.

Mrs. James beckoned. The shape ventured timidly forward, its head dangling. It was surrounded by an inert chill, which fastened on Betty. As Mrs. James turned to the bed, still beckoning, Betty saw her smile. There was more than righteousness in that smile; there was pride.

STAGES

AS RAY EMERGED onto the pavement he heard someone approaching. Before he could retreat to the house, a shadow spilled from the side road. Its figure followed: a large man, stumping rapidly. As his shadow unrolled before him, shrank beneath him and unrolled again, it seemed that the shadow was carrying him. He bore down heavily on Ray, who dwindled within himself, withered by fear. The man knew he was tripping.

The man came abreast of the gate and glanced suspiciously at him. Beneath the streetlamp the man looked unnaturally pink, like a boiled baby; his cheeks trembled a little, gelatinously, as he walked. He was a quaking mass of flesh, contained only by a thin bag of skin. He frowned disapprovingly at Ray and was past, drawing his tail of shadow into him.

He hadn't really known Ray was tripping. That was just paranoia; Ray had had the same experience on acid. Nevertheless Ray almost ran across the bare roadway. If a fuzz should stop him, ask him why he was walking at this hour— He was sure his speech would betray him. The glare of the streetlights faded behind him, like a negative shadow.

At the park he slowed. Behind his shoulder a tower block loomed. The sky was fat with clouds; a sharp-edged full moon cut swiftly through them. An avenue of trees stretched dimming into the vague depths of the park. On either side lawns gleamed, black. He walked forward, beneath the trees.

Their shadows closed over him like shutters, regular as the mechanism of a sleepy camera. Again and again he emerged into the clear pure moonlight. The September morning was warm. His trip seemed to be fading; it moved windless trees a little for him, unfurling their foliage into subtle patterns. He strolled, calm.

He emerged into a stone glade. Paths led from the space, flowing slowly away from him, like streams of luminous mercury. On the central island stood a statue of Peter Pan. Ray caressed the smooth limbs, which felt chill and clean. Around him, in the frosty light, the world seemed perfect.

He strolled toward the widening of the lake. The sky was clearer, scattered with clouds like frozen quiffs of foam, like long many-bellied trumpets of glowing white porcelain. If the clouds moved, they did so imperceptibly. Everything was still; the moon hung, a bright flawless circle, razor-keen. Ray moved amid his own stillness, so quietly he couldn't hear his footsteps.

Where the lake widened, a bat hunted. He could see each beat of its wings as it circled, a dodging tattered scrap of darkness. Ducks bobbed together at the edge of the lake; a solitary duck, startled by his approach, plowed out into the water. Its ripples shattered the reflections of light and clouds.

He stared at the scribbling of light on the ripples. The light formed lines of symbols, changing constantly. He could almost interpret them. As he gazed, trying to open his mind to their sense, they steadied and were reflected light and clouds.

That was their meaning: but what did it mean? This new peak of the trip had taken him unawares. Was it about to lead him again into the undreamed? He waited edgily. Over the bright still lake he heard a sound like breathing. It came from a shelter on the far bank.

He gazed across the lake. Somehow the sound promised the resolution to which the whole trip had been leading. The ground and the water held still, frozen by moonlight. He walked back to a path of stepping stones and crossed the lake.

The door and the panes of the shelter were missing. Rags of paint shone white on the moon-blackened wood: the surface looked like a dead tree patched with mold. He could hear now that the sound was a woman's voice, gasping. He reached the dark gap of a window, and peered in.

In the path of moonlight from the doorway, on a coat spread over the floorboards, a woman lay. Her knees rose, her legs strained wide. Beside her, his back to Ray, knelt a man, naked from the waist down. His hand caressed her beneath her long skirt, his mouth moved over her breasts in the frame of her unbuttoned blouse. Clothes were tangled nearby in the shadows.

Ray gazed. The couple's clothes were black in the moonlight, their bodies gleamed white. It seemed that they were performing an act for him, on the stage of light. As their limbs began to move faster, palely luminous, they seemed like animated statues: almost as if his own sculptures had come to life.

The woman's gasps were faster; her tongue ranged about her lips, thrusting them wider. Her trailing ash-blond hair swayed slightly, like moonlight on the lake. Her knees rose high, her black skirt fell softly away like a shadow, unveiling her legs. They opened, shining white; her curly mat glinted darkly. The man knelt above her; the marble club of his penis plunged into shadow.

As Ray watched the man's first slow lingering thrusts, all the woman's limbs embracing him, the path and the lake receded. There was nothing but the play on the stage of moonlight. He could feel the sensations of the players. It was more than imagination. All sense of his separateness from them had receded with the world.

He could feel the soft sheath clenching, squeezing, urging him on. But simultaneously he felt the urgent thrusts of the penis, throbbing snugly within him, stroking warmth to a blaze. Somehow this wasn't disturbing. He accepted it, let the quickening rhythms work together, leading him toward a resolution, a kind of unity. When it came it was an explosion of light beyond light, a prolonged shout of sensation. It had no form he could perceive, and that was its meaning.

Very slowly his old senses drifted back. In time he would know who and where he was. But something was troubling him. It wasn't worth noticing, it would spoil the perfection—but it snagged his perceptions. It was a dimly gleaming face, peering through a gap in the wood. It was his own face, watching him.

He flooded back into himself with a rush that left him gasping. He was at the window. The couple stared up at him; the man was making to rise to his feet. Ray flinched back, then saw that the man could hardly rise. Was he weakened by the experience too? Ray pushed himself away from the shelter, on which his semen glistened. Light and stillness filled the park; there was no sound of pursuit.

He lay on his bed, content to let the trip fade. He was glad he hadn't taken it with Jane. Dawn gathered. As the trip subsided, he began to wonder what exactly had happened in the park.

Perhaps there had been no couple. Later on Sunday, after he'd slept, that seemed possible; it had been a powerful trip. He hoped Dave had synthesized a large batch, whatever the stuff was. The trip had been the most profound experience of his life. Next day, on his way to the College of Art, he made a detour to the science block.

Dave was working at a bench. His sidelong grin of greeting was unusually wary. There was nobody else in earshot. "Hey, about that stuff," Ray said.

Dave smiled hastily. "Right. I'm sorry about that. You haven't taken any, have you?"

"Yeah, on Saturday. It was amazing."

"You're kidding. We took some over the weekend. It was worse than a bad trip, we were nearly screaming before we found the tranquilizers."

"Yeah? Maybe it's best to take it by yourself. Listen, I can handle it. You haven't promised it to anyone, have you?"

"I was going to push it onto Norman, the guy who gave us that bad acid."

"Hey, don't waste it. I'd really like to try some more." Couldn't Dave see how eager he was? "I'll score it tonight, okay?"

Dave turned back to the bench where he'd synthesized the drug. "You can have it for nothing," he said, shrugging.

Ray crossed the university precinct. A group of students passed, bright and loud. A girl whose drawings he knew greeted him; he grinned vaguely. Most of the students had left for the holidays: perhaps these few had stayed to work—selling their work, like Ray, to eke out their grants. He walked along concrete paths between the white chopped-off planes of buildings. The precinct seemed swept clean of all but a few thin saplings. It interested him that Dave and his friends had had a bad trip. It convinced Ray again that there was no use tripping with others in order to get closer to them.

He'd tried. He had felt he ought to get closer to people. But acid had made his friends swollen, knobbly, oily, sometimes dwarfish or malformed; their faces had looked stupid, spiteful, empty. They'd gazed at him, reading his irrepressible thoughts; the faces had hated him for threatening their good trip, for his contempt; they'd excluded him. Some of his friends he hadn't dared speak to again.

Surely he could trip with Jane. After all, they were living together. But the summer night had closed in, squeezing out sweat, oppressing his thoughts. As he lay encased in sweat, beside Jane's hot rubbery flesh, his mind had boiled muddily with childhood guilts, the furtive sadism of his early adolescence, the failures of young adulthood. He'd glimpsed how Jane must see him: cold, dried-up, wound into himself, a premature crone. She'd turned then to gaze into his eyes, and he had watched her smile die. She had talked; she'd wept, but he couldn't respond. Dawn had drifted toward the window, like thick mist, discoloring the end of the trip.

To try to escape the depression, to act, he'd said indifferently "We'd better split up." That had been a month ago; he hadn't seen her since.

Perhaps acid wasn't right for him. But now there was Dave's invention. On Saturday, for the first time while tripping, Ray had been hardly conscious of himself: that was worth having. He hurried into the College of Art, happy to continue his work.

The sculpture was a large white translucent plastic egg; the tapering end suggested a breast with a smooth hollow instead of a nipple. He worked quickly, anxious to catch Dave before he could change his mind, and finished by mid-afternoon. He turned the egg-breast in his hands. He enjoyed it: it was simple, pure, beautiful. He packed it carefully in a carton, and bore it away. The collector who had admired and bought a similar piece of his might like it. "Arp," the collector had said: he'd been comparing Ray's work with that of a French sculptor, not burping.

Dave's flat overlooked a police station. Pastel blue police cars lurked in the alleys. Ray's feet slashed through the grass which matted the path. Dave opened the front door, frowning. "I was coming to see you later," he said; scoring at his flat made him paranoid.

His wife Chris was breast-feeding their baby; Ray smiled nervously and glanced at Dave. "Is that some of your work?" Chris said.

Ray unpacked the egg. "That's really nice," Chris said. "Yeah, that's pretty good," Dave said. "I'll get you that stuff."

"What stuff? You're not giving him that."

"It's all right, Chris. It gave me a good trip."

"But it's awful shit. Really. Dave wanted to get back at Norman with it. I told him he ought to flush it. He still ought to." Her large moist eyes gazed anxiously at Ray; her breast drooped unnoticed into the baby's toothless mouth. He struggled not to look at her. He packed the tinfoil package in the carton, next to the egg, and hurried away.

Back home he bought a take-away curry. No wonder they'd had

a bad trip if they'd taken it opposite the police station, with the baby screaming. The plastic egg's curve gleamed; its completion made him feel peaceful, content. Should he take a trip while he felt so? Yes—and go and visit friends. Sue and Nick had a balcony overlooking the park: a good place to trip. If they weren't tripping, his trip might help him respond to them. And it might help his work develop. His sculptures resembled fragments of bodies, cleaned and perfected; perhaps this trip would humanize his work. Most of all, he wanted to recapture the intensity of Saturday's experience.

He fished the tinfoil out of a disemboweled fountain pen. Unfolding the package, he gazed at the ten bright green microdots, ready to be magnified by his mind and decoded. He swallowed one and returned the package to its lair. A bitter slightly metallic taste faded from his tongue.

Washing up, he remembered Saturday's trip. Music had become a physical force, a flow of intense energy: its intensity had been its meaning. After an hour he'd gone to the window, to watch the passers-by four stories below. His vision was spectacularly intensified; he could see their faces clearly. Gradually thoughts began to drift through his mind—strange thoughts, often more like memories. Hurrying thoughts, lonely thoughts, emotions trailing images: not his thoughts at all. At last he had begun to locate expressions on the tiny passing faces that matched the passing thoughts. He'd stood there for hours, reading the crowd, feeling closer to people than ever before. When the street became deserted his mind felt clear, surrounded by the unself-conscious being of the view.

He washed and shaved; the cold keen blade slid over his throat. Should he take the egg-breast with him, to look at while tripping? No: Sue and Nick might think he was seeking praise. He hurried himself out, empty-handed.

His hand was on the gate when the world began to shake. Convulsive shudders passed through houses and walls, which undulated like submarine plants. Rapid incessant lightning filled the sky. Passers-by stared at him: his gasp had been almost a shout. Their faces brightened, blazing, about to be transformed into pure energy. He fled into the house.

He climbed the growing staircase, panting. He'd thought he had at least half an hour. Jesus. The stairwell rushed away beneath him, yawning. His door key had become fumbling rubber. He turned it at last and slammed himself into the flat, shouting "Jesus!"

He was safe now. The bright stylized flowers of his wallpaper swayed in a gale, but that was familiar enough. After a while he carried a chair to the window. The sky was a delicate blue, puffed up here and there with clouds. No, not clouds: they were fat cartoonish letters, spelling STRONGER THAN ACID! DEEPER THAN STP! He lay helpless in his chair, giggling.

He watched the sky clearing gradually of cloud, a great steady purification. Slowly it was purified even of light. Below him in the dark hung the backs of the heads of the streetlights, silhouetted snake-heads casting their glare at the roadway.

Faint yellow light lapped over the road. In a moment the car emerged from the side street and parked outside the house opposite Ray's. He heard doors slam. Two figures went into the house; he watched lights climb the stairs. Lights sprang into the window of a flat, opposite and a little lower than his. Two figures appeared between borders of open curtains; it was as though they had made a stage entrance.

His heightened vision closed on them. The man switched on the television and sat on a couch; the girl left the stage, limping slightly, to return with a trolleyload of supper. Ray watched as they shared their coffee. Their minuteness gave each gesture and expression an intense significance. Before long he saw they were moving toward sex.

He studied their mating ritual. They glanced secretly at each other, admiring, tender. The man gestured a splash of coffee into his face, the girl gazed at him with amused resigned affection. When their eyes met, they needed only a slight smile to exchange their private language.

They drew together on the couch and watched a film. A mouth

screamed silently in a shower; a knife hacked. A man fell back-wards down a staircase, his face bloodily cloven. Light stirred in empty dusty eyes, a skull bloomed from a face. The window seemed like a cinema screen now, framing a tinier monochrome screen. The girl flinched, the man put his arm about her shoulders; she nestled her head on his chest. Ray found this part of the ritual frustrating.

As the film ended the girl rose and limped quickly away. The next room lit up orange. Beneath an orange Chinese paper lantern Ray saw a bed. The girl limped to the window. She mustn't draw the curtains! She grasped them; Ray's held breath throbbed in his ears; she pulled the curtains together. But she left a crack, which framed half the distant bed.

The man extinguished the living room. After a while he appeared naked in the distance of the gap, and sat on the bed. She took his hand, as if for a dance. The touch seemed to speak between them. She sat on his lap; he cradled her shoulders. In the orange light their bodies glowed like perfected flesh. Now they were puppets, playing for Ray.

The man's lips moved tenderly over her nipples. Her head strained back, eyes closed, mouth wide. His arm supported her, his free hand stroked her genitals. For a while their faces clung together violently. She looked down; the man's penis was flaccid. She knelt between his legs, her long black hair trailing its shine over his thighs. Her mouth lifted his penis, her head nodded. All at once the man levered himself back on the bed, grasping handfuls of blankets. She followed and mounted him. Ray felt the gasp of her body as she took him into her.

He felt the man's slow heavy rhythm. He felt the mouthing—partly controlled, partly helpless—of the girl's genitals. As their rhythms quickened, his sensations flickered from the girl to the man and back again. He felt the widening waves of the girl's plea-sure, the slowly growing throb of the man's: his mind seemed to dart wherever sensation was most intense, back and forth, faster than their quickening.

Too fast! He tried to slow them. Suddenly, by what was perhaps a misperception, he seemed to do so; he held the man back, retarded his furious movements a little. He seemed to will the girl to clench her thighs more tightly about his back. Perhaps his perceptions were lagging, dislocated, and he was failing to realize that he'd already seen the couple's actions before apparently willing them. He had no chance to wonder. He was shuttling from sensation to sensation, faster than the strobe of acid: the orange puppets rocked together wildly, waves of sensation overwhelmed him, pounding, flickering. The vibration of the flickering became pure energy that flooded him, blazing, blinding, timeless.

The orange room went out. Gradually the street faded back. He could only go to bed and lie gazing at the dark as it filled with memories, increasingly elaborate, of what had happened.

All the next day he wondered whether he had controlled them. Had he really slowed the man, made the girl's legs move? Or could the couple themselves have been a hallucination? His surroundings simplified themselves, as his trip ceased to elaborate them. Gazing from the window, he watched the couple emerge from the house. So they were real. He wiped the stain of his semen from the pane.

That evening he rang the collector. Yes, he was certainly interested in anything Ray had to show. He'd view it tomorrow, if that was convenient. Had Ray any new work in mind? Ray emerged from the long box of stale tobacco-smoke and walked home, musing.

The following day, while waiting for the collector, he made some preliminary sketches. One appealed to him: a kind of idealized penis without orifices, its shaft embedded snugly in fat rings. Should the shaft be curved? Should the whole convey a movement of the rings, or ought they to seem one with the shaft? He lost interest and stood at the window, pondering. But the flat opposite was deserted.

The collector viewed the egg. Yes; yes, he liked it. Strong and clean, yet delicate. Ray showed him the sketches. Interesting; he'd like to see the work when it was completed.

Ray made more sketches. His intuition was clear to itself, but his pencil got in the way. His latest sketch looked like a banana stuffed through doughnuts. Still, there was no hurry, no point in forcing it. The collector had paid him well; that freed him of the need to work for a while. He felt content. He read *Rolling Stone*, listened to Tangerine Dream. He watched the couple opposite.

They read, ate meals at a shiny pine table, watched television. They came on stage from the landing or the kitchen. He wasn't controlling them now, that was certain; he felt as though they were perversely refusing to have sex. As the week passed he became increasingly irritable. He had to know whether he could still make the imaginative leap, to share their experience.

On the fourth night they went into the bedroom. The gap between the curtains was narrower, like a slitted eye standing on its corner. Nevertheless he could see them on the bed, their tiny bodies stained orange. As they coupled he felt only mild stimulation. Without his heightened eyesight he found them blurred, distant, uninvolving. He turned away, depressed.

He had to know. One more trip would tell. He mustn't keep taking it, he had to work. But the collector would wait. Just one more, to make sure; then he'd save the experience for whenever it meant most to him. He drew a group of rapid sketches. The last, in which the phallic shaft lay cradled in muscular swellings, might well be worth sculpting.

For two nights the couple went into the bedroom to sleep. God, Ray thought. They wouldn't get much work in the blue movies. Come on, man, get it up. The third night he watched them emerge from the toy car. The man held the gate open, the girl hurried to the front door with her key. To Ray their actions were annoyingly banal. Come on, come on.

Lights stepped up the house. The couple appeared in the living room. The girl limped away, but to the kitchen. Her trolley nosed into the room, bearing coffee. Ray felt he'd seen it all before. He

left the window to roll a joint; perhaps he'd listen to some elec-
tronics. Licking the cigarette-papers sealed, he glanced toward the
window. The orange room was lit.

Jesus! He ran to peer around the sash. The girl was pulling the
bedspread smooth. She called to the man, who replied without
looking up from his newspaper. She shrugged—a little disappointed
or rebuffed—and sat waiting on the bed. Ray had time. He
snatched the tinfoil out of the pen, and almost spilled the microdots. He lifted one with his wet fingertip, and swallowed the drug
hastily. He switched out the light and sat at the window.

He waited. The girl waited. The man turned pages leisurely.
Come on, Ray urged the chemical. His previous trip had been
unexpectedly swift; he hoped this one would be still quicker. The
girl was stretching her legs, tapping her foot impatiently. She mas-
saged her unsteady leg.

She called again. The man let go of the newspaper lingeringly,
and prepared to stand up. Not yet! The girl was coming toward
the window. She was reaching for the curtains. Ray strained his
mind, groping for the trip; his tongue felt rough and dry. The last
of the dim light in the sky began to jerk rapidly. Don't close the
curtains! His head throbbed. Her face seemed to approach him,
clearing, as though he had focused a microscope. The curtains
closed. Then her hands faltered, and she turned away beyond the
gap, looking puzzled and preoccupied. Ray relaxed; but his forehead
was thick with sweat.

The couple undressed. Around them the frame of the world
shook incessantly. The man sat on the bed. The girl knelt and
stroked the insides of his thighs; her mouth fastened softly on his
hanging penis. Something had gone wrong.

It was only the strain of preventing her from drawing the curtains. Once Ray recovered from that, he'd be fine. But there was
more: a growing dissatisfaction and frustration. The man lifted the
girl gently, holding her hands; he clasped her shoulders with one
arm and caressed her breasts as she moved luxuriously on his lap.
Ray watched, bored. Didn't they ever try anything else?

More than that was frustrating him. He felt excluded from their tenderness. All he could see were two tiny dolls, squirming slowly over each other. God, wouldn't they ever get on? He was surrounded by his own clammy flesh. His mind groped to catch hold of what the dolls felt. He felt dull, empty, grimy, alone: a sticky dusty figure at a window, spying. He sat trembling, paralyzed by the strain of his impotent will. Get on with it! he screamed. You limping cocksucker, you useless dangler, get fucking!

Without warning he felt his will catch hold of them.

Yet still he couldn't experience their tenderness. He felt the excitement dormant in their separate genitals. He felt their bodies moving slowly, cradled in each other's affection. They were deliberately frustrating him. He reached out a hand and, grasping his penis, began to rub the glans against the girl's thigh. On the screen across the road he watched this acted out.

The girl's eyes opened sharply. She smiled, puzzled, shaking her head; she made to kneel. But Ray dug his fingers into her shoulder. The penis was erect now. He shoved her back hastily. She reached to begin caressing him, but he thrust two fingers impatiently deep, opening her for his penis before the thing went down again.

Her frown was of pain now; she began to struggle. He forced his penis deeper, knocking her thighs wider with his pelvis. Sensations were throbbing; light and pleasure merged. Beyond this lurked a shadow of disquiet as his body worked, apparently independent of him yet undeniably giving him pleasure. But the throbbing blotted that out. In a few moments the frantic vibrations were a dazzling uninterrupted flood.

When the tiny room settled back onto his vision, Ray saw the man sitting on the bed, stunned, mouth open. The girl was limping heavily about the room, collecting her clothes, weeping. Perhaps she was exaggerating her limp. The man seemed to think so; he pointed at her leg and said something, cold-faced. The girl curled up on the living room couch, weeping. Ray gazed at the window where dark and the man sat; he stared at the girl's shaking body.

Eventually he leapt up and hurried to the park. Flowers glowed luridly in the ponderous night; his trip shifted them sluggishly. At last two fragments of the moon appeared, floating calmly in the sky and in the lake.

In the morning he gazed from his window. The girl limped out, carrying suitcases. The man hurried after her, trying to take the cases, to persuade her toward his car. But she stood at the bus-stop, gripping the cases tight, turning her back whenever he approached. After a while he went back into the house. Ray gazed indifferently; the scene was distant, uninvolving. Soon a bus bore the girl away.

He craned from the window. Yes, it was. "Dave!" he shouted, in case Dave were headed elsewhere, and hurried downstairs. He opened the front door, grinning broadly. "I was going to come and see you," he said.

"Yeah?" Dave didn't seem anxious to know why. "How's your work going?" he said.

"Pretty good," Ray panted, climbing. "I sold that piece you saw."

"Listen, I can't stay long."

"You've got time for a coffee."

"All right." Dave sounded reluctant. He gazed about the flat. Ray knew the place was a mess: so what? He waited to say so what, but Dave said "Did you sell that piece quickly? Good, great. What have you done since?"

"Oh, I've got something in mind." He waited for Dave to follow him into the kitchen. "Hey, what I wanted to ask you," he said, spooning coffee. "Have you got any more of that stuff?"

"You had it all. You can work without that, can't you?"

"Sure, if I have to," Ray said indignantly. "But I've got something working now that's going to be really good, if I can get it right. You're not turning straight, are you? What was that you said about the first trip you gave me—science helping art?"

"Yeah, but that was acid."

"So? This stuff is better. Listen, can you make me some more?"

"No chance. I threw away the formula."

"Jesus Christ." Ray stared dully; his mind slumped. "Jesus Christ. Why?"

"If you had the trip Chris and I had you'd know why. Anyway, I only discovered the formula by accident. We don't know what the side effects might have been. That was evil shit, I'm sure it was. Listen, if you've got any left throw it away. I'll make you some good acid."

He kept talking, though Ray's back was unreadable. Ray thrust a mug of coffee at him, then turned away. "Chris says Jane was asking for you," Dave said. "She hasn't been with anyone since you split up. Chris says she seems lonely." But Ray seemed uninterested. Dave gulped his coffee, and left.

Ray stared from the kitchen window. Narrow alleys separated cramped yards, which looked to him like stalls in a slaughterhouse. He made himself walk into the living room, and flicked idly through the clutter of sketches. He stared at the shaft and the rings. It depressed him now; its failure did. *In Praise of Quoits*, he'd named it on his last trip.

He unfolded the tinfoil from its wrinkles. Somewhere in the four remaining microdots was what he sought. But his last four trips had been confused, disturbing. At best they'd contained reminiscences of the flood of transcendent energy he had experienced. He had seen something profound and absolute, and now he'd forgotten it; he was left with imperfect glimpses. If only he could see it once more, he would create a masterpiece.

But how? Not on his recent trips. He'd taken to watching the houses opposite, waiting for bedroom curtains to close. He'd found that if he let his mind reach out steadily, his will could penetrate curtains. It wasn't just imagination; in some rooms he found only featureless sleep, or pale floating dreams. Elsewhere he encountered plunging bodies, acceleration of sensation. He became aware of sensation first, only gradually of the participants; this was disturbing, and sometimes exciting. But even here he was a spectator, a passive participant, surrounded by his flickering.

His last trip had been worse than frustrating. In the month since he'd begun to use the drug, tolerance had overtaken him; the drug's effects were weaker. He'd felt like a feeble ghost, fluttering helplessly between his own moist cumbersome flesh and dark half-seen acts in alien rooms. His sight had seemed to retreat from him; he saw, but it meant nothing. He had drifted helplessly for hours, unable to distinguish where he was, from scene to scene: dim movements of flesh in dark rooms, sluggish gropings, clamminess. Often he couldn't make out the sex or sexes of the participants. Some scenes of pain or humiliation he struggled to escape, but that only trapped him more securely, holding him down in his suffocating disgust. Perhaps these scenes were objectively real, perhaps hallucinations and hence part of him: which would be worse? At last the dawn and his stumbling bumping heart slowly recalled him. He had sat panting, staring, hollow.

He gazed at the four microdots. It hadn't been the drug's fault. The setting had been to blame; that, and the underdose. And he had been wrong to leave himself so much at the mercy of his imagination. He needed to see his performers before him, not imagine them. He needed to see them tonight.

Tonight would be perfect. The moon would be full, whitewashing the world. White had always been the color of his best trips. He'd go to the park. There might well be couples there, and if not, it was surrounded by flats; his heightened sight would bring them close. And tomorrow he'd begin his new work; his mind would grasp it this time. Perhaps he'd even sketch while tripping. He felt elated, eager for the night.

He went down to the Wampo Egg and took away a curry. He ate and washed up. He sorted through his latest sketches; some might not be so bad, after all. The city calmed; below, on the road, the slow bullying of traffic moved on, leaving only the occasional rapid car. Banks of cloud parted like curtains on the night sky; the full moon floated leisurely over the roofs. A clock tolled midnight. Smiling at its solemnity, Ray opened the tinfoil.

Not many trips left, and no possibility of more. He must make sure this was a good one. He swallowed a microdot; then, impulsively, another. Apprehension flooded him. He slid the tinfoil into the pen. It was all right. The setting was perfect, he wasn't taking a risk.

He strode toward the park. Sharp white edges of cloud framed the black sky; the lines of trees leading into the park stood thinly, glinting. At the end of the avenue Peter Pan glowed palely. Ray walked along the edge of the lake and lay on the grass overlooking the shelter where he'd seen the couple. He wasn't visible from the path. He felt someone might use the shelter tonight.

His trip began. The moon parted into segments; its reflection opened like a shining anemone. Threads of light vibrated in the lake; soon the water shone white in the frame of absolute dark. Beyond the park, when he looked, windows darted about their buildings like swarms of rectangular fireflies. He watched, engrossed. The world became insubstantial; he was alone with the open universe.

Hours passed. The night grew cold; he was angry with himself for shivering. The shelter stood deserted. Soon he would have passed the peak of his trip. He stared across the park. Windows were lit, but their curtains were drawn tight. Had he wasted this trip? He felt the insidious creeping of depression. He lay on the chilly grass, unable to think what to do.

A light caught his attention. A car had halted on the road beyond the lake. Its headlights went out; he heard doors slam. He held his breath. Please, please. Footsteps. Approaching. Turning aside, fading. No, they'd returned to the main path. He saw the couple catch sight of the shelter. The man's boots crunched on the path, the girl's long skirt billowed gently. Ray watched them enter the shelter. He heard their murmur of approval; their footsteps turned hollow, echoing.

He inched down the slope, over the slippery grass. He dug his fingers into the earth. Suppose he slithered and fell against the shelter! But he was nearly there. The couple were out of sight beneath the windows; his ears were full of the faint brushing of clothes pulled over flesh. He grasped the earth, inching down.

He had nearly reached the shelter when a light sprang on him, trapping him. He gasped; his heart felt pierced. The eye of light hung above the path, behind it a shadow loomed. "Now just what are you up to?" the shadow said.

It was a policeman. Ray felt his throat clench tight. If he spoke he would only scream. The light held his face; the shadow moved closer. In a moment it would see his trip in his eyes, it would take hold of him, engulf him.

Ray lowered his head to escape the probing of the light and pretended to cough, hacking at his throat to clear it of terror, to give himself time. Now he could speak. He could. Speak. "I was just walking," he stammered. "I heard something in there. In the shelter. Something going on."

The light glared at him. At last the shadow went to a window, to peer in. "Oh, that's the way, is it?" it said happily.

Ray backed away, along the path. The shadow stood poking its light into the shelter. Suddenly it turned. "Hey, you!" it shouted. "I didn't say you could go!" But Ray was running, past the shaking blinding lake, past the pale stone boy, into the striped dark avenue. When at last he halted, only silence was following him. He stood sucking at the air. Then his fingers clawed. Christ, no. He clenched his body, but it was no use. Beneath the moon, amid the whispering of the trees, his bowels betrayed him.

He lay. As dawn approached, a cold light settled into the room, like mud. A thought gathered, as slowly and inexorably. Would he ever be able to have sex again, other than alone?

His future stifled him: an endless version of this moment. He would be alone with his own emptiness, with nothing to sustain him: certainly not his work. He was a helpless speck in a void, without even the will to suicide. Reaching down into himself, he found nothing. There was nothing to reach out for.

Except—

At noon he was waiting outside the English department. Amid

the long white frontage, glass doors displayed planes of sunlight. The glass swung, the light slipped; faces emerged, singly or in bobbing bunches. Some, which he knew, greeted him. Sometimes he remembered to smile.

Jane was one of the last to emerge. She strode alone through the sliding light. She shook back her blond hair, presenting her face to the sunlight. He knew that gesture, it was Jane: it looked defiant, self-possessed, but in fact it was a gesture against her own vulnerability. A shiver passed through Ray. Jane glanced at him, and saw him.

She hesitated. Quick masks of emotion passed over her face: exaggerated surprise, aloofness, nonchalance; then she gave a slight neutral smile. She made to walk unhurriedly away, but he'd already reached her, almost running. "Hello, Jane," he said.

"Hello," she said as if he were someone she knew slightly. "What a coincidence."

He couldn't tell if she meant that ironically. "Right. I was just passing," he said. "Shall we go for a drink?"

She shrugged. "If you like."

The campus pub was scattered with students; billiards clicked in an alcove. "Do you want your usual?" Ray said.

"Yes please," but she spoke curtly, as if she resented his sharing her memory.

He drank beer. The last of the trip made it taste metallic, but he could feel that it was helping to bring him down. They chatted awkwardly. Jane was reading Hardy. Laurel too? Her smile at that was genuinely pained; once it wouldn't have been. Did she like the books? He must read some. Which did she recommend? She was finishing her drink. "Listen," he said hurriedly.

She glanced warily at him. "I'm sorry," he stumbled. "For what I said to you that time. I was having a bad trip, that's all. It wasn't our fault, it was the setting. I mean, it was so hot. I was nearly suffocating."

She gazed, waiting patiently for him to finish. "Do you see what I mean?" he demanded.

"Yes, all right," she agreed indifferently. She picked up her hand-bag. "Thank you for the drink. I must go to class."

He felt his hand trembling beneath the table, writhing. He couldn't reach her, she was alien now. Suddenly the last of the trip impelled him to say "I wasn't really passing. I waited for you. I'm lonely."

She stood looking down at him. She allowed no expression to reach her face, but her eyes were moist. He thought she was trying to pull away. "I'm lonely without you," he said. "Come back with me. Please."

After a pause she sat down. "Oh Ray." She sounded helpless.

He chattered on. "I'm really sorry. Look, I do—" (he glanced at the nearby students, felt embarrassment rising in him like bile; he could say it, he must, it was true) "I do love you, you know."

"Do you?" She shook her head sadly; its blond curtains swayed. "I don't know."

"Please let me talk to you tonight," he said desperately. "Come and talk to me. I'll meet you from your class."

"No, don't meet me. All right, I'll come. I haven't forgotten where you live." She stood up before he could reply, and was gone.

She was only asserting her independence. Refusing to be met left her free to choose to come to him; she valued that freedom. But she wouldn't break her word. Nevertheless he suffered nervously throughout the afternoon. Mightn't she decide she had promised too hastily, just to escape him? Might she send a friend to say she'd changed her mind? He stared from his window; cars rattled by, glinting like dusty tin; solitary figures wandered, clutching dilapidated bags and groping in litter-bins. He started to tidy the flat desultorily, but gave up the attempt. Let Jane see how he'd become.

Clouds grew on the sky. Like white mold, he thought. Cars multiplied on the road, hindering each other; people squeezed through the maze of metal. Jane's class must be over by now. She wasn't coming. She hadn't even bothered to let him know. Dull light hung beneath the ceiling of cloud; girls passed below, their colors sullen. There was a blonde. Another. Another. The crowd was full of blond heads, floating sluggishly, infuriatingly. There was Jane.

He had to crane out to make certain. She saw him, but didn't wave until he did; then she raised one hand briefly. He couldn't read her face, his vision seemed frustratingly limited now. He ran downstairs.

"Hello," she said tonelessly. He wasn't sure whether she had come only because she couldn't tell him she had reconsidered. He let her precede him up the stairs. Her hips swung, sketching her buttocks on her long skirt. He remembered her body.

She entered the flat, and balked. She stared at the tangled bed-clothes, the jumble of sketches, the clogged dustpan lurking under a chair, a recumbent mug dribbling cold coffee on the floorboards. He could feel her struggling to select a reaction. All at once she sighed loudly. "Oh, Ray. I can't leave you for five minutes, can I?"

He gasped silently behind her. She'd taken him back. He turned her by the shoulders, to hold her, but she pushed her hands against his chest. "Never mind that. Just you help me to clear up this mess."

He saw the flat as she must see it: abandoned, squalid. He hurried about, ashamed. Still, it was only because he had been alone that he'd let the squalor accumulate; it showed he needed Jane. Together they smoothed out the bed, as they'd often used to. All at once Jane hugged him violently. "I thought you hated me," she said. "Don't ever look at me again like you did, or I really will leave you."

She gazed at him, then she kissed him. But before he could enter her mouth she had slipped away and was leafing through his sketches. "How's your work?"

"All right."

She frowned at his tonelessness. " 'All right', or just 'all right'?"

Abruptly he remembered how it had been between them. Sometimes her concern had stifled him: her anxious questions, her still more anxious silences. If he told her to leave him alone he hurt her, if he didn't respond he was cold, and hurt her; he used to squirm inwardly, helplessly, as she tried to come oppressively close to him. Now he could only shake his head and reply "Just all right."

She put her arms around him, her stiffness softened. "Never mind," she said. "You'll be able to work now."

Slowly her smile opened. She accepted him again, completely. As he gazed down at her, his penis stirred. He pushed her gently backwards onto the bed. He began to push her T-shirt up over her bare breasts, but her fingers light on his wrist halted him. She drew the curtains and undressed herself; then she pushed him back and stripped him.

She wanted them both to be aware that she was giving herself freely. She mounted his body, moving violently over him. He thought her violence was meant to tell him she had had nobody else. He caressed her, his tongue impaled her mouth. But all he could feel was the limpness of his penis.

Had his trips fixated him? Couldn't he respond to Jane now? He closed his eyes, straining inwardly, twitching the muscles around his genitals. But that was simply frustrating. Temporary impotence had always wound him tight within himself.

Jane kissed his clenched eyes. Her warmth moved along his body; her mouth surrounded his glans. He stared down. His penis reminded him of raw sausage, served between his thighs; Jane's mouth hung on it, like a leech. Her head nodded mechanically. He was aware of nothing but his absurd flesh. The rubbing of her mouth, her heavy warmth between his legs, annoyed him. He felt in danger of being engulfed by her dutiful ministering. There was one way he might break through his oppression— He moved his legs restlessly. "Just let me go for a pee," he said.

As he hurried by the table, he palmed the hollow pen. He'd thought he might share the last trip with Jane. In a way that was what he would be doing: perhaps the best way. He emptied both microdots down his throat.

He drummed his fingers on the bath. It shouldn't take long. He padded about the cramped carpet; his hanging glans bumped his thigh, feebly as an infant's fist. He stared at his face in the mirror. Wasn't it beginning to transform—or were his tired eyes betraying him? "What are you doing?" Jane called.

He stared guiltily. "Just coming," he said, and his face grinned savagely under glass, at the cruel inadvertent pun. He knew how she felt: he seemed to have been in the bathroom for hours. He couldn't delay longer, she would feel rebuffed. He unbolted the door and went out.

She lay patiently, legs ajar. She looked a little slighted. Her eyebrows rose, her lips moved: she was going to ask whether he didn't want her. He did, he did! Shrinking from the threat of a discussion, he knelt to kiss her genitals.

As he did so, the world shivered. He glanced up, kneeling. Jane's body was foreshortened; her head, her breasts and her vagina were in conjunction—it was as though she had become a symbol of herself. All at once he felt a surge of calm profound affection.

Her cunt glowed. It was an archway of luminous flesh. Around it shone a dark pubic aura. He touched the archway and it opened, revealing the deep hall of glowing flesh. Jane watched his awe, and he felt her yearning for him. His penis rose at once; its inner light brightened slowly, in the rhythm of its throbbing.

He entered Jane. At once a sense of her spilled over him, overwhelming. She was energies: warmth, compassion, devotion, practicality, sexuality; they flooded him. She offered them, if he should want them. Their flood was dazzling yet calm; it couldn't harm him. Compared to this, his previous trips were dim.

Each of his movements, however tiny, intensified the flood. His eyes were open, yet he was somewhere in a shimmering region beyond sight; his senses had merged. Another movement, and he felt his orgasm rushing closer, closer, until it overtook him. His spasms seemed enormous, violent, prolonged: explosions of energy so intense they were separated by gaps of blinded darkness. Someone was gasping. His heart throbbed more furiously than his penis.

All of him went limp. He was somewhere, content to return to himself in time. He was aware that Jane's orgasm had begun. It was

more violent than his own had been. It was a whirlpool of sensation, engulfing him.

No more! Too much! But the intensity of her sensations sucked
him in, more inexorably than anything he had witnessed before.
Her orgasm assaulted all his senses; he had no chance to be aware
of anything else.

They lay exhausted. Gingerly he reached for his senses. Nothing:
vacancy. Where was he? Senses drifted like dreams, uncontrollably.
What could he feel, weighing him down? What was wrong?

Eyes opened. Stared. Someone gasped, then cried out. A face
stared at him with extinguished eyes: his own face.

His own body lay lifeless on him, weighing him down. Hands
reached upward, thrusting frantically at his body's shoulders, hands
with slim fingers and long nails: Jane's hands. He heard her sobbing, but he couldn't see her face. Yes: he could see her eyes,
blurred as they were. Her rapid eyelids tried to snatch tears from
them. He was looking out through them.

He mustn't panic. He'd been out of his body before, on all these
trips. On the first he'd seen his own face, peering into the shelter.
He could get back. His body had only passed out for a moment,
stunned by its orgasm. But Jane's cries were losing their hold on
words now. She was punching the shoulders of the body, struggling
to free herself.

Don't! Jesus! He must reach her, reassure her. But he was being
carried away by terror, by the sight of his own lifeless face gaping
at him, his own flopping body cut off completely from him, a dead
mindless weight. Her terror was swelling uncontrollably. It burst
and flooded him, crushing him, sweeping away his control, his
identity. As Jane lay screaming and heaving at his body, he dwindled to a thin helpless shriek, lost in hers.

LOVEMAN'S COMEBACK

SURELY SHE WAS DREAMING. She lay in bed, but the blankets felt like damp moss. Her eyes were white and blind. She suffered a muffled twinge of nightmare before she realized that what filled her eyes was moonlight and not cataract. Sitting up hastily, she saw the moon beyond the grubby pane. Against it stood a nearby chimney, a square black horned head.

The light must have awakened her, if she was awake. The moonlit blankets and their shadows retained a faint tousled outline of her. As she gazed at the vague form she felt hardly more present herself. She was standing up, she found, and at some point had dressed herself ready for walking.

Why did she want to go out? Frost glittered on the window, as though the grime were flowering translucently. Still, perhaps even the cold might be preferable to the empty house, which sounded drained of life, rattling with her echoes. It hadn't sounded so when her parents— No point in dwelling on that subject. Walk, instead.

No need to hurry so. Surely she had time to switch on the light above the stairs. Her compulsion disagreed: moonlight reached across the landing from her open bedroom door and lay like an askew fragment of carpet over the highest stairs; that was illumination enough. Her shadow jerked downstairs jaggedly ahead of her. Her echoes ran about the house like an insubstantial stumbling crowd, to remind her how alone she was. To escape them, she hurried blindly down the unclothed stairs, along the thundering hall, and out.

The street was not reassuring. But then so late at night streets seldom were: they reminded her of wandering. Or was that a dream too? Hadn't she wandered streets at night, the more deserted the better, alongside others—friends, no doubt—sharing fat multicolored hand-rolled cigarettes, or locked into the depths of themselves by some chemical? Hadn't houses shrunk as though gnomes were staging illusions, hadn't bricks melted and run together like wax? But she couldn't be sure that she was remembering; even her parents resembled a dream. The urge to walk was more real.

Well, she could walk no faster. Underfoot, the roadway felt cracked: on the pavements dead streetlamps help up their broken heads. At one end of the street she'd glimpsed a street soaked in moonlight; it seemed to her like the luminous skeleton of something unimaginable. But her impulse tugged her the other way, between unbroken ranks of houses whose only garden was the pavement. Moonlight covered the slated roofs with overlapping scales of white ice. As she passed, the dim dull windows appeared to ripple.

She was so numb that she felt only the compulsion to walk. It was a nervousness that must be obeyed, a vague nagging like a threat of pain. Was it like the onset of withdrawal symptoms? She couldn't recall—indeed, wasn't sure whether she had experienced them. Had she gone so far with the needle?

Litter scuttled on the chill wind; something broken scraped a lamp's glass fangs. Terraced houses enclosed her like solid walls. In the darkness, their windows looked opaque as brick; surely nobody could live within. Could she not meet just one person, to convince her that the city hadn't died in the night?

The dimness of her memories had begun to dismay her. Her mind seemed dark and empty. But the streets were brightening. Orange light glared between walls, searing her eyes. A coppery glow hovered overhead, on gathering clouds. When she heard the brisk whirr of a vehicle she knew she was approaching the main road.

Bleak though it was, it heartened her. At least she would be able to see; groping and stumbling along the side streets had reminded her of her worst secret fear. She could walk beside the dual carriageway. Even the drivers, riding in their tins as though on a conveyor belt, would be company. Perhaps one might give her a ride. Sometimes they had.

But she wasn't allowed to walk there. Before she had time even to narrow her eyes against the glare, her impulse plunged her into the underpass, where graffiti were tangled in barbaric patterns. Long thin lights fluttered and buzzed like trapped insects. A car rumbled dully overhead. The middle of the underpass was a muddy pool that drowned the clogged drains. Though she had to walk through it she couldn't feel the water. Didn't that prove she was dreaming?

Perhaps. But as she emerged onto the far pavement she grew uneasy. She knew where she was going— but her mind refused to be more explicit. She was compelled forward, between two hefty gateposts without gates, beneath trees.

Memories were stirring. They peered out, but withdrew before she could tell why she was unnerved. Her compulsion hurried her along the private road, as though to outdistance the memories. But there were things she'd seen before: great white houses standing aloof beyond their gardens, square self-satisfied brick faces cracked by the shadows of branches; families of cars like sleeping beasts among the trees; lamp-standards or ships' steering wheels outside front doors; boats beached far from any sea. When had she been here, and why? In her unwilling haste she slipped and fell on wet dead leaves.

Gradually, with increasing unpleasantness, her mind became strained. Opposing impulses struggled there. She wanted to know why this place was familiar, yet dreaded to do so. Part of her yearned to wake, but what if she found she was not asleep? Oblivious of her confusion, her feet trudged rapidly onward.

Suddenly they turned. She had to fight her way out from her thoughts to see where she was going. No, not here! It wasn't only that a faint threatening memory had wakened; she was walking towards someone's home. She'd be arrested! Christ, what was she planning to do? But her feet ignored her, and her body carried her squirming inwardly towards its goal.

Hedges pressed close to her; leafy fists poked at her face. She slithered on the grassy path that led her away from the road; she saved herself from falling, but the hedge snapped and threshed. Someone would hear her and call the police! But that fear was almost comforting—for it distracted her from the realization that the place towards which she was heading was very much unlike anybody's home.

At a gap in the hedge she halted. Surely she wasn't going— But she forced her way through the creaking gap, into a wider space. Trees stooped over her, chattering their leaves; infrequent shards of moonlight floated on the clouds. She stumbled along what might be a path. After a while she left it and picked her way blindly over mounds, past vertical slabs that scraped her legs; once she knocked over what seemed to be a stone vase, which toppled heavily onto earth.

Dark blocks loomed ahead. One of them was an unlit house; she must be returning towards the road. Was there a window dim as the clouds, and a head peering out at her? This glimpse prevented her from noticing the nearer block until she was almost there. It was a shed that smelled of old damp wood, and her hand was groping for the doorknob.

No. No, she wasn't going in there. Not when the tics of moonlight showed her the unkempt mounds, some of them gaping— But her body was an automaton; she was tiny and helpless within it. Her hand dragged open the scaly door, her feet carried her within. At least please leave the door open, please— But except for trembling, her hand ignored her. It reached behind her and shut her in the dark of the graveyard shed.

It must be a dream. No shed could contain such featureless dark.

She couldn't move to explore, even if she had dared; her body was stopped, switched off, waiting. Wasn't that nightmarish enough to be a dream? Couldn't the same be said of the slow footsteps that came stumbling across the violated graveyard, towards the shed? She must turn; she must see what had opened the door and was standing there silently. But fear or compulsion held her still as a doll. Timid moonlight outlined a low table before her, over which most of the shadow of a head and shoulders was folded, deformed. Then the dark slammed closed around her.

Three paces had taken her into the shed; no more than three would find her. She heard the shuffling feet advance: one pace, two—and fingers clumsy as claws dragged at her hair. They reached for her shoulders. Deep in her a tiny shriek was choking. The hands, which were very cold, lifted her arms. As she stood like a shivering cross in the dark, the hands clutched her breasts.

When they fumbled to unbutton her dress her mind refused to believe; it backed away and hid in a corner, muttering: a dream, a dream. Her breasts were naked beneath the dress. The fingers, cold as the soil through which she'd stumbled, rolled her nipples roughly, as though to rub them to dust. Her mind, eager to distract her, was reminded of crumbling cannabis onto tobacco. When at last her nipples came erect they seemed distant, no part of her at all.

The hands pushed her back against the table. They pulled her own hands down to grip the table's edge, and spread her legs. She might have been a sex doll: she felt she was merely an audience to the antics of her puppet body. When the hands bared her genitals the sensation was less convincing than a dream.

She felt the penis enter her. It seemed unnaturally slippery, and quite large. Her observations were wholly disinterested, even when the fingers teased out her clitoris. The thrusting of the penis meant as little to her as the pounding of a distant drum. The grotesqueness of her situation had allowed her to retreat into a lonely bleak untroubled place in her mind.

She felt the rhythm quicken, and the eventual spurting, without having experienced even the hint of an orgasm; but then, she rarely did. The familiar dissatisfaction was oddly reassuring. Only the nervous gasping of her partner, a gulping as though he'd been robbed of breath, was new.

As soon as he'd finished he withdrew. He shoved her away, discarded. Her hands sprang up to ward off the clammy planks of the walls, but touched nothing. Of course she mightn't, in a dream. She teetered giddily, unprepared to have regained control of her body, and glimpsed the abruptly open doorway, a bow-legged figure stumbling out; its vague face looked fat and hirsute as moldy food. It snatched the door closed as it went.

Perhaps she was imprisoned. But her mind could accept no more; if she were trapped, there was nothing it could do. She dressed blindly, mechanically; the buttons felt swollen, pebble-thick. The door was not locked. Yes, she was surrounded by a graveyard. Her numbed mind let her walk: no reason why she shouldn't go home. She trudged back to the deserted main road, through the flooded underpass. The moon had passed over; the side streets were dark valleys. Perhaps once she reached her bed her dream would merge with blank sleep. When she slumped fully clothed on the blankets, oblivion took her at once.

When she woke she knew at once where she had been.

In her dream, of course. Understandably, the dream had troubled her sleep; on waking she found that she'd slept all day, exhausted. She would have preferred her deserted house not to have been so dark. The sky grew pale with indirect moonlight; against it, roofs blackened. In the emptiness, the creak of her bed was feverishly loud. At least she was sure that she had been dreaming, for Loveman was dead.

But why should she dream about him now? She searched among the dim unwieldy thoughts in her dusty mind. Her parents' death must be the reason. Of all her activities that would have shocked and distressed them had they known, they would have hated Loveman most. After their death she'd kept thinking that now she was free to do everything, without the threat of discovery—but that freedom had seemed meaningless. The thought must have lain dormant in her mind and borne the dream.

Remembering her parents hollowed out the house. She'd felt so small and abandoned during her first nights with the emptiness; she hadn't realized how much she'd relied on their presence. For the first time she'd taken drugs other than for pleasure, in a desperate search for sleep. No doubt that explained why she slept so irregularly now.

She hurried out, not bothering to switch on the lights; she knew the house too well. It wasn't haunted: just dead, cold, a tomb. She fled its dereliction, towards the main road. The light and spaciousness might be welcoming.

Terraces passed, so familiar as to be invisible. Thoughts of Loveman blinded her; she walked automatically. God, if her parents had found out she'd been mixed up in black magic! Not that her involvement had been very profound. She'd heard that he called his women to him, whether or not they were willing, by molding dolls of them. The women must have been unbalanced and cowed by the power of his undeniably hypnotic eyes. But he hadn't needed to overpower her in order to have her—nobody had. He'd satisfied her no more than any other man. So much for black magic!

Then—so she'd gathered from friends—his black magic had been terminated by a black joke. He had been knocked down on the main road, by a car whose driver was a nurse and a devout Christian, no less. Even for God, that seemed a mysterious way to move. Had that happened before her parents' death or after? Her memories were loose and imprecise. Her jagged sleep must have blurred them.

And the rest of her dream— Just a nightmare, just exaggeration. Yes, he had lived in that private road and yes, there had been a graveyard behind his house. No doubt he was buried there; her dream appeared to think so. Why should he be troubled? But she was, and was recalling the night when she'd gone to Loveman's house only to meet him emerging from the graveyard. As he'd glanced sidelong at her he had looked shamefaced, aggressively self-righteous, secretly ecstatic. She hadn't wanted to know what he had been doing; even less did she want to know now.

Here was the main road. Its lights ought to sear away her dream. But it remained, looming at the back of her mind, a presence she was never quick enough to glimpse. Cars sang by; the curtains of the detached houses shone. There was one way she might rid herself of the dream. She could take a stroll along Loveman's road and oust the dream with reality.

But she could not. She reached the mouth of the underpass and found herself unable to move. The tiled entrance gaped, scribbled with several paints, like the doorway of a violated tomb. A compulsion planted too deep in her to be perceived or understood forbade her to advance a step nearer Loveman's road.

Something had power over her. Details of her dream, and memories of Loveman, crowded ominously about her. Suppose the graveyard, which she'd never entered, were precisely as she'd dreamed it? A stray thought of sleepwalking made her flinch away from the cold tiled passage, the muddy pool which flickered with ghosts of the dying lights.

All of a sudden, with vindictively dramatic timing, the road was bare of cars. The lit windows of the houses served only to exclude her. Abruptly she felt cold, perhaps more emotionally than physically, and shuddered. Across the carriageway, ranks of trees that sprouted from both pavements of the private road swayed together overhead, mocking prayer.

She was afraid to be alone. She could no more have returned to the empty house than she would have climbed into a coffin. Driveways confronted her, blocked by watchdog cars. Beyond the smug houses stood a library. She had been in there only once, to score some acid; books had never held her attention for long. But she fled to the building now, like a believer towards a church.

Indeed, there were churchy elements. Women paced quietly, handling romances as though they were missals, tutting at anyone who made a noise. Still, there were tables strewn with jumbled newspapers, old men covertly filling the crosswords, young girls giggling behind the shelves and sharing a surreptitious cigarette. She could take refuge in here without being noticed, she could grow calm—except that as she entered, a shelf of books was waiting for her. *Black Magic. Grimoire. Truth About Witchcraft.* She flinched awkwardly aside.

People moved away from her, frowning. She was used to that; usually they'd glimpsed needle tracks on her arms. She pulled her sleeves down over her hands. Nobody could stop her sitting down—but there was no space: old men sat at all the tables, doodling, growling at the newspapers and at each other.

No: there was one almost uninhabited table, screened from the librarian's view by bookcases. A scrawny young man sat there, dwarfed by his thick shabby overcoat; a wool cap covered his hair. He was reading a science fiction novel. He fingered the pages, rather as though picking at a dull meal.

When she sat down he glanced up, but with no more interest than he would have shown had someone dumped an old coat on her chair. His limp hands riffled the pages, and she caught sight of the needle tracks on his forearm. So that was why this table was avoided. Perhaps he was holding stuff, but she didn't want any; she felt no craving, only vague depression at being thus reminded of the days when she had been on the needle.

But the marks held her gaze, and he glanced more sharply. "All right?" he said, in a voice so bored that the words slumped into each other, blurring.

"Yes thanks." Perhaps she didn't sound so convincing; her fears hovered just behind her. "Yes, I think so," she said, trying to clarify the truth: his stare lay heavily on her, and she felt questioned, though no doubt he simply couldn't be bothered to look away. "I've just been walking. I wanted to sit down," she said, unable to admit more.

"Right." His fingers obsessively rubbed the corner of a page, which grew tattered and grubby. She must be annoying him. "I'm sorry," she said, feeling rebuffed and lonely. "You want to read."

The librarian came and stood near them, disapproving. Eventually, when he could find nothing of which to accuse them, he stalked away to harangue an old man who was finishing a crossword. "What's this, eh, what's this? You can't do that here, you know."

"I'm not reading," the young man said. He might have been, but was perversely determined now to antagonize the librarian. "Go on. You were walking. Alone, were you?"

Was there muffled concern in his voice? Her sudden loneliness was keener than the dully aching emptiness she had been able to ignore. "Yes," she muttered.

"Don't you live with anyone?"

He was growing interested; he'd begun to enunciate his words. Was he concerned for her, or was his anxiety more selfish? "No," she said warily.

"Whereabouts do you live?"

His self-interest was unconcealed now; impatience had given him an addict's shamelessness. "Where do *you* live?" she countered loudly, triumphantly.

"Oh," he said evasively, "I'm moving." His nervous eyes flickered, for her triumph had brought the librarian bearing down on them; the man's red face hovered over the table. "I must ask you to be quieter," the librarian said.

"All right. Fuck off. We're going." The interruption had shattered his control; his words were as jagged as his nerves. "Sorry," he said plaintively at once. "I didn't mean that. We'll be good. We won't disturb you. Let us stay. Please."

She and the librarian stared at him, acutely embarrassed. At last the librarian said "Just behave yourself" and dawdled away, shaking his head. By then she had realized why the young man was anxious not to be ejected: he was waiting to score dope.

"I'll be going in a minute," she whispered. "I'm all right now. I've been having strange dreams, that's all," she added, to explain

why she hadn't been all right before. Only dreams, of course that
was all, just dreams.

"Yeah," he said, and his tone shared with her what dreams meant
to him: he'd seen the marks on her arms. "You don't have to go,"
he whispered quickly; perhaps she'd reminded him of what he
craved, and of the loneliness of his addiction. "You can get a book."
Something about him—the familiar needle tracks, or his concern, however selfish—made her feel less alone. The feeling had
already helped her shrug off her dream; it could do her no harm
to stay with him for a while. She selected books, though none
seemed more attractive than any other. She flicked rapidly through
them, lingering over the sexual scenes, none of which reached her;
they were unreal, posturings of type and paper. Opposite her his
fingertips poked at the novel, letting the pages turn when they
would.

The librarian called "Five minutes, please." The clock's hands
clicked into place on the hour. Only when the librarian came
frowning to speak to him did the young man stand up reluctantly.
Nobody else had visited the table. He hurried to the shelves and
slammed a book home—but she saw that he'd feinted; with a con-
juror's skill, he had vanished the science fiction novel beneath his
coat.

Outside the library he said "Do you want to go somewhere?"

She supposed he meant to score. The proposal was less tempting
than depressing. Besides, she suspected that if she accompanied
him, she wouldn't be able to conceal from him where she lived.
She didn't want him to know; she'd lost control of situations too
often, most recently in the dream. She didn't need him now—she
was rid of the dream. "I've got to go home," she said hastily, and
fled.

Glancing back, she saw him standing inert on the library steps.
His pale young withered face was artificially ruddy beneath the
sodium lamps; his thin frame shivered within the long stained overcoat. She was glad she wasn't like that any more. She dodged into

the nearest side street, lest he follow. It had begun to rain; drops rattled on metal among the streets. The moon floated as though in muddy water, and was incessantly wreathed by black drifting clouds. Though it soaked her dress, the onrush of rain felt clean on her face; it must be cold, but not sufficiently so to bother her. She was cleansed of the dream.

But she was not, for on the far side of a blankness that must have been sleep she found herself rising from her bed. Outside the window, against the moon, the chimney glittered, acrawl with rain. She had time only for that glimpse, for the impulse compelled her downstairs, blinking in the dark, and into the street.

How could she dream so vividly? Everything seemed piercingly real: the multitude of raindrops pecking at her, the thin waves that the wind cast in her face, the clatter of pelted metal. Her ears must be conveying all this to her sleep—but how could she feel the sloshing of cold pools in the uneven pavement, and see the glimmer of the streaming roadway?

Some of the lights in the underpass had died. The deeper pool slopped around her ankles; the chill seized her legs. She hadn't felt that last night. Was her dream accumulating detail, or was her growing terror refusing to allow her to be so unaware?

The private trees dripped. Raindrops, glaring with sodium light, swarmed down trunks and branches. The soft vague hiss of the downpour surrounded her. She could be hearing that in bed—but why should her dream bother to provide a car outside Loveman's house? There was a sign in the window of the car. Before she could make it out she was compelled aside, between the hedges.

All the leaves glistened, and wept chill on her. Her sodden hair slumped down her neck. When she pushed, or was pushed, through the gap, the hedge drenched her loudly. She was too excessively wet for the sensation to be real, this was a dream of drenching— But she was staggering through the dark, among the stones, the unseen holes which tried to gulp her. What had there been in that opened earth? Please let it be a dream. But the cold doorknob, its scales of rust loosened by the rain and adhering to her hands, was no dream. Though she struggled to prevent it, her hand twitched the door shut behind her. She stumbled forward until her thighs collided with the edge of the table. It must be the rain that filled the darkness with a cloying smell of earth, but the explanation lulled her terror not at all. Worse still, the clouds had left the moon alone. A faint glow diluted the dark of the shed. She would be able to see.

The first sound of footsteps was heavy and squelching; the feet had to be dragged out of the earth. She writhed deep in her doll of a body, silently shrieking. The footsteps plodded unevenly to the door, which creaked, slow and gloating. Hands fumbled the door wide. Perhaps their owner was blind—incomplete, she thought, appalled.

Moonlight was dashed over her. She saw her shadow, which was unable even to tremble, hurled into the depths of the shed. The darkness slammed; the footsteps advanced, dripping mud. Wet claws that felt gnarled and soaked as the hedges seized her shoulders. They meant to turn her to face her tormentor.

With an effort that momentarily blinded her, she battled not to turn. At least let her body stay paralyzed, please let her not see, please! In a moment the claws ceased to drag at her. Then, with a shock that startled a cry almost to her lips—the incongruity and degradation—she was shoved face down over the table and beaten. He bared her, and went on. Suddenly she knew that he could have compelled her to turn, had he wanted; he was beating her for pleasure. She felt little pain, but intense humiliation, which was perhaps what had been intended.

All at once he forced her legs urgently wide and entered her from behind. He slithered in, bulging her. She became aware only of her genitals, which felt chilled. The dark grew less absolute: weren't there vague distorted shadows ahead of her, miming copulation? She was not dreaming. Only a sense that she was not entirely awake permitted her to cling to that hope. A dream, a dream, she repeated, borrowing the rhythm of the penis to pound her mind into stupidity. When his orgasm flooded her it felt icy as the rain.

He levered himself away from her, and her sodden dress fell like a wash of ointment over her stinging buttocks. The shed lit up before the slam. The squelching footsteps merged with the hiss of mud and rain. When she buttoned herself up, her dress clung to her like a shroud.

The compulsion urged her home. She stumbled over the gaping earth. Stone angels drooled. She was sobbing, but had to make do with rain for tears. In a pitiful attempt to preserve her hope, she tried to touch as few objects as possible, for everything felt dreadfully real. But the pool in the underpass drowned her shoes while she waited shivering, unable to move until a car had passed.

Rain trickled from her on to the blankets, which felt like a marsh. She lay shuddering uncontrollably, trying to calm herself: it was over now, over for tonight. She needed to sleep, in order to be ready—for she had a plan. As she'd trudged sobbing home it had grown like an ember in her mind, faint but definite. Tomorrow she would move in with one of her friends, any one. She must never be alone again. She was still trying to subdue herself to rest when sleep collapsed over her, black as earth.

She was a doll in a box. Around her other dolls lay, blind and immobile and mindless, in their containers. Her outrage burned through her—like a tonic, or like poison? She wasn't a doll, for she had a mind. She must escape her box, before someone came and bought her. She thrust at the lid that blinded her. Slowly, steadily. Yes, it was moving. It slid away, and the enormous fall of earth suffocated her.

She woke coughing and struggling to scream. The earth was only darkness; she was lying on her back on top of her bed. *Only* darkness? Despite her resolve she had overslept. All right, never mind, she hushed her panic. Some of her friends would surely be at home.

She lay massaging pliability into her stiff chill limbs. Whom would she try first, who was kindest, who had room for her? Her limbs were shaking; the damp bed sounded like a sponge. Just one friend would do, just one good friend— But her whole body was shuddering with panic which she struggled not to put into words. She could remember not a single name or address of a friend.

No longer could she pretend she was dreaming. She had been robbed of every memory that could help her. Perhaps the thing which had power over her made her sleep during the day; perhaps his power was greater at night. Her empty house was a box in which she was kept until she was wanted.

Then she must not stay there. That was the one clear thought her panic allowed her. She ran from the house, hunted by her echoes. The moon skulked behind the roofs. The houses faced her blindly; not a window was lit. Even if there had been—even if she battered at the doors and woke the streets with the scream that threatened to cut her open, like a knife of fear—nobody would believe her. How could they?

She fled along the streets. Deprived of the moon, the sky was so dark that she might have been stumbling along an enclosed passage. Far ahead, the main road blazed with unnatural fire; the sullen clouds glowed orange. Suppose he weren't in the library, the young man? Indeed, suppose he were? He couldn't be much help— in his addiction, he was as helpless as she. She didn't even know his name. But he might be the only living person in the world whom she could recognize.

She struggled with the double doors, which seemed determined to shoulder her out. People turned to stare as she flung the doors wide with a crash and ran into the library. The librarian frowned, and made to stalk her. For a terrified moment she thought he meant to tell her to leave. She outdistanced him, and ran to the concealed table. Nothing would rob her of the vague reassurance of the bright lights. They'd never get her to leave. She'd fight, she'd scream.

The young man was toying with a different book. He glanced

up, but she wasn't the visitor he'd hoped for; his gaze slumped to the pages. "Back again," he said apathetically.

The librarian pretended to arrange books on a nearby shelf. Neither he, nor the young man's indifference, could deter her. She sat down and stared at a scattered newspaper. An item caught her eye, something about violated graves—but an old man hurried to snatch the newspaper, grumbling.

She could only gaze at the young man. He looked less tense; smiles flickered over his lips—he must have obtained something to take him up. Could the same thing help her fight her compulsions? If she were honest, she knew it could not. But she was prepared to do anything in order to stay with him and whatever friends he had. "Are you going somewhere later?" she whispered.

He didn't look up. "Yeah, maybe." He wasn't interested in the book: just less interested in her.

She mustn't risk making him impatient. Read. She went to the shelf next to the spying librarian. He needn't think she was scared of him; she was scared of— Panic welled up like abrupt nausea. She grabbed the nearest book and sat down.

Perhaps she'd outfaced the librarian, for he retreated to his desk. She heard him noisily tidying. She smirked; he had to make a noise to work off his frustration. But at once she knew that was not the point, for he shouted "Five minutes, please."

Oh Christ, how could it be so late? In five minutes the young man would go, she'd be alone! He was preparing to leave, for he'd slipped the book into hiding. When she followed him towards the exit he ignored her. The librarian glared suspiciously at him. Oh God, he would be arrested, taken from her. But though she was streaming and shivering with panic, they escaped unmolested.

She clung gasping to a stone pillar at the foot of the steps. The young man didn't wait for her; he trudged away. God, no! "Are you going somewhere, then?" she called in as friendly a voice as she could manage, trying not to let it shatter into panic.

"Dunno." He halted, but evidently the question annoyed him. She stumbled after him, and glimpsed herself in the dark mirror

of the library window: pale and thin as a bone, a wild scarecrow—
the nightmares in the shed must have done that to her. Her hair
had used to shine. How could she expect to appeal to him? But
she said "I was only thinking that maybe I could come with you."
"Yeah, well. I'm moving," he muttered, gazing away from her.
She mustn't plead; having lost almost all her self-respect in the
shed, she must cling to the scraps that remained. "I could help
you," she said.

"Yeah. Maybe moving isn't quite the word." She could tell that
he bitterly resented having to explain. "I haven't got anywhere to
live at the moment. I was staying with some people. They threw
me out."

Nor must she allow her pride to trick her. The sodium glow
filled the road with fire, but it was very cold. "You can come home
with me if you like," she blurted.

He stared at her. After a pause he said indifferently "Yeah, okay."

She mustn't expect too much of him. All that mattered was that
she mustn't be alone. She took his clammy hand and led him
towards her street. Without warning he said "I never met anyone
like you." It sounded less like a compliment than a statement of
confusion.

They groped along the dark streets, their eyes blinded by lingering orange. "Is this where you live?" he said, almost contemp-
tuously. Where did he expect? The dreadful private road? The
thought convulsed her, made her grip his lank hand.

Thin carpets of moonlight lay over the crossroads, but her road
brimmed with darkness. It didn't matter, for she could feel him
beside her; she wouldn't let go. "You're so cold," he remarked,
speaking a stray thought.

Since she had no drugs, there was only one method by which
she might bind him to her. "In some ways I'm not cold at all," she
dared to say. If he understood, he didn't respond. He held her hand
as though it were something fragile that had been thrust upon him,
that he had no idea how to handle.

Though he didn't comment when they reached her house, she

sensed his feelings: disappointment, depression. All right, she knew it was a bit dismal: the scaly front door, the windows fattened with dusty grime, the ghosts of dust that rose up as she opened the door. She'd had no enthusiasm for keeping the place clean, nor indeed for anything else, since her parents had died. Now she'd enticed him so far, her fear was lightening slightly; she was able to think that he ought to be grateful, she was giving him a place to stay although she didn't even know his name.

She led him straight to her bedroom. Since her parents' death she had been unable to face the other deserted rooms. Moonlight leaked down the stairs from her door. As she climbed the vague treads she could feel him holding back. Suppose he decided not to stay, suppose he fled! "Nearly there now," she blurted, and became nervously still until she heard him clambering.

She pushed the door wide. Moonlight soaked the bed; a trace of her shape lay on the luminous sheets, a specter of virginity. Dust came to meet her. "Here we are," she said, treading on the board which always creaked—now she wasn't alone, she could enjoy such familiar aspects of the room.

He hesitated, a dark scrawny bulk in the doorway. It disturbed her not to be able to see his face. "Isn't there a light?" he muttered.

"Yes, of course." She was surprised both that he should ask and that it hadn't occurred to her to turn it on. But the switch clicked lifelessly; there was no bulb. When had it been removed? "Anyway, it's quite light in here," she said uneasily. "We can see."

He didn't advance, but demanded "What for?"

He wanted to know why she'd brought him here; he expected her to offer him dope. She must persuade him not to leave, but could she? A worse fear invaded her. Even if he stayed, might not the power of the thing in the graveyard drag her away from him?

"No, we don't need to see." She was talking rapidly, to make sure of him before her trembling shook her words to pieces. "I only offered you somewhere to stay." No time for self-respect now; her panic jerked out her words. "Come to bed with me."

Oh Christ, she'd scared him off! But no, he hadn't shifted; only his hands squirmed like embarrassed children. "Please," she said. "I'm lonely."

If only he knew how alone! She felt the great raw gap where her memory had been. She could go to nobody except the thing in the graveyard shed. Her panic made her say "If you don't, you can't stay."

At last he moved. He was heading for the stairs. Her gasp of horror filled her mouth with dust. All at once she saw what his trouble might be. Heroin might have rendered him impotent. "Please," she wailed, clutching his arm. "I'll help you. You'll be all right with me."

Eventually he let her lead him to the bed. But he stared at it, then leaned one hand on the blankets. Disgusted, he flinched back from the squelching. She hadn't realized it was still so damp. "We'll spread your coat on top," she promised. "You haven't got anywhere better to go, have you?"

She unbuttoned his coat. His jeans were the colors of various stains; his drab sweater was spotted with flesh-tinted holes. She undressed him swiftly—naked, he couldn't escape. In the moonlight his penis dangled like the limp tail of a pale animal.

She managed to smile at him, though his ribs ridged his chest with shadows and his limbs were spindly. She didn't need a dream lover, only a companion. But he was stooping to his shoes, perhaps to cover up the inadequacy of his penis.

She hoped he might open her dress. She stood awaiting him. At least she could see his reaction, unlike the face in the shed. But there was no reaction to see. Undressing him had been like stripping a dummy, and it might have been a dummy that confronted her, its face slumped, its hands and penis dangling.

She removed her dress. It was dry; she spread it over his coat. She slid off her panties and dropped them on the small heap of clothes, all friends together. Both of them were shivering, she more from panic than with chill. They must be quick. If the thing reached out of the dark for her she would have to go—but sex with the young man might anchor her here. It would. It must.

She persuaded him on to the bed, though he shuddered as his leg brushed the damp blankets. He lay on his coat and her dress, like a victim of concussion. Then irritability seemed to enliven him. He pushed her back and knelt over her, kissing her nipples, trying to find her clitoris with both hands. She felt her nipples harden, but no pleasure. He fell back abruptly, defeated by his lack of desire. His limp penis struck his thigh as though he were whipping himself.

God, he mustn't fail her! The creaking of the bed was thin and lonely in the deserted house. She was surrounded by empty rooms, dark streets, and—far too close—the shed. What would the thing's call be like? Would she feel her body carrying her away towards the shed before she knew it? She gazed trembling at the young man. "Please try," she pleaded.

He glared at her with something like hatred. She'd succeeded only in reminding him of his failure. She must help him. Her mouth moved down his body, which was very cold. Her head burrowed between his thighs, like a frightened animal; his penis flopped between her lips. She tried every method she could summon to raise it, but it was unresponsive as a corpse.

Please, oh please! The call from the dark was about to seize her, she could feel it lurking near, it would drag her helpless to the shed— The nodding of her head became more frenzied; in panic, her teeth closed on his penis. Then she faltered, for she thought his penis had stirred.

The dark blotch of his face jerked up gasping. It *had* stirred, and he was as surprised as she. She redoubled her efforts, nipping his penis lightly. Come on, oh please! At last—though not before she felt swarming with icy sweat—she had erected him. Terrified lest he dwindle, she mounted his body at once and worked herself around him.

In the moonlight his face lay beneath her, white and gasping as a dead fish. Despite her sense of imminent terror she was almost angry. She'd liven him, she'd make him respond to her. She moved slowly at first, drawing his penis deeper, awakening it gradually.

When the room was loud with his quickened breathing she drove faster. Make him grateful to her, make him stay! His penis jerked within her, lively now. She encouraged its throbbing, until all at once the throbbing cascaded. His gasp was nearly a scream; he clung to her with all his limbs. Though she experienced no pleasure, she was gratified that he had achieved his orgasm. Of this situation at least she was in control.

She lay on him. His cold cheek nuzzled hers. "I didn't think I could," he muttered, amazed and shyly boastful. She stroked his face tenderly, to make sure that he would stay with her. She had embraced his shoulders, hoping that she could sleep in his arms, when the summons came.

She couldn't tell which sense perceived it. Perhaps its appeal was deeper than any sense. She had no time to know what was happening, for her body had risen on all fours, like an instinctively obedient pet. Her consciousness was merely an observer, and could not even voice its scream.

No, it could do more. For the first time she was awake when summoned. Her panic blazed, jagged as lightning, through her nerves. It convulsed her, and made her nails clutch her partner's shoulders. He gasped; then his limbs seized her. He thought she was eager for sex again.

All at once her body sagged. Incredibly, she seemed free. The summons had withdrawn, balked. She slumped on the young man, who embraced her more closely. She'd won! But she was nervous with a thought, urgent yet blurred: the summons might not be the only power with which her tormentor could seize her. She glared wildly about. The horned black head of the chimney loomed against the moon. She was still trying to imagine what might come to her when she felt it: disgust, that spread through her like poison.

At once the young man was intolerable. His gasping fish-lips, his flesh cold and pale as something long drowned, his limbs clutching at her, bony and spider-like, his dull eyes white with moonlight, his moist flabby penis— She tried to struggle free, but he clung to her, unwilling to let her go.

Then she was flooded by another sort of power. It had seized her once before: a slow and steady physical strength, enormous and ruthless. Appalled, she thought of her dream of the boxes. She tore herself free of the young man—but the strength made her go on, though she tried to close her eyes, to shut out the sight of what she was doing. Somewhere she'd read of people being torn limb from limb, but she had thought that was just a turn of phrase. She had never been able to visualize how it could be done—nor that it could be so deafening and messy.

By the time she had finished, her consciousness had almost managed to hide. But she felt the summons marching her downstairs. Rooms resounded with her helplessly regular footsteps. As she heard the emptiness, she remembered how utterly lonely she had felt after her parents' death. One night she had emptied a bottle of sleeping tablets into her hand.

The call dragged her from the house. Moonlight spilled into the street, and she saw that all the houses were derelict, windowed with corrugated tin. She was allowed that glimpse, then she was marching: but not towards the main road—towards the church.

Her mind knew why, and dreaded remembering. But she must prepare herself for whatever was to come. She struggled in her trudging body. The only memory she could grasp seemed at first irrelevant. The words that she'd glimpsed in the window of the car outside Loveman's house had been DISTRICT NURSE.

Loveman wasn't dead. At once she knew that. The rumor of his death had been nothing more. Perhaps he had spread the rumor himself, for his own purposes. He must have married the Christian nurse; no doubt she had nursed him back to health. But married or not, he would have been unable to forgo his surreptitious visits to the graveyard. He still preferred the dead to the living.

She knew what that meant. Oh Christ, she knew! She didn't need to be shown! But the power forced her past the massive bland church and into the graveyard. She was rushed forward, stumbling and sobbing inwardly, past funereal dildoes of stone. If she could move her hand just a little, to grab one, to hold herself back—

But she'd staggered to a halt, and was forced to gaze down at a fallen headstone surrounded by an upheaval of earth.

Still he must have felt that she was insufficiently convinced. She was forced to burrow deep into her grave, and to lie there blindly. It was a long time before he allowed her to scrabble her way out and to trudge, convulsively shaking herself clean of earth, towards the shed.

MERRY MAY

AS KILBRIDE LEFT the shadow of the house whose top floor he owned, the April sunlight caught him. All along this side of the broad street of tall houses, trees and shrubs were unfurling their foliage minutely. In the years approaching middle age the sight had made him feel renewed, but now it seemed futile, this compulsion to produce tender growth while a late frost lay in wait in the shadows. He bought the morning paper at the corner shop and scanned the personal columns while his car warmed up.

Alone and desperate? Call us now before you do anything else . . . There were several messages from H, but none to J for Jack. Deep down he must have known there wouldn't be, for he hadn't placed a message for weeks. During their nine months together, he and Heather had placed messages whenever either of them had had to go away, and the day when that had felt less like an act of love to him than a compulsion had been the beginning of the end of their relationship. The thought of compulsion reminded him of the buds opening moistly all around him, and he remembered Heather's vulva, gaping pinkly wider and wider. The stirring of his penis at the memory depressed and angered him. He crumpled the newspaper and swung the car away from the curb, deeper into Manchester.

He parked in his space outside the Northern College of Music and strode into the lecture hall. So many of his female students reminded him of Heather now, and not only because of their age. How many of them would prove to be talented enough to tour with even an amateur orchestra, as she had? How many would suffer a nervous breakdown, as she had? The eager bright-eyed faces dismayed him: they'd drain him of all the knowledge and insight he could communicate, and want more. Maybe he should see himself as sunlight to their budding, but he felt more like the compost as he climbed onto the stage.

"Sonata form in contemporary music . . ." He'd given the lecture a dozen times or more, yet all at once he seemed to have no thoughts. He stumbled through the introduction and made for the piano, too quickly. As he sat down to play an example there wasn't a note of living music in his head except his own, his thoughts for the slow movement of his symphony. He hadn't played that music to anyone but Heather. He remembered her dark eyes widening, encouraging him or yearning for him to succeed, and his fingers clutched at the keys, hammered out the opening bars. He'd reached the second subject before he dared glance at his students. They were staring blankly at him, at the music.

Surely they were reacting to its unfamiliarity; or could it be too demanding or too esoteric in its language? Not until a student near the back of the hall yawned behind her hand did it occur to Kilbride that they were simply bored. At once the music sounded intolerably banal, a few bits of second-hand material arranged in childishly clever patterns. He rushed through the recapitulation and stood up as if he were pushing the piano away from him, and felt so desperate to talk positively about music that he began another lecture, taking the first movement of Beethoven's Ninth to demonstrate the processes of symphonic breakdown and renewal. As the students grew more visibly impatient he felt as if he'd lost all his grasp of music, even when he realized that he'd already given this lecture. "Sorry, I know you've heard it all before," he said with an attempt at lightness.

It was his only lecture that Friday. He couldn't face his colleagues, not when the loss of Heather seemed to be catching up with him all at once. There was a concert at the Free Trade Hall, but by the time he'd driven through the lunchtime traffic clogged with roadworks, the prospect of Brahms and early Schoenberg seemed to have nothing to do with him. Perhaps he was realizing at last how little he had to do with music. He drove on, past the Renaissance arcades of the Hall, past some witches dancing about for a camera crew outside the television studios, back home to Salford.

The road led him over the dark waters of the Irwell and under a gloomy bridge to the near edge of Salford. He had to stop for traffic lights, so sharply that the crumpled newspaper rustled. He wondered suddenly if as well as searching for a sign of Heather he'd been furtively alert for someone to replace her. He made himself look away from the paper, where his gaze was resting leadenly, and met the eyes of a woman who was waiting by the traffic lights.

Something in her look beneath her heavy silvered eyelids made his penis raise its head. She wasn't crossing the road, just standing under the red light, drumming silver fingernails on her hip in the tight black glossy skirt. Her face was small and pert beneath studiedly shaggy red hair that overhung the collar of her fur jacket. "Going my way?" he imagined her saying, and then, before he knew he meant to, he reached across the passenger seat and rolled the window down.

At once he felt absurd, aghast at himself. But she stepped toward the car, a guarded smile on her lips. "Which way are you going?" he said just loud enough for her to hear.

"Whichever way you want, love."

Now that she was close he saw that she was more heavily made up than he'd realized. He felt guilty, vulnerable, excited. He fumbled for the catch on the door and watched her slip into the passenger seat, her fishnet thighs brushing together. He had to clear his throat before he could ask "How much?"

"Thirty for the usual, more for specials. I won't be hurt, but I'll give you some discipline if that's what you like."

"That won't be necessary, thank you."

"Only asking, love," she said primly, shrugging at his curtness. "I reckon you'll still want to go to my place."

She directed him through Salford, to a back street near Peel Park. At least this wasn't happening in Manchester itself, where the chief constable was a lay preacher, where booksellers were sent to jail for selling books like *Scared Stiff* and the police had seized *The Big Red One* on videocassette because the title was suggestive, yet he couldn't quite believe that it was happening at all. Children with scraped knees played in the middle of the street under clotheslines stretched from house to house; when at first they wouldn't get out of the way, Kilbride was too embarrassed to sound his horn. Women in brick passages through pairs of terraced houses stared at him and muttered among themselves as he parked the car and followed the silvered woman into her house.

Beyond the pink front door a staircase led upward, but she opened a door to the left of the stairs and let him into the front room. This was wedge-shaped, half of an already small room that had been divided diagonally by a partition. A sofa stood at the broad end, under the window, facing a television and video recorder at the other. "This is it, love," the woman said. "Don't be shy, come in."

Kilbride made himself step forward and close the door behind him. The pelt of dark red wallpaper made the room seem even smaller. Presumably there was a kitchen beyond the partition, for a smell of boiled sprouts hung in the air. The sense of invading someone else's domesticity aggravated his panic. "Relax now, love, you're safe with me," the woman murmured as she drew the curtains and deftly pulled out the rest of the sofa to make it into a bed.

He watched numbly while she unfolded a red blanket that was draped over the back of the sofa and spread it over the bed. He could just leave, he wasn't obliged to stay—but when she patted the bed, he seemed only able to sit beside her while she kicked off her shoes and hitched up her skirt to roll down her stockings. "Want to watch a video to get you in the mood?" she suggested.

"No, that isn't . . ." The room seemed to be growing smaller and hotter, which intensified the smell of sprouts. He watched her peel off the second stocking, but then the shouts of children made him glance nervously behind him at the curtains. She gave him an unexpected lopsided smile. "I know what *you* want," she said in the tone of a motherly waitress offering a child a cream cake. "You should've said."

She lifted a red curtain that had disguised an opening in the partition and disappeared behind it. Kilbride dug out his wallet hastily, though an inflamed part of his mind was urging him just to leave, and hunted for thirty pounds. The best he could do was twenty-seven or forty. He was damned if he would pay more than he'd been quoted. He crumpled the twenty-seven in his fist as she came back into the room.

She'd dressed up as a schoolgirl in gymslip and knee socks. "Thought as much," she said coyly. As she reached for the money she put one foot on the bed, letting her skirt ride up provocatively, and he saw that her pubic hair was dyed red, like her hair. The thought of thrusting himself into that graying crevice made him choke, red dimness and the smell of sprouts swelling in his head. He flung himself aside and threw the money behind her, to gain himself time. He fumbled open the inner door, then the outer, and fled into the street.

It was deserted. The women must have called in their children in case they overheard him and their neighbor. She'd thought when he glanced at the window that the children were attracting him, he thought furiously. He stalked to his car and drove away without looking back. What made it worse was that her instincts hadn't been entirely wrong, for now he found himself obsessively imagining Heather dressed as a schoolgirl. Once he had to stop the car in order to drag at the crotch of his clothes and give his stiffening penis room. Only the fear of crashing the car allowed him to interrupt the fantasy and drive home. He parked haphazardly, limped groaning upstairs to his flat, dashed into the bathroom and came violently before he could even masturbate.

It gave him no pleasure, it was too like being helpless. His penis remained pointlessly erect, until he was tempted to shove it under the cold tap, to get rid of his unfulfilling lust that was happier with fantasy than reality. Its lack of any purpose he could share or even admit to himself appalled him. At least now that it was satisfied, it wouldn't hinder his music.

He brewed himself a pot of strong coffee and took the manuscript books full of his score to the piano. He leafed through them, hoping for a spark of pleasure, then he played through them. When he came to the end he slammed his elbows on the keyboard and buried his face in his hands while the discord died away.

He thought of playing some Ravel to revive his pianistic technique, or listening to a favorite record, Monteverdi or Tallis, whose remoteness he found moving and inspiring. But now early music seemed out of date, later music seemed overblown or arid. He'd felt that way at Heather's age, but then his impatience had made him creative: he'd completed several movements for piano. Couldn't he feel that way again? He stared at the final page of his symphony, Kilbride's Unfinished, The Indistinguishable, Symphony No. −1, Symphony of a Thousand Cuts, not so much a chamber symphony as a pisspot symphony. . . . Twilight gathered in the room, and the notes on the staves began to wriggle like sperm. When it was too dark to see he played through the entire score from memory. The notes seemed to pile up around him like the dust of decades. He reached out blindly for the score and tore the pages one by one into tiny pieces.

He sat for hours in the dark, experiencing no emotion at all. He seemed to see himself clearly at last, a middle-aged nonentity with a yen for women half his age or even younger, a musical pundit with no ability to compose music, no right to talk about those who had. No wonder Heather's parents had forbidden him to visit her or call her. He'd needed her admiration to help him fend off the moment when he confronted himself, he realized. The longer he sat in the dark, the more afraid he was to turn on the light and see how alone he was. He flung himself at the light switch, grabbed handfuls of the torn pages and stuffed them into the kitchen bin. "Pathetic," he snarled, at them or at himself.

It was past midnight, he saw. He would never be able to sleep: the notes of his symphony were gathering in his head, a cumulative discord. There was nowhere to go for company at this hour except nightclubs, to meet people as lonely and sleepless as himself. But he could talk to someone, he realized, someone who wouldn't see his face or know anything about him. He tiptoed downstairs into the chilly windswept night and snatched the newspaper out of the car.

Alone and desperate? Call us now before you do anything else . . . The organization was called Renewal of Life, with a phone number on the far side of Manchester. The distance made him feel safer. If he didn't like what he heard at first he needn't even answer.

The phone rang for so long that he began to think he had a wrong number. Or perhaps they were busy helping people more desperate than he. That made him feel unreasonably selfish, but he'd swallowed so much self-knowledge today that the insight seemed less than a footnote. He was clinging stubbornly to the receiver when the ringing broke off halfway through a phrase, and a female voice said "Yes?"

She sounded as if she'd just woken up. It *was* a wrong number, Kilbride thought wildly, and felt compelled to let her know that it was. "Renewal of Life?" he stammered.

"Yes, it is." Her voice was louder, as if she was wakening further, or trying to. "What can we do for you?"

She must have nodded off at her post, he thought. That made her seem more human, but not necessarily more reassuring. "I—I don't know."

"You've got to do something for me first, and then I'll tell you."

She sounded fully awake now. Some of what he'd taken for drowsiness might have been something else, still there in her voice: a hint of lazy coyness that could have implied a sexual promise. "What is it?" he said warily.

"Swear you won't hang up on me."

"All right, I swear." He waited for her to tell him what was being offered, then felt absurd, embarrassed into talking. "I don't know what I was expecting when I called your number. I'm just at a low ebb, that's all, male menopause and all that. Just taking stock of myself and not finding much. Maybe this call wasn't such a good idea. Maybe I need someone who's known me for a while to show me if there's anything I missed about myself."

"Well, tell me about yourself then." When he was silent she said quickly, "At least tell me where you are."

"Manchester."

"Alone in the big city. That can't be doing you any good. What you need is a few days in the country, away from everything. You ought to come here, you'd like it. Yes, why don't you? You'd be over here for the dawn."

He was beginning to wonder how young she was. He felt touched and amused by her inexpertness, yet the hint of an underlying promise seemed stronger than ever. "Just like that?" he said laughing. "I can't do that. I'm working tomorrow."

"Come on Saturday, then. You don't want to be alone at the weekend, not the way you're feeling. Get away from all the streets and factories and pollution and see May in with us."

Sunday was May Day. He was tempted to go wherever she was inviting him—not the area to which the telephone number referred, apparently. "What sort of organization are you, exactly?"

"We just want to keep life going. That's what you wanted when you rang." She sounded almost offended, and younger than ever. "You wouldn't have to tell us anything about yourself you didn't want to or join in anything you didn't like the sound of."

Perhaps because he was talking to her in the middle of the night, that sounded unambiguously sexual. "If I decide to take you up on that I can call you then, can't I?"

"Yes, and then I'll give you directions. Call me even if you think you don't want to, all right? Swear."

"I swear," Kilbride said, unexpectedly glad to have committed himself, and could think of nothing else to say except "Good night." As soon as he'd replaced the receiver he realized that he should have found out her name. He felt suddenly exhausted, pleasantly so, and crawled into bed. He imagined her having been in bed while she was talking to him, then he saw her as a tall slim schoolgirl with a short skirt and long bare thighs and Heather's face. That gave him a pang of guilt, but the next moment he was asleep.

The morning paper was full of oppression and doom. He scanned the personal columns while he waited for his car engine to rouse itself. He no longer expected to find a message from Heather, but there was no sign of the Renewal of Life either.

That was his day for teaching pianistic technique. Some of his students played as if passion could replace technique, others played so carefully it seemed they were determined not to own up to emotion. He was able to show them where they were going wrong without growing impatient with them or the job, and their respect for him seemed to have returned. Perhaps on Tuesday he'd feel renewed enough to teach his other classes enthusiastically, he thought, wondering if the printers had omitted the Renewal of Life from today's paper by accident.

One student lingered at the end of the last class. "Would you give me your opinion of this?" She blushed as she sat down to play, and he realized she'd composed the piece herself. It sounded like a study of her favorite composers—cascades of Debussy, outbursts of Liszt, a token tinkle of Messiaen—but there was something of herself too, unexpected harmonic ideas, a kind of aural punning. He remarked on all that, and she went out smiling with her boyfriend, an uninspired violinist who was blushing now on her behalf. She had a future, Kilbride thought, flattered that she'd wanted his opinion. Maybe someday he'd be cited as having encouraged her at the start of her career.

A red sky was flaring over the turrets and gables of Manchester. Was he really planning to drive somewhere out there beyond the sunset? The more he recalled the phone conversation, the more dreamlike it seemed. He drove home and made sure he had yesterday's paper, and thought of calling the number at once—but the voice had said Saturday, and to call now seemed like tempting fate. The success of the day's teaching had dampened his adventurousness; he felt unexpectedly satisfied. When he went to bed he had no idea if he would phone at all.

Birdsong wakened him as the sky began to pale. He lay there feeling lazy as the dawn. He needn't decide yet about the weekend, it was too early—and then he realized that it wasn't, not at all. He wriggled out of bed and dialed the number he'd left beside the phone. Before he could even hear the bell at the other end a voice said "Renewal of Life."

It was brisker than last time. It had the same trace of a Lancashire accent, the broad vowels, but Kilbride wasn't sure if it was the same voice. "I promised to call you today," he said.

"We've been waiting. We're looking forward to having you. You are coming, aren't you?"

Perhaps the voice sounded different only because she had clearly not just woken up. "Are you some kind of religious organization?"

She laughed as if she knew he was joking. "You won't have to join in anything unless you want to, but whatever you enjoy, you'll find it here."

She could scarcely be more explicit without risking prosecution, he thought. "Tell me how to get to you," he said, all at once fully awake.

Her directions would take him into Lancashire. He bathed and dressed quickly, fueled the car and set out, wondering if her route was meant to take him through the streets and factories and pollution the first call had deplored. Beyond the city center streets of small shops went on for miles, giving way at last to long high almost featureless mills, to warehouses that made him think of terraced streets whose side openings had been bricked up. Their shadows shrank back into them as the sun rose, but he felt as if he would never be out of the narrow streets under the grubby sky.

At last the road began to climb beyond the crowding towns. Lush green fields spread around him, shrinking pools shone through the half-drowned grass. The grimy clouds were washed clean and hung along the horizon, and then the sky was clear. He drove for miles without meeting another car on the road. He was alone with the last day of April, the leaves opening more confidently, hovering in swarms in all the trees.

Half an hour or so into the countryside he began to wonder how much further his destination was. "Drive until you get to the Jack in the Green," she'd said, "and ask for us." He'd taken that to be a pub, or was it a location or a monument? Even if he never found it, the sense of renewal he had already derived from the day in the open would be worth the journey. The road was climbing again, between banks of ferns almost as large as he was. He'd find a vantage point and stop for a few minutes, he thought, and then the road led over a crest and showed him the factory below.

The sight was as unexpected as it was disagreeable. At least the factory was disused, he saw as the car sped down the slope. All the windows in the long dull-red facade had fallen in, and so had part of the roof. Once there had been several chimneys, but only one remained, and even that was wobbling. When he stared at it, it appeared to shift further. He had to strain his eyes, for something like a mist hung above the factory, a darkening of the air, a blurring of outlines. The chimney looked softened, as did all the window openings. That must be an effect of the air here in the valley— the air smelled bad, a cold slightly rotten stench—but the sight made him feel quiverish, particularly around his groin. He trod hard on the accelerator, to be out from among the drab wilting fields.

The car raced up into the sunlight. He blinked the dazzle out of his eyes and saw the village below him, on the far side of the crest from the factory. A few streets of limestone cottages led off the main road and sloped down to a village green overlooked by an inn and a small church. Several hundred yards beyond the green, a forest climbed the rising slopes. Compared with the sagging outlines of the ruin, the clarity of the sunlit cottages and their flowery gardens was almost too intense. His chest tightened as he drove past them to the green.

He parked near the inn and stared at its sign, the Jack in the Green, a jovial figure clothed and capped with grass. He hadn't felt so nervous since stage fright had seized him at his first recital. When he stepped out of the car, the slam of the door unnerved him. A dog barked, a second dog answered, but there was no other sound, not even of children. He felt as if the entire village was waiting to see what he would do.

A tall slim tree lay on the green. Presumably it was to be a maypole, for an axe gleamed near it in the grass, but its branches had still to be lopped. Whoever had carried it here might be in the inn, he thought, and turned toward the building. A woman was watching him from the doorway.

She sauntered forward as his gaze met hers. She was tall and moderately plump, with a broad friendly face, large gray eyes, a small nose, a wide very pink mouth. As she came up to him, the tip of her tongue flickered over her lips. "Looking for someone?" she said.

"Someone I spoke to this morning."

She smiled and raised her eyebrows. Her large breasts rose and fell under the clinging green dress that reached just below her knees. He smelled her perfume, wild and sweet. "Was it you?" he said.

"Would you like it to be?"

He would happily have said yes, except that he wondered what choices he might be rejecting. He felt his face redden, and then she touched his wrist with one cool hand. "No need to decide yet. When you're ready. You can stay at the Jack if you like, or with us."

"Us?"

"Father'll be out dancing."

He couldn't help feeling that she meant to reassure him. There was an awkward pause until she said, "You're wondering what you're supposed to do."

"Well, yes."

"Anything you like. Relax, look around, go for a walk. Tomorrow's the big day. Have some lunch or a drink. Do you want to work up an appetite?"

"By all means."

"Come over here then and earn yourself a free lunch."

Could he have been secretly dreaming that she meant to take him home now? He followed her to the maypole, laughing inwardly and rather wildly at himself. "See what you can do about stripping that," she said, "while I bring you a drink. Beer all right?"

"Fine," he said, reflecting that working on the maypole would be a small price to pay for what he was sure he'd been led to expect. "By the way, what's your name?"

"Sadie." With just the faintest straightening of her smile she added, "Mrs. Thomas."

She could be divorced or a widow. He picked up the axe, to stop himself brooding. It was lighter than he expected, but very sharp. When he grasped a branch at random and chopped experimentally at it, he was able to sever it with two blows.

"Not bad for a music teacher," he murmured, and set to work systematically, starting at the thin end of the tree. Perhaps he should have begun at the other, for after the first dozen or so branches the lopping grew harder. By the time Sadie Thomas brought him a pint of strong ale, his arms were beginning to ache. As she crossed the green to him he looked up, wiping sweat from his forehead in a gesture he regretted immediately, and found that he had an audience, several men sitting on a bench outside the inn.

They were Kilbride's age, or younger. He couldn't quite tell, for their faces looked slack, blurred by indolence—pensioned off, he thought, and remembered the factory. Nor could he read their expressions, which might be hostile or simply blank. He was tempted to step back from the maypole and offer them the job—it was their village, after all—but then two of them mopped their foreheads deliberately, and he wondered if they were mocking him. He chopped furiously at the tree, and didn't look up until he'd severed the last branch.

A burst of applause, which might have been meant ironically, greeted his laying down the axe. He felt suddenly that the phone conversations and the rest of it had been a joke at his expense. Then Sadie Thomas squatted by him, her green skirt unveiling her strong thighs, and took his hands to help him up. "You've earned all you can eat. Come in the Jack, or sit out if you like."

All the men stood up in case he wanted to sit on the bench. Some looked resentful, but all the same, they obviously felt he had the right. "I'll sit outside," he said, and wondered why the men exchanged glances as they moved into the inn.

He was soon to learn why. A muscular woman with cropped gray hair brought out a table which she placed in front of him and loaded with a plateful of cheese, a loaf and a knife and another tankard of ale, and then Sadie came to him. "When you're done eating, would you do one more thing for us?"

His arms were trembling from stripping the maypole; he was only just able to handle the knife. "Nothing strenuous this time," she said reassuringly. "We just need a judge, someone who isn't from around here. You've only to sit and choose."

"All right," Kilbride said, then felt as if his willingness to please had got the better of him. "What am I judging?"

She gave him a coy look that reminded him of the promise he thought he'd heard in the telephone voice. "Ah, that'd be telling."

Perhaps the promise would be broken if he asked too many questions, especially in public. It still excited him enough to be worth his suffering some uncertainty, not least over how many of the villagers were involved in the Renewal of Life. His hands steadied as he finished off the cheese, and he craned to watch Sadie as she hurried into the village, to the small schoolhouse in the next street. He realized what they must want him to judge at this time of the year as the young girls came marching from the school and onto the green.

They lined up in front of the supine maypole and faced him,

their hands clasped in front of their stomachs. Some gazed challengingly at him, but most were shy, or meant to seem so. He couldn't tell if they knew that besides casting their willowy shadows toward him, the sun was shining through their uniforms, displaying silhouettes of their bodies. "Go closer if you like," Sadie said in his ear.

He stood up before his stiffening penis could hinder him, and strode awkwardly toward the girls. They were thirteen or fourteen years old, the usual age for a May Queen, but some of them looked disconcertingly mature. He had to halt a few yards short of them, for while embarrassment was keeping his penis more or less under control, every step rubbed its rampant tip against his fly. Groaning under his breath, he tried to look only at their faces. Even that didn't subdue him, for one girl had turned her head partly away from him and was regarding him through her long dark eyelashes in a way that made him intensely aware of her handfuls of breasts, her long silhouetted legs. "This one," he said in a loud hoarse voice, and stretched out a shaky hand to her.

When she stepped forward he was afraid she would take his hand in front of all of them. But she walked past him, flashing him a sidelong smile, as the line of young girls broke up, some looking relieved, some petulant. Kilbride pretended to gaze across the green until his penis subsided. When he turned, he found that several dozen people had gathered while he was judging.

The girl he'd chosen had joined Sadie. Belatedly he saw how alike they were. Even more disconcerting than that and the silent arrival of the villagers was the expression he glimpsed on Sadie's face as she glanced at her daughter, an expression that seemed to combine pride with a hint of dismay. The schoolgirls were dispersing in groups, murmuring and giggling. Some of the villagers came forward to thank Kilbride, so hesitantly that he wasn't sure what he was being thanked for; the few men who did so behaved as if they had been prodded into approaching him. Close up their faces looked flabbier than ever, almost sexless.

Sadie turned back from leading away her daughter to point along the street behind the inn. "You're staying with us, aren't you? We're at number three. Dinner's at seven. What are you going to do in the meantime?"

"Walk, I should think. Find my way around."

"Make yourself at home," said a stocky bespectacled woman, and her ringleted stooping companion added, "Anything you want, just ask."

He wanted to think, though perhaps not too deeply. He sat on the bench as the shadows of the forest crept toward the green. He was beginning to think he knew why he'd been brought here, but wasn't he just indulging a fantasy he was able at last to admit to himself? He stood up abruptly, having thought of a question he needed to ask.

The inn was locked, and presumably he wasn't meant to go to Sadie's before seven. He strolled through the village in the afternoon light, flowers in the small packed gardens glowing sullenly. People gossiping outside cottages hushed as he approached, then greeted him heartily. He couldn't ask them. Even gazing in the window of the only shop, a corner cottage whose front room was a general store, he felt ill at ease.

He was nearly back at his starting point after ten minutes' stroll when he noticed the surgery, a cottage with a doctor's brass plaque on the gatepost, in the same row as Sadie's. The neat wizened gnomish man who was killing insects on a rockery with precise bursts from a spray bottle must be the doctor. He straightened up as Kilbride hesitated at the gate. "Is there something I can do for you?" he said in a thin high voice.

"Are you part of the Renewal of Life?"

"I certainly hope so."

Kilbride felt absurd, though the doctor didn't seem to be mocking him. "I mean, are all of you here in the village part of that?"

"We're a very close community." The doctor gave a final lethal squirt and stood up. "So don't feel as if you aren't welcome if anyone seems unfriendly."

That was surely a cue for the question, if Kilbride could frame it carefully enough. "Am I on my own? That's to say, was anyone else asked to come here this weekend?"

The doctor looked straight at him, pale eyes gleaming. "You're the one."

"Thank you," Kilbride said and moved away, feeling lightheaded. Passing the church, where a stone face with leaves sprouting from its mouth and ears grinned from beneath the steep roof, he strolled toward the woods. The doctor's reply had seemed unequivocal, but questions began to swarm in Kilbride's mind as he wandered through the fading light and shade. Whether because he felt like an outsider or was expected to be quite the opposite, he skulked under the trees until he saw the inn door open. As he returned to the village, a hint of the stench from the factory met him.

The bar was snug and darkly paneled. The flames of a log fire danced in reflections on the walls, where photographs of Morris dancers hung under the low beams. Kilbride sat and drank and eventually chatted to two slow men. At seven he made his way to Sadie Thomas' house, and realized that he couldn't remember a word of the conversation in the pub.

Sadie's cottage had a red front door that held a knocker in its brass teeth. When Kilbride knocked, a man came to the door. He was taller and bulkier than Kilbride, with a sullen almost circular face. A patchy moustache straggled above his drooping lips. He stared with faint resentment at the suitcase Kilbride had brought from the car. "Just in time," he muttered, and as an afterthought before Kilbride could step over the threshold, "Bob Thomas."

When he stuck out his hand Kilbride made to shake it, but the man was reaching for the suitcase. He carried it up the steep cramped stairs, then stumped down to usher Kilbride into the dining kitchen, a bright room the width of the house, its walls printed with patterns of blossoms. Sadie and her daughter were sitting at a round table whose top was a single slice of oak. They smiled at Kilbride, the daughter more shyly, and Sadie dug a ladle into a steaming earthenware pot. "Sit there," Bob Thomas said gruffly when Kilbride made to let him have the best remaining chair.

Sadie heaped his plate with hotpot, mutton stewed with pota-
toes, and he set about eating as soon as seemed polite, to cover
the awkwardness they were clearly all feeling. "Good meat," he
said.

"Not from around here," Sadie said as if it was important for
him to know.

"Because of the factory, you mean?"

"Aye, the factory," Bob Thomas said with unexpected fierceness.
"You know about that, do you?"

"Only what I gathered over the phone—I mean, when I was
told to get away from factories."

Bob Thomas gazed at him and fingered his moustache as if he
were trying to conjure more of it into existence. Kilbride froze
inside himself, wondering if he'd said too much. "Daddy doesn't
like to talk about the factory," the daughter murmured as she raised
her fork delicately to her lips, "because of what it did to him and
all the men."

"Margery!"

Kilbride couldn't have imagined that a father could make his
child's name sound so like a curse. Margery flinched and gazed at
the ceiling, and Kilbride was searching for a way to save the conversation when Margery said, "Did you notice?"

She was talking to him. Following her gaze, he saw that the
rounded beam overhead seemed more decorative than supportive.
"It's a maypole," he realized.

"Last year's."

She sounded prouder than he could account for. "You believe
in keeping traditions alive, then," he said to Bob Thomas.

"They'll keep theirselves alive whatever I believe in, I reckon."

"I mean," Kilbride floundered on, "that's why you stay here, why
you don't move away."

Bob Thomas took a deep breath and stared furiously at nothing.
"We stay here because family lived here. The factory came when
we needed the work. Him who owned it was from here, so we
thought he was doing us a kindness, but he poisoned us instead.

We found work up road and closed him down. Poisoned we may be, we'll not be driven out on top of it. We'll do what we have to to keep place alive."

It was clearly an unusually sustained speech for him, and it invited no response. Kilbride was left wondering if any of it referred to himself. Sadie and her daughter kept up the conversation during the rest of the meal, and Kilbride listened intently, to their voices rather than to their words. "Father isn't like this really, it's just the time of year. Don't let him put you off staying," Sadie said to Kilbride as she cleared away the plates.

"Swear you won't," Margery added.

He did so at once, because now he was sure he'd spoken to her on the phone at least the first time. Bob Thomas lowered his head bull-like, but said nothing. His inertia seemed to sink into the house; there was little to say, and less to do—the Thomases had neither a television nor a radio, not even a telephone as far as Kilbride could see. He went up to his bedroom as soon as he reasonably could.

He stood for a while at the window that was let into the low ceiling, which followed the angle of the roof, and watched the moon rise over the woods. When he tired of that he lay on the bed in the small green room and wished he'd brought something to read. He was loath to go out of the room again, in case he met Bob Thomas. Eventually he ventured to the bathroom and then retired to bed, to watch an elongating lozenge of moonlight inch down the wall above his feet. He was asleep before it reached him.

At first he thought the voices were calling him, dozens of voices just outside his room. They belonged to all the girls who had paraded for his judgment on the green, and now they were here to collect a consolation prize. They must be crowded together on the steep staircase—he'd have no chance of escaping until they had all had a turn, even if he wanted to. Besides, his penis was swelling so uncontrollably that he was helpless; already it was thicker than his leg, and still growing. If he didn't answer the voices the girls would crowd into the room and fall on him, but he was unable to make any sound at all. Then he realized that they couldn't be calling him, because nobody in the village knew his name.

The shock wakened him. The voices were still calling. He shoved himself into a sitting position, almost banging his head on the ceiling, and peered wildly about. The voices weren't calling to him, nor were they in the house. He swung his feet off the bed, wincing as a floorboard creaked, and gazed out of the window.

The moon was almost full. At first it seemed to show him only slopes coated with moonlight. Nothing moved except a few slow cows in a field. Not only the cows but the field were exactly the color of the moon. The woods looked carved out of ivory, so still that the shifting of branches sent a shiver through him. Then he saw that the trees which were stirring were too far apart for a wind to be moving them.

He raised the window and craned out to see. He stared at the edge of the woods until the trunks began to flicker with his staring. The voices were in the woods, he was sure. Soon he glimpsed movement in the midst of the trees, on a hillock that rose above the canopy of branches. Two figures, a man and a woman, appeared there hand in hand. They embraced and kissed, and at last their heads separated, peering about at the voices. The next moment they disappeared back into the woods.

They were early, Kilbride thought dreamily. They ought to wait until the eleventh, May Day of the old calendar, the first day of the Celtic summer. In those days they would be blowing horns as well as calling to one another, to ensure that nobody got lost as they broke branches and decorated them with hawthorn flowers. Couples would fall silent if they wanted to be left alone. He wondered suddenly whether he was meant to be out there—whether they would be calling him if they knew his name.

He opened the bedroom door stealthily and tiptoed onto the tiny landing. The doors of the other bedrooms were ajar. His heart quickened as he paced to the first and looked in. Both rooms were empty. He was alone in the cottage, and he suspected that he might be alone in the village.

Surely he was meant to be in the woods. Perhaps tradition forbade anyone to come and waken him, perhaps he had to be wakened by the calling in the trees. He closed his bedroom window against the stench that seeped down from the factory, then he dressed and hurried downstairs.

The front door wasn't locked. Kilbride closed it gently behind him and made for the pavement, which was tarred with shadow. Less than a minute's walk through the deserted village took him into the open, by the church. Though only the stone face with leaves in its ears and mouth seemed to be watching him, he felt vulnerable in the moonlight as he strode across the green, past the supine maypole, and into the field that was bordered by the woods. Once he started, for another stone face with vegetation dangling from its mouth was staring at him over a gate, but it was a cow. All the way from the cottage to the woods, he heard voices calling under the moon.

He hesitated at the edge of the trees, where the shadow of a cloud crept over bleached knuckly roots. The nearest voices were deep in the woods. Kilbride made his way among the trees, his feet sinking into leaf-mold. He stopped and held his breath whenever he trod on a twig, however muffled the sound was, or whenever he glimpsed movement among the pale trunks etched intricately with darkness. All the same, he nearly stumbled over the couple in the secluded glade, having taken them for moving shadows.

Kilbride dodged behind a tree and covered his mouth while his breathing grew calmer. He didn't want to watch the couple, but he dared not move until he could measure his paces. The woman's skirt was pushed above her waist, the man's trousers were around his ankles; Kilbride could see neither of their faces. The man was tearing at the mossy ground with his hands as his buttocks pumped wildly. Then his shoulders sagged, and the woman's hands cupped his face in a comforting gesture. The man recommenced thrusting at her, more and more desperately, and Kilbride was suddenly convinced that they were Bob and Sadie Thomas. But the man's head jerked back, his face distorted with frustration, and Kilbride saw that he was no more than twenty years old.

In that moment a good deal became clear to Kilbride. What was happening in the woods wasn't so much a celebration of Spring as a desperate ritual. Now he saw how total the effect of the pollution by the factory had been, and he realized that he hadn't seen or heard any young children in the village. He hid behind the tree, his face throbbing with embarrassment, and tiptoed away as soon as he thought he could do so unnoticed. All the way out of the woods he was afraid of intruding on another scene like the one he'd witnessed. He was halfway across the moonlit field, and almost running for fear that someone would see him and suspect that he knew, when he realized fully what they must expect of him.

He stood in the shadow of the inn to think. He could fetch his suitcase and drive away while there was nobody to stop him—but why should he fear that they would? On the contrary, the men seemed anxious to see the last of him. He wouldn't be driven out, he promised himself. It wasn't just that he'd been invited, it was that someone needed him. All the same, back in the green bedroom he lay awake for hours, wondering when they would send for him, listening to the distant voices calling in the dark. They sounded plaintive to him now, almost hopeless. It was close to dawn before he fell asleep.

This time his dreams weren't sexual. He was at a piano in an empty echoing concert hall, his fingers ranging deftly over the keys, drawing music from them that he'd never heard before, music calm as a lingering sunset then powerful as a mountain storm. The hands on the keys were his hands as a young man, he saw. He looked for pen and paper, but there was none. He'd remember the music until he could write it down, he told himself. He must remember, because this music was the whole point of his life. Then a spotlight blazed into his eyes, which jerked open, and the dream and the music were gone.

It was the sun, shining through the window in the roof. He

turned away from it and tried to grasp the dream. Sunlight groped over his back and displayed itself on the wall in front of him. Eventually he gave up straining, in the hope that the memory would return unbidden. The silence made itself felt then. Though it must be midday at least, the village was silent except for the lowing of a cow and the jingle of bells. The sound of bells drew him to the window.

The maypole was erect in the middle of the green. The villagers were standing about on the grass. The young women wore short white dresses, and garlands in their hair. Half a dozen Morris dancers in uniform—knee-breeches, clogs, bracelets of bells at their wrists—stood near the inn, drinking beer. At the far side of the green were two empty seats. Kilbride blinked sleepily toward these, and then he realized that one of them must be his—that the whole village was waiting for him.

They might have wakened him, then. Presumably they had no special costume for him. He bathed hastily, dressed and hurried out. As he reached the green, the villagers turned almost in unison to him.

The Morris man who came over to him proved to be Bob Thomas. Kilbride found the sight of him in costume disconcerting in a variety of ways. "Ready, are you?" Bob Thomas said gruffly. "Come on, sit you down." He led Kilbride to the left-hand of the chairs, both of which were made of new wood nailed together somewhat roughly. As soon as Kilbride was seated, two of the garlanded girls approached him with armfuls of vines, wrapping them around his body and then around his limbs, which they left free to move, to his relief. Then Margery came forward alone and sat by him.

She wasn't wearing much under the long white dress. As she passed in front of him, shyly averting her eyes, her nipples and the shadows around them appeared clearly through the linen. Kilbride gave her a smile which was meant to reassure her but which he suspected might look lecherous. He turned away as the girls approached once more, bearing a crown composed of blossoms on a wiry frame, which they placed on Margery's head.

The festivities began then, and Kilbride was able to devote himself to watching. When Sadie Thomas brought him and Margery
a trayful of small cakes, he found he was ravenous. The more he
ate, the stranger and more appealing the taste seemed: a mixture
of meat, apple, onion, thyme, rosemary, sugar and another herbal
taste he couldn't put a name to. Margery ate a token cake and left
the rest for him.

The young girls danced around the maypole, holding onto ribbons that dangled from the tip. The patterns of the dance and the
intricate weaving of the ribbons gradually elaborated themselves in
Kilbride's mind, a kind of crystallizing of the display on the green,
the grass reaching for the sunlight, the dazzling white dresses ex-
posing glimpses of bare thighs, the girls glancing at himself and
Margery with expressions he was less and less sure of. How long
had they been dancing? It felt like hours to him and yet no time
at all, as though the spring sunlight had caught the day and
wouldn't let it go.

At last the girls unweaved the final pattern, and the Morris
dancers strode onto the green. Bob Thomas wasn't the leader, Kilbride saw, feeling unaccountably relieved. The men lined up face-
to-face in two rows and began to dance slowly and deliberately,
brandishing decorated staves two feet long, which they rapped together at intervals. The patterns of their turns and confrontations
seemed even more intricate than the maypole dance; the muscu-
larity of the dancing made his penis feel thickened, though it
wasn't erect. The paths the dancers described were solidifying in
his mind, strengthening him. He realized quite calmly that the
cakes had been drugged.

The shadows of the Morris men grew longer as he watched,
shadows that merged and parted and leapt toward the audience of
villagers on the far side of the green. Shouldn't shadows be the
opposite of what was casting them? he thought, and seemed unable
to look away from them until the question was resolved. He was
still pondering when the dancing ended. The shadows appeared to
continue dancing for a moment longer. Then the Morris men

clashed their staves together and danced away toward the nearest field.

Kilbride watched bemused as all the males of the village followed them. Several boys and young men glared at him, and he realized that his time was near. Led by the Morris dancers, the men and boys disappeared over the slope toward a green sunset. The jingling of bells faded, and then there was only the sound of birdsong in the woods behind him.

He supposed he ought to turn to Margery, but his head was enormous and cumbersome. He gazed at the dimming of the green, which felt like peace, imperceptibly growing. His awareness that Sadie and another woman were approaching wasn't enough to make him lift his head. When they took hold of his arms he rose stiffly to his feet and stood by the chair, his body aching from having sat so long, while they unwound the vines from him. Then they led him away from Margery, past the maypole and its willowy garlands, past the clods the Morris dancers' heels had torn out of the ground. The women beside the green parted as he reached them, their faces expressionless, and he saw that Sadie and her companion were leading him to the church.

They led him through the small bare porch and opened the inner door. Beyond the empty pews the altar was heaped with flowers. A few yards in front of the altar, a mattress and pillows lay on the stone floor. The women ushered Kilbride to the mattress and lowered him onto it, so gently that he felt he was sinking like an airborne seed. They walked away from him side by side without looking back, and closed the doors behind them.

The narrow pointed windows darkened gradually as he lay waiting. The outlines of pews sank into the gathering dark. The last movements he'd seen, the women's buttocks swaying as they retreated down the aisle, filled his mind and his penis. His erection felt large as the dark, yet not at all peremptory. He had almost forgotten where he was and why he was waiting when he heard the porch door open.

The inner door opened immediately after. He could just see the night outside, shaped by the farther doorway. Against the outer darkness stood two figures in white dresses. Their heads touched to whisper, and then the slimmer figure ventured hesitantly forward.

Kilbride pushed himself easily to his feet and went to meet her. He hadn't reached her when her companion stepped back and closed the inner door. A moment later the porch door closed. Kilbride paced forward, feeling his way along the ends of the pews, and as he gained the last he made out the white dress glimmering in front of him. He reached out and took her hand.

He felt her stiffen so as not to flinch, heard her draw a shaky breath. Then she relaxed, or made herself relax, and let him lead her toward the altar. Though the dark had virtually blinded him, his other senses were unusually acute; the warmth of her flesh seemed to course into him through her hand; her scent, more delicate than Sadie's, seemed overwhelming. He hardly needed to touch the pews to find his way back to the mattress. Once there he pushed her gently down on it and knelt beside her. The next moment she reached clumsily for him.

Her hands groped over his penis, fumbling at his fly. He stroked her hair, which was soft and electric, to soothe her, slow her down, but she dragged at his clothes all the more urgently. She'd eaten one of the cakes, he remembered; it might well have been an aphrodisiac. He wriggled out of his clothes and left them on the stone floor, then he found her again in the dark.

Her hands closed around his swelling penis, her nervous fingers traced its length. He stroked her narrow shoulders, ran his hands down her slim body, over her firm buttocks, which tensed as his hands slid down her thighs and back up under her dress. She raised herself so that he could pull the dress over her head, then her hands returned to his penis, more confidently. When he stroked her buttocks, which were clad in thin nylon, she moaned under her breath.

As soon as he began to ease her knickers down she pulled them off and kicked them away, then grabbed his hand and closed her thighs around it. He ran his thumb through her wiry pubic bush, and her thighs opened wide to him. The lips of her sex closed over his fingers, gulping them moistly, more and more greedily, and then she curled herself catlike and took his penis in her mouth.

As her tongue flickered over the tip his erection grew suddenly urgent. His penis felt like pleasure incarnate, pleasure so intense it made the darkness blaze and throb behind his eyes. He put one hand under her chin to raise her head. Before he could move she climbed over him and lowered herself onto his penis, thrust him deep into her.

He couldn't tell if her cry expressed pain or pleasure: perhaps both. She pressed herself fiercely against him as her body grasped his penis moistly, sucking him deeper. Despite the urgency, each crescendo of sensation was longer and slower and more lingering. Her arms began to tremble with supporting herself above him, and he rolled her over and plunged himself as deep as he could. When he came, it seemed to last forever. He was intensely aware of her and of the church around them, and the slow flowering of himself seemed an act of worship of both.

As he dwindled within her, sensations fading slowly as a fire, he felt capable of embracing the world. All at once the path of his life, leading through it to this moment, grew clearer to him. He viewed it with amused tolerance, even the music in his dream, which he remembered now. It wasn't that good, he saw, but it might be worth transcribing. Just now this sense of all-embracing peace was enough.

Or almost enough, for the girl was shivering. He could see the outline of her face now, in the moonlight that had begun to seep through the narrow windows. He lay beside her, his penis still in her, and stroked her face. "It was the first time for Renewal of Life too, wasn't it? I hope it achieves what it was meant to. I just want to tell you that I've never experienced anything like it, ever. Thank you, Margery."

He must be speaking more loudly than he intended, for his voice was echoing. He thought that was why she jerked away from him, lifted herself clear and fled along the glimmering aisle—and then he realized what he'd done to make her flee. He'd used her name, he'd betrayed that he knew who she was. They would never let him go now. The notion of dying at this point in his life was unexpectedly calming. He felt as if he'd achieved the best he was capable of. He dressed unhurriedly and paced along the aisle, through stripes of moonlight. As he stepped into the darkness of the porch he heard a muffled sobbing outside the church. He hoped it wasn't Margery. He grasped the iron ring and opened the outer door.

The moon was high above the green. From the porch it looked impaled by the rearing maypole. The sound of renewed sobbing made him turn toward the inn. Several women had gathered outside, and in their midst was Margery, weeping behind her hands. Someone had draped a black coat over her white dress. Sadie Thomas glanced at Kilbride, regret and resignation and a hint of sympathy on her face, as the Morris men who had been waiting outside the church moved toward him.

Bob Thomas was leading them. For the first time Kilbride saw power in his eyes, though the man's face was expressionless. All the men had taken off their bracelets of bells, but they still carried the decorated staves two feet long they'd used in the dance. Their clogs made no sound on the grass. As Bob Thomas raised his stave above his head Kilbride closed his eyes and hoped it would be the last thing he would see or feel.

The first blow caught him across the shoulders. He gritted his teeth, squeezed his eyes tighter, prayed that the next blow wouldn't miss. But the stave struck him across his upper arm, agonizingly. He opened his teary eyes in protest and saw that the women had gone. He turned to Bob Thomas, to try belatedly to reason with him, and read on the man's face that they didn't mean to kill him—not yet, at any rate.

They began to beat Kilbride systematically, driving him away from the church, heading him off when he tried to dodge toward his car. He fled toward the woods, his bruised body aching like an open wound. With their clogs they wouldn't be able to keep up with him, he told himself, and once he was far enough out of reach he could double back to the car. But they drove him into the woods, where he tripped over roots in the dark. Soon he was limping desperately. When he saw that they were herding him toward a hut beside a glade he lurched aside, but they caught him at once. One shoved a stave between his legs and felled him in the glade.

Kilbride struggled around on the soft damp ground to face them. He was suddenly afraid that they meant to stamp him to death with their clogs, especially when four of them seized his arms and legs. As Bob Thomas stooped to him, jowls dangling, Kilbride realized that someone had followed the chase, a small figure in the shadows at the edge of the glade. "Never experienced anything like it, haven't you?" Bob Thomas muttered. "You've not experienced the half of what you're going to, my bucko."

Kilbride tried to wrench himself free as he heard metallic sounds in the shadows, saw the glint of a knife. Bob Thomas moved aside as the doctor came forward, carrying his bag. He might never have seen Kilbride before, his wizened face was so impassive. "Our women make us feel small but our friend here won't, I reckon," Bob Thomas said and stood up, rubbing his hands. "We'll feed him and nurse him and keep him hidden safe, and comes Old May Day we'll have our own Queen of the May."

THE LIMITS OF FANTASY

AS SID PYM PASSED HIS DOOR and walked two blocks to look in the shop window, a duck jeered harshly in the park. March frost had begun to bloom on the window, but the streetlamp made the magazine covers shine: the schoolgirl in her twenties awaiting a spanking, the two bronzed men displaying samples of their muscles to each other, the topless woman tonguing a lollipop. Sid was looking away in disgust from two large masked women flourishing whips over a trussed victim when the girl marched past behind him.

Her reflection glided from cover to cover, her feet trod on the back of the trussed man's head. Despite the jumbling of images, Sid knew her. He recognized her long blond hair, her slim graceful legs, firm breasts, plump jutting bottom outlined by her ankle-length coat, and as she glanced in his direction, he saw that she recognized him. He had time to glimpse how she wrinkled her nose as her reflection left the shop window.

He almost started after her. She'd reacted as if he was one of the men who needed those magazines, but he was one of the people who created them. He'd only come to the window to see how his work shaped up, and there it was, between a book about Nazi war crimes and an Enid Stone romance. He'd given the picture of Toby Hale and his wife Jilly a warm amber tint to go with the title *Pretty Hot*, and he thought it looked classier than most of its companions.

He didn't think Toby needed to worry so much about the rising costs of production. If Sid had gone in for that sort of thing he would have bought the magazine on the strength of the cover.

The newspapers had to admit he was good, one of the best in town. That was why the *Weekly News* wanted him to cover Enid Stone's return home, even though some of the editors seemed to dislike accepting pictures from him since word had got round that he was involved in *Pretty Hot*. Why should anyone disparage him for doing a friend a favor? It wasn't even as though he posed, he only took the photographs. There ought to be a way to let the blonde girl know that, to make her respect him. He swung away from the shop window and stalked after her, telling himself that if he caught up with her he'd have it out with her. But the street was already deserted, and as he reached his building her window, in the midst of the house opposite his rooms, lit up.

He felt as if she had let him know she'd seen him before pulling the curtains—as if she'd glimpsed his relief at not having to confront her. He bruised his testicles as he groped for his keys, and that enraged him more than ever. A phone which he recognized as his once the front door was open had started ringing, and he dashed up the musty stairs in the dark.

It was Toby Hale on the phone. "Still free tomorrow? They're willing."

"A bit different, is it? A bit stronger?"

"What the punters want."

"I'm all for giving people what they really want," Sid declared, and took several quick breaths. The blonde girl was in her bathroom now. "I'll see you at the studio," he told Toby, and fumbled the receiver into place.

What was she trying to do to him? If she had watched him come home she must know he was in his room, even though he hadn't had time to switch on the light. Besides, this wasn't the first time she'd behaved as if the frosted glass of her bathroom window ought to stop him watching her. "Black underwear, is it now?" he said through his teeth, and bent over his bed to reach for a camera.

God, she thought a lot of herself. Each of her movements looked like a pose to Sid as he reeled her towards him with the zoom lens. Despite the way the window fragmented her he could distinguish the curve of her bottom in black knickers and the black swellings of her breasts. Then her breasts turned flesh-colored, and she dropped the bra. She was slipping the knickers down her bare legs when the whir of rewinding announced that he'd finished the roll of Tri-X. "Got you," he whispered, and hugged the camera to himself.

When she passed beyond the frame of the window he coaxed his curtains shut and switched the room light on. He was tempted to develop the roll now, but anticipating it made him feel so powerful in a sleepy generalized way that he decided to wait until the morning, when he would be more awake. He took *Pretty Hot* to bed with him and scanned the article about sex magic, and an idea was raising its head in his when he fell asleep.

He slept late. In the morning he had to leave the Tri-X negatives and hurry to the studio. Fog slid flatly over the pavements before him, vehicles nosed through the gray, grumbling monotonously. It occurred to him as he turned along the cheap side street near the edge of town that people were less likely to notice him in the fog, though why should he care if they did?

Toby opened the street door at Sid's triple knock and preceded him up the carpetless stairs. Toby had already set up the lights and switched them on, which made the small room with its double bed and mock-leather sofa appear starker than ever. A brawny man was sitting on the sofa with a woman draped face down across his knees, her short skirt thrown back, her black nylon knickers more or less pulled down.

Apart from the mortarboard jammed onto his head, the man looked like a wrestler or a bouncer. He glanced up as Sid entered, and the hint of a warning crossed his large bland reddish face as Sid appraised the woman. She was too plump for Sid's taste, her mottled buttocks were too flabby. She looked bored—more so when she glanced at Sid, who disliked her at once.

"This is Sid, our snapshooter," Toby announced. "Sid, our friends are going to model for both stories."

"All right there, mate," the man said, and the woman grunted.

Sid glanced through the viewfinder, then made to adjust the woman's knickers; but he hadn't touched them when the man's hand seized his wrist. "Hands off. I'll do that. She's my wife."

"Come on, the lot of you," the woman complained. "I'm getting a cold bum."

It wouldn't be cold for long, Sid thought, and felt his penis stir unexpectedly. But the man didn't hit her, he only mimed the positions as if he were enacting a series of film stills, resting his hand on her buttocks to denote slaps. For the pair of color shots Toby could afford the man rubbed rouge on her bottom.

"That was okay, was it, Sid?" Toby said anxiously. "It'd be nice if we could shoot *Slave of Love* tomorrow."

"Wouldn't be nice for us," the woman said, groaning as she stood up. "We've got our lives to lead, you know."

"We could make it a week today," her husband said.

"They look right for the stories, I reckon," Hale told Sid when they'd left. "I'm working on some younger models, but those two'll do for that kind of stuff. The perves who want it don't care."

Sid thought it best to agree, but as he walked home he grew angrier: how could that fat bitch have given him a tickle? Working with people like her might be one of Sid's steps to fame, but she needed him more than he needed her. "I'll retouch you, but I won't touch you," he muttered, grinning. Someone like the blonde girl over the road, now—she would have been Sid's choice of a model for *Spanked and Submissive*, and it wouldn't all have been faked, either.

That got his penis going. He had to stand still for a few minutes until its tip went back to sleep, and the thought of the negatives waiting in his darkroom didn't help. He would have her in his hands, he would be able to do what he liked with her. He had to put the idea out of his head before he felt safe to walk.

After the fog, even the dim musty hall of the house seemed like a promise of clarity. In his darkroom he watched the form of the blonde girl rise from the developing fluid, and he felt as if a fog of dissatisfaction with himself and with the session at the studio were leaving him. The photographs came clear, and for a moment he couldn't understand why the girl's body was composed of dots like a newspaper photograph enlarged beyond reason. Of course, it was the frosting on her bathroom window.

Having her in his flat without her knowing excited him, but not enough. Perhaps he needed her to be home so that he could watch her failure to realize he had her. He opened a packet of hamburgers and cooked himself whatever meal it was. The effort annoyed him, and so did the eating: chew, chew, chew. He switched on the television, and the little picture danced for him, oracular heads spoke. He kept glancing at the undeveloped frame of her window.

By the time she arrived home the fog was spiked with drizzle. As soon as she had switched on the light she began to remove her clothes, but before she'd taken off more than her coat she drew the curtains. Had she seen him? Was she taking pleasure in his frustration at having to imagine her undressing? But he already had her almost naked. He spread the photographs across the table, and then he lurched towards his bed to find the article about sex magic.

By themselves the photographs were only pieces of card, but what had the article said? Toby Hale had put in all the ideas he could find about images during an afternoon spent in the library. The Catholic church sometimes made an image of a demon and burned it to bring off an exorcism. . . . Someone in Illinois killed a man by letting rain fall on his photograph . . . Here it was, the stuff Tony had found in a book about magic by someone with a degree from a university Sid had never heard of. The best spells are the ones you write yourself. Find the words that are truest to your secret soul. Focus your imagination, build up to the discharge of psychic energy. Chant the words that best express your desires. Toby was talking about doing that with your partner, but it had

given Sid a better idea. He hurried to the window, his undecided
penis hindering him a little, and shut the curtains tight.

As he returned to the table he felt uneasy: excited, furtive, ridiculous—he wasn't sure which was uppermost. If only this could
work! You never know until you try, he thought, which was the
motto on the contents page of *Pretty Hot.* He pulled the first photograph to him. Her breasts swelled in their lacy bra, her black
knickers were taut over her round bottom. He wished he could see
her face. He cleared his throat, and muttered almost inaudibly, "I'm
going to take your knickers down. I'm going to smack your bare
bum."

He sounded absurd. The whole situation was absurd. How could
he expect it to work if he could barely hear himself? "By the time
I've finished with you," he said loudly, "you won't be able to sit
down for a week."

Too loud! Nobody could hear him, he told himself. Except that
he could, and he sounded like a fool. As he glared at the photograph, he was sure that she was smiling. She had beaten him. He
wouldn't put it past her to have let him take the photographs
because they had absolutely no effect on her. All at once he was
furious. "You've had it now," he shouted.

His eyes were burning. The photograph flickered, and appeared
to stir. He thought her face turned up to him. If it did, it must be
out of fear. His penis pulled eagerly at his fly. "All right, miss," he
shouted hoarsely. "Those knickers are coming down."

She seemed to jerk, and he could imagine her bending reluctantly beneath the pressure of a hand on the back of her neck. Her
black knickers stretched over her bottom. Then the photograph
blurred as tears tried to dampen his eyes, but he could see her more
clearly than ever. By God, the tears ought to be hers. "Now then,"
he shouted, "you're going to get what you've been asking for."

He seized her bare arm. She tried to pull away, shaking her head
mutely, her eyes bright with apprehension. In a moment he'd
trapped her legs between his thighs and pushed her across his knee,
locking his left arm around her waist. Her long blond hair trailed

to the floor, concealing her face. He took hold of the waistband of her knickers and drew them slowly down, gradually revealing her round creamy buttocks. When she began to wriggle, he trapped her more firmly with his arm and legs. "Let's see what this feels like," he said, and slapped her hard.

He heard it. For a moment he was sure he had. He stared about his empty flat with his hot eyes. He almost went to peer between the curtains at her window, but gazed at the photograph instead. "Oh no, miss, you won't get away from me," he whispered, and saw her move uneasily as he closed his eyes.

He began systematically to slap her: one on the left buttock, one on the right. After a dozen of these her bottom was turning pink and he was growing hot—his face, his penis, the palm of his hand. He could feel her warm thighs squirming between his. "You like that, do you? Let's see how much you like."

Two slaps on the left, two on the right. A dozen pairs of those, then five on the same spot, five on the other. As her bottom grew red she tried to cover it with her hands, but he pinned her wrists together with his left hand and forcing them up to the dimple above her bottom, went to work in earnest: ten on the left buttock, ten on its twin . . . She was sobbing beneath her hair, her bottom was wriggling helplessly. His room had gone. There was nothing but Sid and his victim until he came violently and unexpectedly, squealing.

He didn't see her the next day. She was gone when he wakened from a satisfied slumber, and she had drawn the curtains before he realized she was home again. She was making it easier for him to see her the way he wanted. Anticipating that during the days which followed made him feel secretly powerful, and so did Toby Hale's suggestion when Sid rang him to confirm the *Slave of Love* session. "We're short of stories for number three," Toby said. "I don't suppose you've got anything good and strong for us?"

"I might have," Sid told him.

He didn't fully realize how involving it would be until he began to write. He was dominating her not only by writing about her but also by delivering her up to the readers of the magazine. He made her into a new pupil at a boarding school for girls in their late teens. "Your here to lern disiplin. My naime is Mr Sidney and dont yoo forgett it." She would wear kneesocks and a gymslip that revealed her uniform knickers whenever she bent down. "Over my nee, yung lady. Im goaing to give you a speling leson." "Plese plese dont take my nickers down, Ill be a good gurl." "You didnt cawl me Mr Sidney, thats two dozin extrar with the hare brush . . ." He felt as if the words were unlocking a secret aspect of himself, a core of unsuspected truth which gave him access to some kind of power. Was this what they meant by sex magic? It took him almost a week of evenings to savor writing the story, and he didn't mind not seeing her all that week; it helped him see her as he was writing her. Each night as he drifted off to sleep he imagined her lying in bed sobbing, rubbing her bottom.

At the end of the story he met her on the bus.

He was returning from town with a bagful of film. She caught the bus just as he was lowering himself onto one of the front seats downstairs. As she boarded the bus she saw him, and immediately looked away. Even though there were empty seats she stayed on her feet, holding onto the pole by the stairs.

Sid gazed at the curve of her bottom, defining itself and then growing blurred as her long coat swung with the movements of the bus plowing through the fog. Why wouldn't she sit down? He leaned forwards impulsively, emboldened by the nights he'd spent in secret with her, and touched her arm. "Would you like to sit down, love?"

She looked down at him, and he recoiled. Her eyes were bright with loathing, and yet she looked trapped. She shook her head once, keeping her lips pressed so tight they grew pale, then she turned her back on him. He'd make her turn her back tonight, he thought, by God he would. He had to sit on his hands for the rest of the journey, but he walked behind her all the way from the bus stop to her house.

"You're not tying me up with that," the woman said. "Cut my wrists off, that would. Pajama cord or nothing, and none of your cheap stuff neither."

"Sid, would you mind seeing if you can come up with some cord?" Toby Hale said, taking out his reptilian wallet. "I'll stay and discuss the scene."

There was sweat in his eyebrows. The woman was making him sweat because she was their only female model for the story, since Toby's wife wouldn't touch anything kinky. Sid kicked the fog as he hurried to the shops. Just let the fat bitch give him any lip.

Her husband bound her wrists and ankles to the legs of the bed. He untied her and turned her over and tied her again. He untied her and tied her wrists and ankles together behind her back, and poked his crotch at her face. Sid snapped her and snapped her, wondering how far Tony had asked them to go, and then he had to reload. "Get a bastard move on," the woman told him. "This is bloody uncomfortable, did you but know."

Sid couldn't restrain himself. "If you don't like the work we can always get someone else."

"Can you now?" The woman's face rocked towards him on the bow of herself, and then she toppled sideways on the bed, her breasts flopping on her chest, a few pubic strands springing free of her purple knickers like the legs of a lurking spider. "Bloody get someone, then," she cried.

Toby had to calm her and her suffused husband down while Sid muttered apologies. That night he set the frosted photograph in front of him and chanted his story over it until the girl pleaded for mercy. He no longer cared if Toby had his doubts about the story, though Sid was damned if he could see what had made him frown over it. If only Sid could find someone like the girl to model for the story . . . Even when he'd finished with her for the evening, his having been forced to apologize to Toby's models clung to him. He was glad he would be photographing Enid Stone tomorrow. Maybe it was time for him to think of moving on.

He was on his way to Enid Stone's press conference when he saw the girl again. As he emerged from his building she was arriving home from wherever she worked, and she was on his side of the road. The slam of the front door made her flinch and dodge to the opposite pavement, but not before a streetlamp had shown him her face. Her eyes were sunken in dark rings, her mouth was shivering; her long blond hair looked dulled by the fog. She was moving awkwardly, as if it pained her to walk.

She must have female trouble, Sid decided, squirming at the notion. On his way to the bookshop his glimpse of her proved as hard to leave behind as the fog was, and he had to keep telling himself that it was nothing to do with him. The bookshop window was full of Enid Stone's books upheld by wire brackets. Maybe one day he'd see a Sid Pym exhibition in a window.

He hadn't expected Enid Stone to be so small. She looked like someone's shrunken crabby granny, impatiently suffering her hundredth birthday party. She sat in an armchair at the end of a thickly carpeted room above the bookshop, confronting a curve of reporters sitting on straight chairs. "Don't crowd me," she was telling them. "A girl's got to breathe, you know."

Sid joined the photographers who were lined up against the wall like miscreants outside a classroom. Once the reporters began to speak, having been set in motion by a man from the publishers, Enid Stone snapped at their questions, her head jerking rapidly, her eyes glittering like a bird's. "That'll do," she said abruptly. "Give a girl a chance to rest her voice. Who's going to make me beautiful?"

This was apparently meant for the photographers, since the man from the publishers beckoned them forwards. The reporters were moving their chairs aside when Enid Stone raised one bony hand to halt the advance of the cameras. "Where's the one who takes the dirty pictures? Have you let him in?"

Even when several reporters and photographers turned to look at Sid he couldn't believe she meant him. "Is that Mr Muck? Show him the air," she ordered. "No pictures till he goes."

The line of photographers took a step forwards and closed in front of Sid. As he stared at their backs, his face and ears throbbing as if from blows, the man from the publishers took hold of his arm. "I'm afraid that if Miss Stone won't have you I must ask you to leave."

Sid trudged downstairs, unable to hear his footsteps for the extravagant carpet. He felt as if he weren't quite there. Outside, the fog was so thick that the buses had stopped running. It filled his eyes, his mind. However fast he walked, there was always as much of it waiting beyond it. Its passiveness infuriated him. He wanted to feel he was overcoming something, and by God, he would once he was home.

He grabbed the copy of the story he'd written for Toby Hale and threw it on the table. He found the photograph beside the bed and propped it against a packet of salt in front of him. The picture had grown dull with so much handling, but he hadn't the patience to develop a fresh copy just now. "My name's Mister Sidney and don't you forget it," he informed the photograph.

There was no response. His penis was as still as the fingerprinted glossy piece of card. The scene at the bookshop had angered him too much, that was all. He only had to relax and let his imagination take hold. "You're here to learn discipline," he said soft and slow.

The figure composed of dots seemed to shift, but it was only Sid's vision; his eyes were smarting. He imagined the figure in front of him changing, and suddenly he was afraid of seeing her as she had looked beneath the streetlamp. The memory distressed him, but why should he think of it now? He ought to be in control of how she appeared to him. Perhaps his anger at losing control would give him the power to take hold of her. "My name's Mr Sidney," he repeated, and heard a mocking echo in his brain. His eyes were stinging when it should be her bottom that was. He closed his eyes and saw her floating helplessly towards him. "Come here if you know what's good for you," he said quickly, and then he thought he knew how to catch her. "Please," he said in a high panicky voice, "please don't hurt me."

It worked. All at once she was sprawling across his lap. "What's my name?" he demanded, and raised his voice almost to a squeak. "Mr Sidney," he said.

"Mr Sidney sir," he shouted, and dealt her a hefty slap. He was about to give the kind of squeal he would have loved her to emit when he heard her do so—faintly, across the road.

He blinked at the curtains as if he had wakened from a dream. It couldn't have been the girl, and if it had been, she was distracting him. He closed his eyes again and gripped them with his left hand as if that would help him trap his image of her. "What's my name?" he shouted, and slapped her again. This time there was no mistaking the cry which penetrated the fog.

Sid knocked his chair over backwards in his haste to reach the window. When he threw the curtains open he could see nothing but the deserted road boxed in by fog. The circle of lit pavement where he'd last seen the girl was bare and stark. He was staring at the fog, feeling as though it was even closer to him than it looked, when he heard a door slam. It was the front door of the building across the road. In a moment the girl appeared at the edge of the fog. She glanced up at him, and then she fled towards the park.

It was as if he'd released her by relinquishing his image of her and going to the window. He felt as though he was on the brink of realizing the extent of his secret power. Suppose there really was something to this sex magic? Suppose he had made her experience at least some of his fantasies? He couldn't believe he had reached her physically, but what would it be like for her to have her thoughts invaded by his fantasies about her? He had to know the truth, though he didn't know what he would do with it. He grabbed his coat and ran downstairs, into the fog.

Once on the pavement he stood still and held his breath. He heard his heartbeat, the cackling of ducks, the girl's heels running away from him. He advanced into the fog, trying to ensure that she didn't hear him. The bookshop window drifted by, crowded with posed figures and their victims. Ahead of him the fog parted for a moment, and the girl looked back as if she'd sensed his gaze closing around her. She saw him illuminated harshly by the fluorescent tube in the bookshop window, and at once she ran for her life.

"Don't run away," Sid called. "I won't hurt you, I only want to talk to you." Surely any other thoughts that were lurking in his mind were only words. It occurred to him that he had never heard her speak. In that case, whose sobs had he heard in his fantasies? There wasn't time for him to wonder now. She had vanished into the fog, but a change in the sound of her footsteps told him where she had taken refuge: in the park.

He ran to the nearest entrance, the one she would have used, and peered along the path. Thickly swirling rays of light from a streetlamp splayed through the railings and stubbed themselves against the fog. He held his breath, which tasted like a head cold, and heard her gravelly footsteps fleeing along the path. "We'll have to meet sooner or later, love," he called, and ran into the park.

Trees gleamed dully, wet black pillars upholding the fog. The grass on either side of the path looked weighed down by the slow passage of the murk which Sid seemed to be following. Once he heard a cry and a loud splash—a bird landing on the lake which was somewhere ahead, he supposed. He halted again, but all he could hear was the dripping of branches laden with fog.

"I told you I don't want to hurt you," he muttered. "Better wait for me, or I'll—" The chase was beginning to excite and frustrate and anger him. He left the gravel path and padded across the grass alongside it, straining his ears. When the fog solidified a hundred yards or so to his right, at first he didn't notice. Belatedly he realized that the dim pale hump was a bridge which led the path over the lake, and was just in time to stop himself striding into the water.

It wasn't deep, but the thought that the girl could have made him wet himself enraged him. He glared about, his eyes beginning to sting. "I can see you," he whispered as if the words would make it true, and then his gaze was drawn from the bridge to the shadows beneath.

At first he wasn't sure what he was seeing. He seemed to be watching an image developing in the dark water, growing clearer and more undeniable. It had sunk, and now it was rising, floating under the bridge from the opposite side. Its eyes were open, but they looked like the water. Its arms and legs were trailing limply, and so was its blond hair.

Sid shivered and stared, unable to look away. Had she jumped or fallen? The splash he'd heard a few minutes ago must have been her plunging into the lake, and yet there had been no sounds of her trying to save herself. She must have struck her head on something as she fell. She couldn't just have lain there willing herself to drown, Sid reassured himself, but if she had, how could anyone blame him? There was nobody to see him except her, and she couldn't, not with eyes like those she had now. A spasm of horror and guilt set him staggering away from the lake.

The slippery grass almost sent him sprawling more than once. When he skidded onto the path the gravel ground like teeth, and yet he felt insubstantial, at the mercy of the blurred night, unable to control his thoughts. He fled panting through the gateway, willing himself not to slow down until he was safe in his rooms; he had to destroy the photographs before anyone saw them. But fog was gathering in his lungs, and he had a stitch in his side. He stumbled to a halt in front of the bookshop.

The light from the fluorescent tubes seemed to reach for him. He saw his face staring out from among the women bearing whips. If they or anyone else knew what he secretly imagined he'd caused . . . His buttocks clenched and unclenched at the thought he was struggling not to think. He gripped his knees and bent almost double to rid himself of the pain in his side so that he could catch his breath, and then he saw his face fit over the face of a bound victim.

It was only the stitch that had paralyzed him, he told himself, near to panic. It was only the fog which was making the photograph of the victim appear to stir, to align its position with his.

"Please, please," he said wildly, his voice rising, and at once tried to take the words back. They were echoing in his mind, they wouldn't stop. He felt as if they were about to unlock a deeper aspect of himself, a power which would overwhelm him.

He didn't want this, it was contrary to everything he knew about himself. "My name is—" he began, but his pleading thoughts were louder than his voice, almost as loud as the sharp swishing which filled his ears. He was falling forwards helplessly, into himself or into the window, wherever the women and pain were waiting. For a moment he managed to cling to the knowledge that the images were nothing but the covers of magazines, and then he realized fully that they were more than that, far more. They were euphemisms for what waited beyond them.

THE BODY IN THE WINDOW

BACK AT THE HOTEL on the Rembrandtsplein, Woodcock wanted only to phone his wife. He let himself into his room, which was glowing with all the colours of tulips rendered lurid. Once he switched on the light the tinges of neon retreated outside the window, leaving the walls of the small neat room full of twining tulips which were also pressed under the glass of the dressing table mirror. He straightened his tie in the mirror and brushed his thinning hair before lowering himself, one hand on the fat floral quilt of the double bed, into the single chair.

The pinkish phone seemed to be doing its best to deny its nature, the receiver was flattened so thin. He'd barely typed his home number, however, when it trilled in his ear and produced his wife's voice. "Please do help yourself to a refill," she said, and into the mouthpiece "Brian and Belinda Woodcock."

"I didn't realize you had company. What's the occasion?"

"Does there have to be one?" She'd heard a rebuke, a choice which these days he tended to leave up to her. "I'm no less of a hostess because you're away," she said, then her voice softened. "You're home tomorrow, aren't you? Have you seen all you wanted to see?"

"I didn't want to see anything."

"If you say so, Brian. I still think I should have come so you'd have had a female view."

"I've seen things today no decent woman could even dream of."

"You'd be surprised." Before he had a chance to decide what that could possibly mean, Belinda went on "Anyway, here's Stan Chataway. He'd like a word."

No wonder she was being hospitable if the guest was the deputy mayor, though Woodcock couldn't help reflecting that he himself hadn't even touched the free champagne on the flight over. He squared his shoulders and adopted a crouch not unlike a boxer's on the edge of the chair as he heard the phone being handed over. "What's this I'm getting from your good lady, Brian?" Chataway boomed in his ear. "You're never really in Amsterdam."

"Not for much longer."

"But you didn't want to make the trip with the rest of us last month."

"Quite a few of my constituents have been saying what I said they'd say, that they don't pay their council tax for us to go on junkets. And you only saw what you were supposed to see, from what I hear."

"I wonder who you heard that from." When the implied threat failed to scare out a response, Chataway sighed. "It's about time you gave up looking after the rest of us so much."

"I thought that was our job."

"Part of the job is forging foreign links, Brian, and most of the people who matter seem to think twinning Alton with Amsterdam is a step forward for our town."

"Maybe they won't when they hear what I have to describe at the next council meeting."

Chataway's loudness had been causing the earpiece to vibrate, but when he spoke again his voice was quieter. "Your lady wife may have something, you know."

"Kindly keep her out of it. What are you implying, may I ask?"

"Just that the papers could make quite a lot of your jaunt, Brian, you cruising the sex joints and whatever else you've been taking in all on your lonesome. If I were you I'd be having a word with my better half before I opened my mouth."

"I'll be speaking to my wife at length, thank you, but in private." Woodcock was so enraged that he could barely articulate the words. "Please assure her I'll be home tomorrow evening," he managed to grind out, and slammed the phone down before it could crack in his grip.

He was sweating—drenched. He felt even grubbier than his tour of inspection had made him feel. He squeezed the sodden armpits of his shirt in his hands, then sprang out of the chair and tore off the shirt and the rest of his clothes before tramping into the bathroom. As he clambered into the bath, the swollen head of the shower released a drop of liquid which shattered on the back of his hand. He twisted the taps open until he could hardly bear the heat and force of the water, and drove his face into it, blinding himself. It was little use; it didn't scour away his thoughts.

What had Belinda meant about dreaming? Could she have intended to imply that he was no longer discharging his marital duty as he should? His performance had seemed to be enough for her throughout their more than twenty years together, and certainly for him. Sex was supposed to be a secret you kept, either to yourself or sharing it with just your partner, and he'd always thought he did both, kissing Belinda's mouth and then her breasts and finally her navel in a pattern which he sometimes caught himself envisioning as a sign of the cross. Wasn't that naughty enough for her? Wasn't it sufficient foreplay? What did she want them to do, perform the weekly exercise in a window with the curtains open wide?

He knuckled his stinging eyes and groped around the sink for the shampoo. Surely he was being unfair to her: she couldn't really have meant herself. He fished the sachet through the plastic curtains and gnawed off a corner, and tried to spit out the acrid soapy taste. He squeezed the sachet, which squirted a whitish fluid onto his palm. A blob of the fluid oozed down his wrist, and he flung the sachet away, spattering the tiles above the taps as he lurched out of the bath to towel himself as roughly as he could. If he couldn't rub away his disgust, at least he could put it to use. He was going to find something that would convince Belinda he'd had reason to protect her from the place—that no reporter would dare accuse him of enjoying—that would appall the council so much there would be no further talk of implicating Alton with Amsterdam.

He wasn't prepared for the revulsion he experienced at the sight of his clothes scattered across the floor, the kind of trail it seemed half the films on television followed to the inevitable bedroom activity or, on the television in this room, much worse, to judge by the single moist closeup of no longer secret flesh he'd glimpsed before switching it off. He dumped the clothes in his suitcase where no chambermaid would see them. Having dressed himself afresh, he grabbed the key and killed the lights, and saw the room instantly become suffused with colours like bruised and excited flesh—made himself stare at it until his gorge rose, because as long as he kept his revulsion intact, nothing could touch him.

He thrust the key across the counter at the blond blue-eyed receptionist before managing to rein in his aggression. "I'm going out," he confided.

"Enjoy our city."

Woodcock forced himself to lean across the counter, and lowered his voice. "I'm looking for, surely I don't need to tell you, we're both men of the world. Something special."

"Involving girls or boys, sir?"

The calm blue eyes were hinting that these weren't the only possibilities, and Woodcock had to overcome an impulse to cosh him with the brass bludgeon attached to the key of his room. "Girls, of course," he snarled, and was barely able to hear or believe what he said next. "A girl doing the worst you can think of."

"To you, would that be, sir?"

"What do you think I—" The man's opinion of him couldn't be allowed to matter, not if that interfered with his mission, Woodcock made himself think. "A girl who'll do anything," he mumbled. "Anything at all."

The receptionist nodded, keeping his gaze level with Wood-cock's, and his face became a tolerant mask. "I recommend you go behind the Oude Kerk. If you would like—"

Woodcock liked nothing about the situation, let alone any further aid the receptionist might offer. "Thank you," he said through his clenched teeth, and shoved himself away from the counter. Seizing the luxuriant handles of the twin glass doors, he launched himself out of the hotel.

The riot of multicoloured neon, and the July sultriness, and the noise of the crowd strolling through the square and seated in their dozens outside every café, hit him softly in the face. Losing himself among so many people who didn't know what he'd just asked came as a relief until he recalled that he had to find out where he'd been advised to go. When he noticed a man sitting not quite at a table, a guidebook in one hand and an extravagantly tall glass of lager in the other, Woodcock sidled up to him and pointed at the book. "Excuse me, could you tell me wh—" He almost asked where, but that was too much of an admission. "—what the Oude Kerk is?"

"Come?"

He'd expended his effort on a tourist who didn't speak English. The nearest of a group of young blond women at the table did, however. "The Old Church? You should cross the Amstel, and then—"

"Appreciated," Woodcock snapped, and strode away. One of his fellow councillors had told him about the church in the depths of the red light district—she'd come close to suggesting that its location justified or even sanctified the place. It was further into that district than Woodcock had ventured earlier. He had to find whatever would revolt his colleagues, and so he sent himself into the night, where at least nobody knew him.

A squealing tram led him to the Muntplien, a junction where headlights competed with neon, from where a hairpin bend doubled back alongside the river. He was halfway across a bridge over the Amstel when a cyclist sped to meet him, a long-legged young

woman in denim shorts and a T-shirt printed with the slogan MARY
WANNA MARY JANE. He didn't understand that, nor why she was
holding her breath after taking a long drag at a scrawny cigarette,
until she gasped as she came abreast of him and expelled a cloud
of smoke into his face. "Sor-ree," she sang, and pedaled onwards.
The shock had made him suck in his breath, and he couldn't
speak for coughing. He made a grab at her to detain her, but as he
swung round, the smoke he'd inhaled seemed to balloon inside his
skull. He clung to the fat stone parapet and watched her long bare
legs and trim buttocks pumping her away out of his reach. The
sight reminded him of his daughter, when she had still been living
at home—reminded him of his unease with her as she grew into
a young woman. The cyclist vanished into the Muntplien, beyond
which a street organ had commenced to toot and jingle. The wriggling of neon in the river appeared to brighten and become deliberate, a spectacle which dismayed him, so that his legs carried him
across the bridge before he was aware of having instructed them.

The far side promised to be quieter. The canal alongside which
a narrow road led was less agitated than the river, and was overlooked by tall houses unstained by neon. Few of the windows,
which were arranged in formal trios on both storys of each house,
were curtained even by net, and those interiors into which he
could see might have been roped-off rooms in a museum; nobody
was to be seen in them, not that anyone who saw him pass could
be sure where he was going. Only the elaborate white gables above
the restrained facades looked at all out of control, especially when
he observed that their reflections in the canal weren't as stable as
he would have liked. They were opening and closing their trian-
gular lips which increasingly, as he tried to avoid seeing them,
appeared to be composed of pale swollen flesh. A square dominated
by a medieval castle interrupted the visible progress of the canal.
In front of the castle trees were rustling, rather too much like an
amplified sound of clothes being removed for his taste. A bridge
extended from the far corner of the square, and across it he saw
windows with figures waiting in them.

He had to see the worst, or his stay would have been wasted; he might even lay himself open to the accusation of having made the trip for pleasure. His nervous legs were already carrying him to the bridge. His hand found the parapet and recoiled, because the stone felt warm and muscular, as though the prospect ahead was infiltrating everything around itself. Even the roundness of the cobblestones underfoot seemed to be hinting at some sly comparison. But now he was across the bridge, and hints went by the board.

Every ground floor window beside the canal was lit, and each of them contained a woman on display, unless she was standing in her doorway instead, clad only in underwear. Closest to the bridge was a sex shop flaunting pictures of young women lifting their skirts or even baring their buttocks for a variety of punishments. Worse still, a young couple were emerging hand in hand from the shop, and the female reminded Woodcock far too much of his daughter. Snarling incoherently, he shoved past them into a lane which ought to lead to the old church.

The lane catered for specialized tastes. A woman fingering a vibrator in a window tried to catch his eye, a woman caressing a whip winked at him as he tried to keep his gaze and himself to the middle of the road, because straying to either side brought him within reach of the women in doorways. His mind had begun to chant "How much is that body in the window?" to the tune of a childhood song. Other men were strolling through the lane, surveying the wares, and he sensed they took him for one of themselves, however fiercely he glowered at them. One bumped into him, and he brushed against another, and felt in danger of being engulfed by lustful flesh. He dodged, and found himself heading straight for a doorway occupied by a woman who was covered almost from head to foot in black leather. As she creaked forward he veered across the lane, and an enormous old woman whose wrinkled belly overhung her red panties and garter belt held out her doughy arms to him. "Oude Kerk," he gabbled, and floundered past three sailors who had stopped to watch him. Ahead, across a square at the end of the lane, he could see the church.

The sight reassured him until he saw bare flesh in windows flanking the church. A whiff of marijuana from a doorway fastened on the traces of smoke in his head. The street tilted underfoot, propelling him across the softened cobblestones until he came to a swaying halt in the midst of the small square. Above him the bell tower of the Oude Kerk reared higher against a black sky streaked with white clouds, one of which appeared to be streaming out of the tip of the tower. The district had transformed everything it contained into emblems of lust, even the church. Revulsion and dizziness merged within him, but he hadn't time to indulge his feelings. He had to see what was behind the church.

He drew a breath so deep it made his head swim, then he walked around the left-hand corner of the building. The nearest windows on this side of the square were curtained, but what activities might the curtains be concealing? He hurried past and stopped with his back to the church.

By the standards of the area, nothing out of the ordinary was to be seen. Some of the windows that were glowing pink as lipstick exposed women, others were draped for however long they had to be. Woodcock ventured a few paces away from the church before a suspicion too unspeakable to put into words caused him to glance at its backside. That was just a church wall, and he let his gaze drift over the houses in search of whatever he'd glimpsed as he'd turned.

It hadn't been in any of the windows. A gap between two houses snagged his attention. The opening looked hardly wide enough to admit him, but at the far end, which presumably gave onto an adjacent street, he made out the contours of a thin female body, which looked to be pinned against a wall.

He paced closer, staying within the faint ambiguous multiple shadow of the church. Now he could distinguish that all her limbs were stretched wide, and in the dimness which wasn't quite dim enough, it became clear that she was naked. Another reluctant step, and he saw the glint of manacles at her wrists and ankles, and the curve of the wheel to which she was bound. Her face was a smudged blur.

Woodcock stared about, desperate to find someone to whom he could appeal on her behalf. Even if a policeman came in sight, what would be the use? Woodcock had seen policemen strolling through the red light district as if it was of no concern to them. The thought concentrated his revulsion, and he lunged at the gap.

It was so much broader than it had previously seemed that he had to suppress an impression of its having widened at his approach. He pressed his arms against his sides, his fingers shifting with each movement of his thighs, a sensation preferable to discovering that the walls felt as fleshy as the bridges and cobblestones had. That possibility was driven out of his mind once he was surrounded by darkness and could see the girl's face. It looked far too young—as young as his daughter had been when she'd stopped obeying him—and terrified of him.

"It's all right," he protested. "I only want . . ." The warm walls pressed close to him, confronting him with his voice, which sounded harsher than he'd meant it to sound. Her mouth dragged itself into a grimace as though the corners of her lips were flinching from him. As he crept down the alley, trying to show by his approach that he was nothing like whoever her helplessness was intended to attract, her large eyes, which were the colour of the night sky, began to flicker, trapped in their sockets. "Don't," he said more sharply. "I'm not like that, don't you understand?"

Perhaps she didn't speak English, or couldn't hear him through the pane of glass. She was shaking her head, flailing her cropped hair, which shone as darkly as the tuft at the parting of her legs. He knew teenagers liked to be thin, but she looked half starved. Had that been done to her? What else? He stepped out of the alley and stretched his upturned empty hands towards her, almost pleading.

He couldn't tell whether he was in a square or a street, if either. The only light came between the glistening walls of the gap between the houses and cast his shadow over the manacled girl. Her mouth was less distorted now, possibly because the grimace was too painful to sustain, but her eyes were rolling. They'd done so several times before he realized they were indicating a door to the left of the window; her left hand was attempting to jerk in that direction too. He wavered and then darted at the heavy paneled door.

He'd fitted his hand around the nippled brass doorknob when he caught himself hoping the door would be locked. But the knob turned easily, and the door drew him forward. Beyond it was a cramped cell which was in fact the entrance to a cell, although it reminded him of his own toolshed, with metal items glinting on the wall in front of him. There was an outsize pair of pliers, there was what appeared to be a small vise; there were other instruments whose use, despite his commitment to seeing the worst, he didn't want to begin to imagine. He lifted the pliers off their supports and paced to the door into the cell.

Despite his attempts to sound gentle, the floorboards turned his slow footsteps menacing. Through the grille he saw the girl staring at the door and straining as much of her body away from it as she could, an effort which only rendered her small firm breasts and bristling pubis more prominent. "No need for that, no need to be afraid," Woodcock muttered, so low that he might have been talking to himself. Grasping the twin of the outside doorknob, he twisted it and admitted himself to the cell.

The door screeched like a bird of prey, and the girl tried to jerk away from him, so violently that the wooden disc shifted, raising her left hand as though to beckon him. When she saw the pliers, however, her body grew still as a dummy in a shop window, and she squeezed her eyes tight shut, and then her lips. "These aren't what you think. That's to say, I'm not," Woodcock pleaded, and raised the pliers as he took a heavy resonating step towards her.

They were within inches of her left hand when her eyes quivered open. She clenched her hand into the tightest fist he'd ever seen, all the knuckles paling with the effort to protect her fingernails from him. There wasn't much more she could do, and he had a sudden overwhelming sense of her helplessness and, worse, of the effect that was capable of having on him. The pliers drooped in his grasp as though, like his crotch, they were putting on weight— as if one might be needed to deal with the other. "Don't," he cried and, gripping the pliers in both hands, dug them behind her manacle where it was fastened to the disc.

The wood was as thick as his hands pressed together. When he levered at the manacle with all his strength, he was expecting this first effort to have little if any effect, particularly since he was standing on tiptoe. But wood splintered, and the girl's arm sprang free, the manacle and its metal bolt jangling at her wrist. The force he'd used, or her sudden release, spun the wheel. Before he could prevent it she was upside down, offering him her defenseless crotch.

He felt as though he'd never seen that sight before—a woman's secret lips, thick and pink and swollen, bearing an expression which seemed almost smug in its mysteriousness. "Mustn't," he cried in a voice he hardly recognized, younger than he could remember ever having been, and grabbed the rim of the wheel to turn it until her face swung up to meet his. Her mouth had opened, and her eyes were also wide and inviting. As they met his she clasped her freed arm around his neck.

"No, no. Mustn't," he said, sounding like his father now. He had to take hold of her wrist next to the manacle in order to pull her arm away from him. Although her wrist was thin as a stick, he had to exert almost as much strength to move her arm as he had to lever out the manacle. Her eyes never left his. The manacle clanged on the wood beside his hip, and he thrust his knees against the wheel between her legs, to keep it still while he released her other arm. He couldn't bear the prospect of her being upturned to him again. Forcing the jaws of the pliers behind the second manacle and bruising his elbows against the wheel on either side of her arm, he heaved at the handles.

He felt the jaws dig into the wood, which groaned, but that was all. His heart was pounding, the handles were slipping out of his sweaty grasp. Renewing his grip, he levered savagely at the manacle. All at once the wood cracked, and the manacle jangled free, so abruptly that the pliers flew out of his hand and thudded on the floor. Only then did he become aware of the activity in the region of his penis, which was throbbing so unmanageably that he had been doing his best to blot it from his consciousness. While he was intent on releasing her arm, the girl had unbuttoned his trousers at the belt and unzipped his fly. As his trousers slithered down his legs she closed her hand around his penis and inserted it deftly into herself.

"No," Woodcock cried. "What are you—what do you think I—" She'd wrapped her arms around his waist, tight as a vise. She didn't need to; he was swollen larger than he'd been for many years, swollen inside the warm slickness of her beyond any hope of withdrawing. Once, early in their marriage, that had happened to him with Belinda, and it had terrified him. There was only one way he could free himself. He closed his eyes and gritted an inarticulate prayer through his teeth, and made a convulsive thrust with his hips. The manacles at her ankles jangled, her body strained upwards, and her arms around his waist lifted him onto his toes. Perhaps it was this shift of weight which set the wheel spinning.

As his feet left the ground he lost all self-control. He was a child on a carnival ride, discovering too late that he wanted to be anywhere but there. When he tried to pull away from the girl the movement intensified the aching of the whole length of his penis, and his reaction embedded him even deeper in her. He groped blindly for handholds as he swung head downward and then up again, and managed to locate the splintered holes left by the manacles. He pumped his hips, frantic to be done and out of her, but the sensations of each thrust contradicted his dismay, and he squeezed his eyes shut in an attempt to deny where he was and what he was doing. The jangling of the manacles had taken on the rhythm of the girl's cries intermixed with panting in his ear. The wheel spun faster, twirling him and his partner head over heels, until the only sense of stability he had was focused on the motions of his hips and penis. Were the girl's cries growing faster and more musical, or was he hearing a street organ playing a carnival tune? He was beyond being able to wonder; the sensations in his penis were mushrooming. As he strained his head back and gave vent to a roar as much of despair as of pleasure, light blazed into his eyes. He could do nothing but thrust and thrust as the vortex in which he was helplessly whirling seemed to empty itself through his penis as though it might never stop.

At last it did, and the girl's arms slackened around his waist as his penis dwindled within her. He kept his eyes shut and tried to calm his breathing as the wheel wavered to a stop. When he was sure he was upright he lowered himself until his toecaps found the boards, and let go of the holes in the wood, and fumbled to pull his trousers up and zip them shut. His eyes were still closed; from what he could hear, he thought he might not be able to bear what he would see when he opened them. After a good many harsh deep breaths he turned and looked.

The window-frame was ablaze with colored lightbulbs. Speakers at each corner of the window were emitting a street organ's merry tune. In the street which the lights had revealed outside the window, dozens of people had gathered to watch: sailors, young couples and some much older, even a brace of policemen in the local uniform. Woodcock stared appalled at the latter, then he stalked out of the cell, wrenching both doors as wide as they would go. Even here the law surely couldn't allow what had just been done to him, and nobody was going to walk away with the idea that he'd been anything other than a victim.

When the audience, policemen included, began to applaud him, however, he forced his way to the gap between the houses and took to his heels. "Bad, bad. The worst," he heard himself declaring—he had no idea how loudly. From the far end of the gap he looked back and saw the girl raising her manacled wrists to the position in which he'd first seen them. As the lights which framed her started to dim, he gripped the corners of the walls as though he could pull the gap shut; then he flung himself away and dashed through the streets choked with flesh to his hotel.

In the morning he almost went back, having spent a sleepless night in trying to decide how much of the encounter could have been real. He felt emptied out, robbed of himself. As the searchlight of the sun crept over the roofs, turning the luminous neon tulips on the walls of his room back into paper, he sneaked downstairs and out of the hotel, averting his face from the receptionist, gripping the brass club in his pocket rather than relinquish that defense.

He left the whines of early trams and the brushing of street cleaners behind as he crossed the river, on which neon lay like a trace of petrol. He followed the canal as far as the lane to the Oude Kerk. Under his hands the parapets were as cold and solid as the cobblestones underfoot. He strode hastily past the occupied windows and halted in sight of the church.

He could see the gap between the houses but not, without venturing closer, how wide it was. One step further, and he froze. The question wasn't simply whether he had encountered the girl or imagined some if it not all of the incident, but rather which would be worse? That such things could actually happen, or that he was capable of inventing them?

A movement beside the church caught his eye. One of the women in the windows was nibbling breakfast and sipping tea from a tray on her lap. An aching homesickness overwhelmed him, but how could he go back now? He turned away from the church and trudged in the direction of the canal, with no sense of where he was going or coming from.

Then his walk grew purposeful before he quite knew why. There was something he ought to remember, something that had to help. The face of the girl on the wheel: no, her eyes . . . Hadn't he seen at least a hint of all those expressions before, at home? It had to be true, he couldn't have imagined them. The bell tower of the Oude Kerk burst into peals, and he quickened his pace, eager to be packed and out of the hotel and on the plane. As never before that he could remember, he was anxious to be home.

KILL ME HIDEOUSLY

"I DON'T READ this kind of stuff myself, but could you sign it for my son?"

As Lisette clenched her fists on his behalf, Willy Bantam raised his heavy eyelids and gave the man ahead of her a full-lipped smile almost as wide as his plump face. "What's his name?" he said.

The man told him, and Bantam sent the son his best wishes on the title page of *The Smallest Trace of Fear*. Lisette swung her tapestry bag off her shoulder as the man retrieved the book, and the volumes in the bag nudged him none too gently at the base of his spine. She made sure he saw her place them in front of their author, who greeted her and them with exactly the smile he'd produced for her predecessor. "Sins of my youth," he remarked.

"They're not sins, and you aren't so old. I don't want them for anyone but me."

"Shall I sign them to . . ."

"Lisette."

"That's a pretty unusual name."

"Thank you," she breathed, and managed not to simper as she watched him begin to inscribe the title page of *Ravage!*. She took a breath that tasted of saliva. "Would you put it in . . ."

"I am, look."

"I don't mean that. I mean, do sign them for me, I'll hold them even dearer then, but when you've finished, Willy can I call you that . . ."

"That's who I was before I was William."

"You were when you wrote these, so will you be for me?"

"Anything for an old supporter."

He meant old in the sense of faithful, Lisette thought as he signed his original name. She was certain his pen was moving more fluently, happy to rediscover what it used to write. She waited for him to open *Writhe!* before she said "The thing I was going to ask you—when you write another book like these, will you put me in it?"

He didn't look up until he'd finished wishing her the best above his zippy signature, and then he gave her a straightened smile. "I'll see if I can find somebody called Lisette a role in one of the kind I write now."

"Don't be insulted, but that's no good. Shall I tell you why?"

"There are people behind you, but please."

"Because in this new one you never describe what happens to the girls who disappear."

"There's the scene where the policewoman has to try and say what she found."

"She doesn't even say three whole sentences. You used to write at least a chapter. The first girl in *Writhe!* got thirteen pages in the hardcover and sixteen in the paperback."

"My agent and my editor persuaded me you could imagine worse than I could ever describe."

Lisette saw the manager of Book Yourself frown at the queue behind her and direct more of the expression at her. "I'm not paying to imagine, I'm paying you to," she said.

"Then I hope these old excesses of mine give you your money's worth."

"I've read them. Thanks for them," Lisette said, and once they were nestling safely in her bag, hugged it to her as she marched out of the shop.

Beyond her Renault, which she'd had to park several hundred yards away, the lights of the department stores and fast-food eateries were padded with November fog. The street was deserted except for a man in a dark raincoat whose length and looseness put her in mind of a slaughterhouse. The lights lent his stiff expressionless face all the colors of a lurid paperback. As she stooped to unlock the car he arrived behind her, and she sensed a cold presence at the back of her neck: his breath as chill as his intentions, the imminent clutch of his hand? It was only the fog.

Five minutes' driving through the blurred streets of the city took her home. She lived in the middle of a row of youthful houses, each of them little wider than the garage that occupied most of the ground floor—no more than a slice of a house, she often thought, but all she needed. Having let herself into and closed the garage with the remote control, she unlocked the door that led from the garage into the house.

A narrow staircase lit by bulbs in cut-glass flowers ascended to the middle floor, half of it a kitchen and dining area, the rest solemnly described by the estate agent as a compact living space. In Lisette's case it was a library, its walls hidden by shelves stuffed with books. She crossed it to the farther staircase and climbed to the solitary bedroom.

She gave her secrets time to glimmer before she fingered the switch. The light seemed to draw the contents of the wall beyond the foot of the bed into a pattern she alone might sometime be able to interpret. The wall was covered with jackets of second-hand Willy Bantam novels and pages torn from them, framed by two female mouths stretched wide by screams, posters for *Ravage!* and *Writhe!* which Lisette had saved from a bookshop bin. She loved the mouth from *Writhe!* most—you could see the tongue starting to grow bigger and longer and harder.

She hung her coat on the back of the door and lay on the bed, her shoulders against the headboard. She placed one of the autographed books on either side of her on the fat quilt, then she opened *Ravage!* and read the inscription, running her fingers over the back of the page to feel how it was embossed by his signature. She was making herself wait, causing all her lips to tingle with anticipation, before she turned to her favourite scene.

". . . Sally had never known why he called them his ghoulies until she kicked him there. When he went into a crouch she thought she had put him out of action long enough for her to run, and then he jerked his head up, gleefully licking his lips. His hands came for her, except they were no longer just hands. His thumbs had stiffened and swelled huge. One moist throbbing thumb forced her mouth open, and the member slid over her tongue. The shock was so intense it was beyond shock, it was an experience she wouldn't have dared admit even to herself she'd dreamed of. She felt his other hand push her skirt above her waist and slide her panties down her helpless legs, and then the pulsing erection that was his other thumb slid deep into her. She would have gasped if she'd been able, and not only because of that—because a slick lengthening finger had found her nether orifice and wormed its way in. The rhythmic penetration was reaching for her deepest self from too many directions to withstand, and as wave after wave of forbidden ecstasy swept away the last of her control she fell back on the bed. When his face above hers began to change there was nothing she could do . . ."

There was plenty Lisette could if she put her mind to it. She pushed one thumb in and out of her mouth, she bit down on it as the other stroked her clitoris and forged deeper while a finger poked between her buttocks. She moaned, she gasped, she writhed on the bed, raising her knees high and flinging her legs wide. She came within an inch of convincing herself.

When she was too exhausted to counterfeit any more pleasure she let all her muscles sag. For just a moment that state considered feeling like the release she'd labored to achieve, and then the dead weight of frustration settled on her. It was waiting in the night whenever she lurched awake, and she was hardly aware of having slept when the bedside clock began to squeak at her to get ready for work.

Her car felt like a helmet not a great deal more metallic than her head. It gave her only just enough protection from the traffic, cars and lorries battling to be first past holes in the roads. All the workers crowding into the city were of a single mind that compelled them to rush along the pavements and bunch at crossings and flock across the roadways whenever lights summoned them. She parked as close to the glass doors of the Civic Coordination building as she could, then she buzzed to be let in.

A blank-walled lift carried her to the fifth floor. The switchboard room might as well have been windowless, since supervisor Bertha insisted on pulling down the blind as soon as the sun appeared in the window. Though the lines weren't due to open for five minutes, the girls were at their boards. "Here's Lisette," Vi said, blowing on her nails. "Bet she doesn't care if Tommo lives or dies."

"Double bet she's never seen him in her life," said Doris, appraising her face in a pocket mirror.

Bertha held up a hand as if to check it was as pale as the unsunned sky. "Hush now, ladies. She may not even know who our favorite gentleman is."

"Of course I do. He's one of your soapy people who's on every night. I wouldn't be watching him even if I had a television," Lisette said, and once the chorus of incredulity had passed its crescendo "I've a date with a man at a bookshop."

"I thought you saw him last night," protested Doris.

"That's why I am tonight."

"Is he one of your horrors?"

"He's the best there's ever been or will be," said Lisette, switching on her computer terminal as her board winked at her.

The caller was desperate for the times of a bus that had changed its route, the sort of call she and her colleagues dealt with every day. The world was full of people trying to catch up with it, and everybody had to find their own way of coping. Perhaps her work-mates managed by doing away with their imaginations, she thought, and had to pity them for their need to care about someone who didn't exist. The point was to find out all you could about yourself, to store up that secret until you were alone with it, the prize you gave yourself at the end of the day—except that tonight she meant to win herself a bonus.

She dined swiftly at a Bunny Burger opposite the car park, then she drove to the next town. She was able to park almost outside another branch of Book Yourself that appeared to have brought many of its neighbors with it from her town for company. She let herself into the shop, and Willy Bantam saw her at once.

He didn't look at her again until the dozen people ahead of her had taken turns to linger. A fat man with a stammer moved aside at last, leaving her the aroma of his armpits, and the author met her eyes. "Back again," she said.

He was producing his smile when he saw the books she'd brought. "That's right, I signed these for you."

"Are you truly not going to write any more like them?"

"Nothing's changed since yesterday."

"Then I shouldn't make you. I've thought what you can do for me instead."

"What's that?"

She opened *Ravage!* at her chapter and turned it towards him. "Put me in this one."

"Put you . . . How . . ."

"Cross Sally out and put my name instead. The way you describe her you could have been thinking of me. Here, use my pen."

When he didn't take it she planted it between his thumb and forefinger, and pressed her thighs together to contain an inadver-tent stirring. "You only use her name five times. It won't take long," she said to enliven him. "She's Nell in *Writhe!* too, isn't she? Could she be your girlfriend?"

"It doesn't work like that."

"Here I am, then. Just this one," Lisette said, nudging the book towards him. "Don't worry, I won't sue."

He raised the pen, but only to level it at her. "For what?"

"Using me for the worst you could think of."

He laid the pen at the very edge of the table and pulled his hand back. "That's yours."

"Can't you use that kind of pen?"

"I can't use any for what you want."

"No, you don't understand. I said I wouldn't sue you, as if I could when it's me who asked for it. I won't be any trouble, I promise."

"Then please don't be," the author said, and looked past her.

"Are you embarrassed? Hasn't anyone ever told you why they read your books? All us girls want to be his victims," Lisette said, turning to the next in line, "don't we?"

The girl seemed in danger of blushing, even though that would upset her color scheme—face white as bone and not much meatier, spiky hair the black of her gloves and boots and long tube of an overcoat—but managed to respond with no more than a series of alarmed blinks. "We do even if we won't say," Lisette told the author, and had to regain her voice, because he'd closed her book and was sliding it towards her with his fingertips. "Couldn't you just . . ."

"Your name's in it. You can't ask more than that."

"Oh, thank you." It seemed hardly possible that he could have substituted her name five times while she was busy with the other girl, but it would be worse than ungrateful of her to inspect the book in his presence. One acknowledgment of herself had to be all the magic Lisette needed. She bore her broad smile past the queue and smiled all the way home.

The garage closed itself behind her, the stairs lit the way to her bedroom. She took her time over removing her coat and unbuttoning the front of her dress, enjoying the delicious tension. She lay on the bed and took out *Ravage!*, which parted its pages at her chapter as though it was as eager to open as her body. Then her mouth widened, but no longer in a smile. Sally; Sally; Sally, Sally— Sally. Not a single use of the name had been changed to hers. He'd lied to her, she thought shrilly as a scream, and then she saw he might only have told her he'd already signed the book. If he'd taken advantage of her willingness to trust him, that was worse than lying. Everything of importance in her room—the Willy Bantam books, the fragments of them on the walls—seemed implicated in the betrayal; the mouths were jeering at her. She flung herself off the bed and was on her way to the stairs before she realized the bookshop would be shut by the time she drove back.

She'd been made to look enough of a fool. That wasn't her kind of victim. When she felt calm enough she reopened the book and read the description of herself—long slim legs, trim waist, full breasts, blond hair halfway down her back. Only the name was false. "Not for long," she promised, and kept repeating it as she lay at the edge of sleep.

Next morning she was at the office twenty minutes ahead of Bertha and the girls. She might as well not have bothered: at that hour Bassinet Press was represented only by an answering machine. She left a message for someone who was privy to Willy Bantam's movements to call her at the inquiry office by name, then waited most of the morning while nobody did. No doubt whoever should have called would be going for an extended lunch as Lisette understood everyone in publishing did, and so she had to contact them before they turned into a machine. The moment Bertha wasn't there to see her phoning out Lisette dialled Bassinet Press and spoke low. "I left a message for Willy Bantam's person. Can I have them now?"

"I'll give you publicity," the receptionist said, which struck Lisette as a generous offer until another voice announced "Publicity."

"Are you Willy Bantam's girl?"

"Mr Bantam's publicist is on the road with him. Can she call you next week?"

"What road are they on? Where is he tonight?"

"Nowhere, I believe. May I ask who's calling?"

"I'm an old friend he used in one of his books. Where's he on next?"

"I think he's reading at a library tomorrow afternoon."

"Have you got the address? I want to surprise him."

There was a pause that might have denoted reluctance, so that Lisette was searching the depths of herself for some further persuasiveness when her informant returned with the address, followed by a question: "Can I just take your—"

"Don't spoil the surprise," Lisette said as she saw Bertha returning from her customary five-minute visit to the toilet. "Thank you for calling," she added, she hoped not too suspiciously loud.

She had apparently fooled the supervisor, but perhaps not Vi or Doris. She didn't say a word to any of her colleagues until she'd had lunch amid the tinny clattering of the basement canteen, followed by several strolls around the car park in pursuit of her clouds of breath to use up the rest of her lunch break. As soon as she was back at her desk, releasing Vi from hers, she said to Bertha "I know it's short notice, but could I have tomorrow afternoon off?"

Bertha turned from adjusting the blind, an irregularity of which had dared to admit a scrap of muffled sunlight. "Is it an emergency?"

Lisette grew aware that Doris was idle and listening. "It wouldn't seem like one to everybody, but—"

"Then we can't treat it as one, can we?" Bertha said with what might even have been a hint of genuine regret. "You know the rules as well as anyone. Forty-eight hours notice of leave except in cases of absolute emergency."

This had never made sense to Lisette—it wasn't as though a substitute worker would be brought in. "I know you wouldn't want to be made an exception of and cause bad feeling," Bertha said, at which Doris gave a nod of agreement so meaningful it might well have contained a threat of telling tales.

Lisette pressed her headphones to her ears as an inquiry summoned her. Her professional voice sounded detached from her, entering her head from outside, but that wasn't new. A worse impression was, however—a sense that instead of being the role she played in order to afford her real life, this empty unfulfilled automaton serving a faceless public would soon be the whole of herself. It wouldn't be while she had any imagination left, she vowed, and remembered Willy Bantam's novels waiting on her bed. Her imagination wouldn't let her down so long as she refrained from wasting it on trying to concoct excuses she didn't need.

She'd hardly reached her bedroom and thrown off her coat when she opened *Ravage!* on her lap, its hard rounded spine digging into her crotch. From her bag she took the pen Willy Bantam had held. It felt cold, but grew warmer as she ran a finger up and down it while she used it to cross out the name that had supplanted hers in *Ravage!* Once she had written her own name everywhere it belonged she found the description of her in *Writhe!* and made it hers too, then she hugged the books to her and rocked back and forth on the edge of the bed.

That night her sleep was uninterrupted, even by dreams. The clock had to repeat its squeak to rouse her. She dressed at her leisure and strolled to the phone box at the end of the road, where she told Doris she was too ill to go to work. Back home she sat on her bed and stroked the Willy Bantam books until it was time to go to him.

She would have left earlier except for not wanting to be conspicuous when she arrived, but the two hours she gave herself proved not to be enough. Winds like tastes of a blizzard threw her car about the motorway and thwarted her even approaching the speed she would have risked. When at last she found the library, she was twenty minutes late.

It was one of several concrete segments surrounding a circular parking area, a plate that might have held a cake the segments had been part of. Besides the library there was a church, a police station, a fraud investigation office. Though the plate was several hundred yards around, it was almost covered with cars, so that Lisette was growing sweaty with desperation when she saw a space outside the library. It was reserved for the Disability Advisement Executive, but Lisette felt her need was greater. She parked as straight as she had time for and dashed into the library, where a notice board tried to confuse her with a list of the day's events: a sale of videocassettes, a meeting of a writers' group, a demonstration of origami, a seminar for teenage parents, a course called "The Koran Can Be Fun" . . . The guest of the writers' group was William Bantam. Far better, the girl at Bassinet Press had misinformed Lisette. He wasn't due to start for five minutes.

Lisette hurried to the end of a corridor papered with posters for counseling services and found herself a seat in the midst of the large loud audience. She squeezed her bag of books between her thighs as a murmur of appreciation greeted the appearance of their author. He wasn't even bothering to look for her: he must believe she was either satisfied with his autograph or overcome by his trick. Then he rounded the table at the end of the room and saw her.

His jaw didn't quite drop, but his lips parted audibly before they snapped together. He poured himself a glass of water and downed half of it, then he set about reading from *The Smallest Trace of Fear*. He read the scene in which a willowy brunette became obsessed with the idea that she was being followed by the same car with different licsense plates and was pitifully grateful to be picked up by her new boyfriend until she heard the rattle of several metal rectangles from behind her seat . . . "Dot dot dot is about the size of it," Lisette muttered, convinced he'd selected the chapter as a gibe at her. "Drip drip drip, more like." That everyone else present seemed impressed struck her as not merely a joke but a bad influence on him. She listened while people praised his subtlety and restraint and went on about his technique, all of them presumably writers so unsuccessful they had nothing better to do than sit at his new clay feet. Soon she was waving her hand, but Bantam and the librarian who was choosing questioners ignored her. As the author finished telling a woman that he didn't think publishers were biased against her or her class or her gender, Lisette sprang to her feet. "Can I speak now?"

Dozens of heads turned to find her wanting. "Are you a writer?" a long-faced shaky bald man demanded on behalf of all of them.

"Yes I am, and I wouldn't be except for Willy Bantam."

Bantam was searching for somebody else to recognize, but all the hands except hers had gone down. "What's your question?" the librarian said.

"I want to read you how it ought to be." Lisette pulled out the book: not her favourite—she was keeping that all for herself—but *Writhe!* "Lisette had been dreaming Frank was still alive," she read, raising her voice as people who could see the book began to murmur. "When she felt her calf being stroked she thought he had come back, and in a way he had. As the caress passed over her knee she parted her thighs. The long soft object squirmed between them, and that was when she knew something was wrong. But the worm that had crawled into her bed had stiffened, and as she gasped it thrust deep into her, spattering her with graveyard earth . . ."

The murmur of the audience had grown louder and more defined—tuts, throat-clearings, embarrassed coughs—and at this point it produced a voice. "You should save that kind of thing for reading when you're by yourself."

A girl brandished a copy of *Writhe!* "That's Mr Bantam's story, only she's not called that in it."

"She should be," Lisette said.

The girl gaped at her. "Is she supposed to be you?"

"Do you need to ask when you've read the book?"

The girl looked away, and so did everyone else. Lisette might have borne that much disbelief, but then she heard a muffled titter. "She's me all right. She always was," Lisette declared. "Willy put me in even if he didn't know he did. You heard him say he doesn't know where some of his ideas come from. You can't deny it's me when everyone can see me, Willy Bantam."

The bald man, shaking more than ever, broke the silence. "Did you have anyone in mind as your victim, Mr Bantam?"

"I'm glad you asked me that. There's only one person an author ever really writes about, and that's himself."

"That's stupid. How can he make out any of the girls are him?" Lisette protested, attempting to provoke a laugh with hers. "He's a Willy, not a Connie. Not a Cunty. Not a Pussy," she said, louder as the librarian gestured urgently at a uniformed guard. "Don't bother, I'm going," she said, grinning at the pairs of knees that flinched out of her way as she made for the aisle. "Just you remember everybody here knows I was in your books when you were Willy Bantam. I'll always be in them now."

She'd marched only a few yards out of the room when she heard hoots of incredulous laughter. What was he saying about her? She might have gone back to find out if the guard hadn't been following her, his face a doleful warning. She strode away, hugging her bagful of books so tightly they seemed to throb in time with her heart, to be transforming themselves into her flesh.

Long before she arrived home the fog was beckoning the night. The lights in her garage and upstairs were harsher than she was expecting. The one in her bedroom spotlighted her on the bed, naked except for *Ravage!* between her legs. "I'm there now, Willy Bantam," she murmured, and rubbed herself against the book as she crouched forward to read her scene. She didn't know how many times she read it before she had to acknowledge it was no use. He'd intervened between her and the book—his smug indifferent face and his words in public had, and the jeering of his audience.

It wasn't until the binding gave an injured creak that she observed she was about to rip the book in half. Instead she closed it slowly as though it, or some thought it was capable of prompting, would tell her how to proceed. The notion kept her company in bed, and as the night settled into the depths of itself she saw what she must do.

The alarm had to make several efforts to waken her. Since the staff at Bassinet Press started work later than she did, her tardiness hardly mattered. She reached the office at least a minute before the switchboards were due to open, but Bertha frowned hard enough to darken her sunless face. "We'd given up on you. Are you better?"

"Getting there."

"We didn't think it was like you to have to stay off with a case of the girlies."

"Maybe I'm becoming a woman," Lisette said, and closed herself in with her headphones, ignoring the looks Vi and Doris exchanged. She dealt with inquiries until Bertha waddled off to relieve herself and remake her makeup, at which point Lisette suffered the next call to carry on twitching its light on her board while she rang Bassinet Press. "Will you put me through to William Bantam's editor, please."

"May I have a name?"

"Someone they'll want to speak to."

Quite soon a deeper female voice said "Mel Daunton."

"Are you the editor Mr Bantam has to talk to?"

"I'm the one he does. Sorry, can I ask who's calling?"

"You ought to be sorry. You should know who I am. He talked to you about me."

"You'll forgive me if I don't—"

"You and his agent and him got together to talk about what I could imagine before he wrote his new book."

"I don't know where you could have got that impression, Miss, Mrs—"

"He said it in front of witnesses at the bookshop here in town, so don't bother trying to tell me it isn't true. You can't take advantage of me any more than he can. Do you know what he wanted me to believe when I saw him yesterday? That the description of me in his books isn't me."

"I did hear something about that. If I can—"

"I'll bet he didn't tell you he said he was me. Even I haven't got the imagination to believe that."

"I'm glad to hear it. Can I ask what you actually—"

"I want compensation for the way he used me and then said he never did. I'm not talking about money. As long as you and his

agent tell him what to write, I want us all to agree how he can
put me in his next book."

"That might take some arranging. Give me your number and I'll
call you back."

"It doesn't matter when we all have to meet, I'll come," said
Lisette, ignoring Vi and Doris, both of whom were staring at her.
It wasn't until they turned to gaze past her that she realized what
was wrong, not that she cared. A glance over her shoulder revealed
Bertha in the doorway, hands on hips. "I'll call you tomorrow,"
Lisette said into the mouthpiece.

"I may not be here then, so if you could give me your—"

"I know what you're up to. Never mind trying to send someone
to shut me up. I'll be there when you're discussing his next book,"
Lisette said, and cut her off.

She waited for Bertha to move into her view. The supervisor
looked so unhappy and reluctant to speak that Lisette stood up at
once. "You needn't say it. I'm fired," she cried, flinging the ear-
phones at the switchboard. "Don't worry, I'm going to a better
place," she said, snatching her coat off its hook, and stamped on
whatever Bertha attempted to say to her back.

She was out of the only job she'd ever had, and already forget-
ting it. She knew who she really was, and before long everybody
would. On her way home she parked in a side street she would
previously have found too unpatrolled to brave and bought a tape
recorder in a pawnbroker's. One of several men who were huddled
under sacks in the doorway of a derelict pub erected his bottle at
her for lack of anything more manageable. "I'll have worse in me
than that," she told him.

It was almost noon, but it might as well have been dusk. Swollen
lumps of light hovered above the pavements, thick glowing veils
hung before the shops. The world had grown soft and remote from
her, and the interior of her house seemed as distant: the closing of
the garage, the climbing of the stairs, the crossing of the room full
of redundant books. Only her bedroom was alive for her, and once
she was naked she pressed herself against the wall that was papered

with samples of Willy Bantam. She ran her fingertips around the screaming lips, she licked the pages of *Ravage!*. The faint taste of ink seemed more nourishing than any meal. When she felt entirely ready she switched on the tape recorder and held in her hand the pen he'd touched, and widened her legs on the bed.

"Willy? Willy Bantam? I know you're going to hear this. I'm not angry with you any more. I can't be angry when we're going to collaborate. This is how I'll die in your next book. You won't be able to resist me. Are you listening?"

When she saw the flare of red that indicated the machine was, she closed her eyes. "Lisette pulled the cap off the famous horror writer's pen. No protection for her. She traced the contours of her full breasts with the tip, she ran it over her flat trim stomach and up and down her long slim thighs, oh, and then she thrust it deep, ah . . ."

Before too long she was able to form words again, and meanwhile her other sounds kept the tape recorder working. "She felt it penetrate her virginity," she gasped, and steadied her voice. "She felt the ink that was his essence flow into her, tingling through her body. She felt herself starting to imagine like him, see into the depths of him, see things he would never have dared to see by himself. Now if she could just . . . just put them into words . . ."

"That's as much as she managed to say," the policeman said, and switched off the tape. "By the sound of it she passed out shortly after."

"And then . . ." Bantam prompted.

"And then she lay there for weeks before anyone found her. She hadn't any friends or family, just books."

"I hope nobody's going to blame me for that."

"Most of them weren't yours," said the policeman, and paused long enough for his gaze to become heavily ambiguous. "We shouldn't need to trouble you further. Nobody can say you encouraged her."

"They better hadn't try." For an instant the author saw the

woman as the sound of her taped voice had conjured her up—an unwelcome presence in the midst of his audience, at least middle-aged and already grey, flat-chested, thick-limbed, less than five feet tall and almost half as broad. "I wish someone else had," he said.

The policeman pushed himself out of the only chair and held up the tape recorder. "Will you want this when we've finished with it?"

"For what? No thanks."

"You won't be doing what she wanted."

"Writing about her? Too many of the papers already have."

"I can see you wouldn't want to get yourself a worse reputation," the policeman said.

Bantam saw him out of the apartment and out of his mind. He'd survived remarks more pointed than that in the course of his career. The woman on the tape was harder to forget, but a large glass of brandy helped, and put him in a working mood. Working cured anything. He sat on the bed with his lap-top word processor and reached out to turn towards him the photograph of his ex-wife, faded by years of sunlight and dust. He could almost feel her breasts filling his hands, feel her slim waist, long slim legs. "Bitch," he said almost affectionately, and began to write.

AFTERWORD

NOBODY REBELS LIKE a good Catholic boy, and I spent quite
a stretch of my childhood in fighting the repressiveness of my up-
bringing. I needed to. At an early age I was infected by my mother's
blushes at anything that might conceal a double meaning, and
anything more explicit than that made me horribly uncomfortable:
I squirmed when Bluebottle and Eccles in the *Goon Show* looked
up someone's trousers to see who he was, and felt physically ill
when Victor Borge introduced the messy soprano who came in a
single pile. I couldn't go through life like that, though I'm sure too
many people do, and by the time I reached adolescence at a gram-
mar school run by Christian Brothers I was beginning to grow
mutinous. I'd no time for the spinsterish way one master wrinkled
his nose at sex in pop songs and denied us a hearing of the Porter
scene in a recording of *Macbeth*. No doubt I resented his disapproval partly because pop songs and dirty jokes, some of which
would have taken a David Cronenberg to visualise, were all the
sexual experience I had. Sex education was thoroughly absent, except for a talk on the ways of the world, delivered on one of my
last days at school by a visiting monk who referred to girls' "head-
lamps" and boys' "spouts". Still, perhaps the beatings that were
frequent at the school were popular with some; in that year's issue
of the magazine a school governor reminisces at unhealthy length
about them. Myself, I agree with Gore Vidal (and quite a few of
its practitioners) in approving of corporal punishment only between consenting adults, a theme I'll return to later.

But my strongest resentment against the church and my upbring-
ing at that time was over the forbidding of books. I had the im-

pression—how accurate I can't say—that as a Catholic I was prevented from reading all sorts of things on pain of some unspecified and therefore daunting penalty. Having persuaded my mother over the years to let me borrow adult ghost books from the library, and eventually, when I was ten, to allow me to buy science fiction magazines and even *Weird Tales*, I now felt ready to confront censoriousness—or at least, I thought I did. This was the year *Lady Chatterley's Lover* was first published in Britain, and while I don't think any of my schoolmates were brave enough to bring a copy to school, quite a few claimed to have read it; undoubtedly some of them had. The best I could do, however, was to skulk near bookstalls where it was displayed and clutch the three and sixpence in my pocket in a vain attempt to goad myself into picking up the book. It wasn't until I left school that I determined to make up for lost time by reading whatever I liked.

So I bought Nabokov's *Lolita*, having seen it recommended by Graham Greene, and found it liberating in several ways, not least as a writer. In order to write anything lively enough for publication I'd needed to unlearn some of the restrictions I'd been taught at school—you couldn't contract "I had" to "I'd", for instance—but the effect of reading Nabokov was an instant lightening of my style and a greatly enhanced enjoyment of language (a pleasure which, I fear, at least one teacher of English literature had had no apparent time for). Meanwhile my first published stories, imitations of Lovecraft, had begun to appear. Pat Kearney, a friend who published the very first in his fanzine *Goudy*, told me about the Olympia Press, *Lolita's* original publisher. A house devoted to publishing books banned in Britain sounded fine to me, particularly since I was incensed to discover that so many books were banned, and so with the advance paid on publication of my first book, I took my mother and myself to Paris, whence I returned with William Burroughs' *The Soft Machine* and *The Ticket That Exploded* and a copy for Pat Kearney of a book of bawdy ballads pseudonymously edited by Christopher Logue. How I intended to bluff my way through Customs I have no idea, but a rough and protracted Channel crossing came to what I was able to regard retrospectively as my aid. Faced with the sight of me, wavering and pale-faced and be-spattered with remains of that morning's croissants, the Customs officer waved me through. In the introduction to his bibliography of the Olympia Press, Pat Kearney celebrates this incident with a description that makes me think of Anthony Cronin's last grisly sight of Brendan Behan.

Another source of banned books was August Derleth, my friend and mentor and (in the days when Arkham House was pretty well his one-man operation) first professional publisher, who sent me Henry Miller's *Tropics* and Lawrence Durrell's *Black Book*. This led me to assume he wouldn't mind if I introduced a different kind of shock into my Lovecraft imitations, but he took the shit out of a line of dialogue. I still think it's what the character would have said, but I see that that may not be relevant to such a stylised form as Lovecraft pastiche. I therefore tried writing for the Olympia Press, who were then publishing a magazine. "A Third-Floor With-drawal" was an attempt to deal with my adolescent sexual turmoil, and the editor of *Olympia* gave me the impression that it might have been published except for its brevity (it was about a thousand words in length). I tried again with "The Folding Socket", a plotless fantasy influenced by William Burroughs, which I wrote at my Civil Service desk in the lunch hours. This, I imagine, was too gross for the magazine, which was aimed at the British and American book-stalls. Both stories are lost, and certainly the latter need not be mourned.

Years later—1969, I think—I had a different sort of experience involving Olympia Press. In the first newsletter of a short-lived Liverpool underground film society, I advertised for sale the Olym-pia edition of de Sade's *120 Days of Sodom*, whose three volumes I'd found somewhat tedious. Of course the nondescript fellow who called at the house to examine the books proved to be a plain-clothes policeman, who had no doubt been planted in the film society so as to keep an eye on things, though I didn't realize this until he returned with three of his colleagues and a warrant to search the house. They were unfailingly courteous, and seemed to be impressed by both my naïveté and my having been published. Weeks later I was invited to the police station to be given a cup of tea and the news that the Director of Public Prosecutions had decided not to prosecute, and almost everything they had seized was returned to me, including Kenneth Patchen's *Memoirs of a Shy Pornographer* and Samuel Beckett's *Imagination Dead Imagine*, in which page 12 had been marked in pencil, apparently because it begins with "the arse" ("the arse against the wall at A, the knees against the wall at B and C, the feet against the wall between C and A, that is to say inscribed in the semicircle ACB . . ."). I don't think Beckett had previously been regarded as a pornographic writer. I had to sign away my rights only to the de Sade, a book which caused the policeman to wrinkle his nose in exactly the way pop songs had affected my old schoolmaster.*

By then I had completed *Demons by Daylight*, my second book, though it wasn't published until 1973. It may not seem especially radical now, but it certainly was then, not least in dealing with characters whose guilts and fears and sexuality and, especially, emotional clumsiness were based on my experience. Indeed, if I hadn't felt driven by the need to bring horror fiction up to date, in line with the contemporary fiction I was reading, I might not have had the courage to continue; I felt that these stories were unlikely to receive August Derleth's approval—so much so that when I'd finished typing the book I fell into a horrible depression, because I both regarded Arkham House as my only market (as Lovecraft regarded *Weird Tales* as his) and was convinced that Arkham wouldn't touch it. But Derleth bought it, though he never gave me his opinion of it, and I was set on my course.

It is sometimes suggested (by Paul Schrader, for instance, in an attempt to justify his vulgar remake of *Cat People*) that all horror fiction is about sex. This is nonsense, and unhelpfully reductionist

---

*How times change! These days not only the novel but Pasolini's bleak and distressing film of it are openly on sale in Britain.

even when applied to tales with sexual themes: it's too easy to slide from "that's what the story is about" to "that's all the story is about." But it's true that many horror stories have a sexual subtext, and I think many of us in the field tended to assume that if the underlying sexual theme was made explicit, it would rob the fiction of its power.

It was the anthologist Michel Parry, an old friend, who gave me the chance to test this theory, though I don't think he quite realised what he was helping to create. After editing three volumes of black magic stories for Mayflower, he complained to me that nobody was submitting tales on a sexual theme. Aroused by the suggestion, I wrote "Dolls," which enabled me both to explore what happened to the supernatural story when the underlying sexual theme (not always present, of course) became overt and to write a long short story that was stronger on narrative than atmosphere, a useful preparation for writing my first novel. Michel hadn't expected anything quite so sexually explicit, and I was amused when his publishers, Mayflower, felt compelled to show "Dolls" to their lawyers for advice. The lawyers advised them to publish, and over the next few years Michel commissioned several more such tales, all of which are included here.

My original title for this book was *Horror Erotica*. The one it bears was the inspiration of Jeff Conner at Scream/Press. At least we didn't call it *Wanking Nightmares*. My correspondent Keith B. Johnston of Goshen came up with *Eldritchly Erect*, and Poppy Z. Brite suggested I should write a second such collection set in Liverpool and called *Mersey Beat-Off*, though admittedly that was after I proposed she call a book *The Phantom of the Okra*.

I don't know if much need be said about most of the following stories. "The Other Woman" has offended some readers, and I probably wouldn't write it that way now if at all, but I think it's a story about fantasies of rape rather than merely being such a fantasy itself. I believe "The Seductress" was filmed for the cable television show *The Hunger*, but although I was paid for it I've never seen the episode. "Merry May" (which was written to tumefy the first edition of this book) became transformed into "Merry Way" on the cover of the American Warner paperback, which also toned the original subtitle ("Tales of Sex and Death") down to "Seven Tales of Seduction and Terror." "The Body in the Window" was written for the *Hot Blood* paperback anthology series, while "Kill Me Hideously" suggested itself as soon as I agreed at a British science fiction convention to offer as an auction item the chance for the highest bidder to appear in my next novel. That was *The Last Voice They Hear*, but the charming bidder had nothing in common with the unlucky Lisette in the present book.

"The Other Woman" and "Loveman's Comeback" were written for the short-lived *Devil's Kisses* series of anthologies of erotic horror Michel edited as Linda Lovecraft, who was in fact the owner of a chain of sex shops and who is one more reason why asking for Lovecraft in a British bookshop may earn you a dubious look. Perhaps the anthologies were ahead of their time, because the second in the series was pulped shortly after publication, apparently in response to objections from Scotland Yard. Rumour had it that the problem was a tale reprinted from *National Lampoon*, involving a seven-year-old girl and a horse. Michel held on to "Stages" for a possible anthology about drugs, but after the above incident the story went into limbo. I confess to being more amused than irritated by the banning of *More Devil's Kisses*, much as I felt upon learning that my first novel had been seen (in a television documentary) on top of a pile of books for burning by Christian fundamentalists—something of a compliment as far as I'm concerned. On reflection, though, I think I wasn't entitled to feel quite so superior about censorship. Though my sexual tales had been, on the whole, progressively darker and more unpleasant, I'd suppressed the third of them, "In the Picture." It was the initial draft of the story published here as "The Limits of Fantasy."

At the time (May 1975) I believed I had decided not to revise and submit the story because it wasn't up to publishable standard, and that was certainly the case. However, the reasons were more personal than I admitted to myself. All fiction is to some extent the product of censorship, whether by the culture within which it is produced or by the writer's own selection of material, both of which processes tend to be to some extent unconscious. Perhaps the most insidious form of censorship, insofar as it may be the most seductive for the writer, is by his own dishonesty. For me the most immediate proof is that it wasn't until Barry Hoffman asked me if I had any suppressed fiction he could publish in *Gauntlet* that I realized, on rereading "In the Picture," that my dishonesty was its central flaw.

One mode of fiction I dislike—one especially common in my field—is the kind where the act of writing about a character seems designed to announce that the character has nothing to do with the author. On the most basic level, it's nonsense, since by writing about a character the writer must draw that personality to some extent from within himself. More to the present point, it smells of protesting too much, and while that may be clear to the reader, for the writer it's a kind of censorship of self. I hope that "In the Picture" is the only tale in which I succumb to that temptation.

"In the Picture" follows the broad outline of "The Limits of Fantasy," though much more humourlessly, up to the scene with Enid Stone, and then Sid Pym begins to indulge in fantasies of rape and degradation which I believe are foreign to his sexual makeup and which are contrived simply to demonstrate what a swine he is—in other words, that he is quite unlike myself. Nothing could be further from the truth. In response to Barry Hoffman I treated "In the Picture" as the first version of the story and rewrote it exactly as I would any other first draft, and I had the most fun writing Pym's boarding-school fantasy, which is at least as much my fantasy as his. For me his presentation of it is both comic and erotic.

It seems to me that even the most liberal of us employ two definitions of pornography: the kind that turns ourselves on, which we're more prone to regard as erotic, and the kind which appeals to people with sexual tastes unlike our own and which we're more likely to condemn as pornographic. In my case the absurdity is that the group of scenarios which I sum up as the boarding-school fantasy (which is obviously as much fetishistic as sadistic) is the only species of pornography I find appealing, and it was therefore especially dishonest of me to include no more than a hint of it when I collected my sexual tales in *Scared Stiff*. I suppose, then and in my original suppression of "In the Picture," I was afraid of losing friends, but that really isn't something writers should take into account when writing. I suspect I was assuming that my readers and people in general are squarer when it comes to erotic fantasy than is in fact the case. Since the publication of *Scared Stiff* I've heard from readers of various sexes that they found parts of the book erotic, and a female reader gave me a copy of *Caught Looking*, a polemic published by the Feminist Anti-Censorship Taskforce, in which one of the illustrations (all chosen by the FACT designers on the basis that they themselves found the images erotically appealing) is a still from *Moral Welfare*, a British spanking video. (The Spankarama Cinema in Soho, rather unfairly chastised in the winter 1982/83 *Sight and Sound* and touched on by association in *Incarnate*, is long gone; perhaps I should have had a publicity photograph taken under the sign while it was there.) Incidentally, perhaps one minor reason for my reticence was the notion that this sexual taste is peculiarly British, but a few minutes on the Internet will give the lie to that. I keep feeling there's a novel in the theme, to be called *Adult Fun*, but who would publish it? Meanwhile "The Limits of Fantasy" adds variety to this collection, which has sometimes struck me as too mechanically including the standard variations in tale after tale.

So I trust this hasn't been too embarrassing. I haven't found it so, but then I may sometimes lack tact in these areas: I once greeted a friend I met in a sex shop, who immediately fled. Still, I'm committed to telling as much of the truth as I can, as every writer should be. If we can't tell the truth about ourselves, how can we presume to do so about anyone or anything? Secretiveness is a weakness, whereas honesty is strength.

If I'm told my field is incapable of something, I'll give it a try—

hence these and others of my tales. No doubt the irritation of censorship also has something to do with it: here it seems to have behaved like Spanish fly. On that basis I should like to thank censors, especially the self-appointed, for helping me write. I love them all. After all, as they must recognize, we hate most in others what we can't admit about ourselves.

RAMSEY CAMPBELL
Wallasey, Merseyside
28 May 2001